RUPERT TH

Katherine Carlyle

corsair

CORSAIR

First published in Great Britain in 2015 by Corsair
1 3 5 7 9 10 8 6 4 2

A CIP catalogue record for this book
is available from the British Library.

ISBN: 978-1-4721-5061-5 (hardback)
ISBN: 978-1-4721-5062-2 (airport/export)
ISBN: 978-1-4721-5063-9 (ebook)

Typeset in Baskerville MT by Hewer Text UK Ltd, Edinburgh

Printed and bound in Great Britain by Clays Ltd, St Ives plc

Papers used by Corsair are from well-managed forests and other responsible sources.

Corsair
An imprint of
Little, Brown Book Group
Carmelite House
50 Victoria Embankment
London EC4Y 0DZ

An Hachette UK Company
www.hachette.co.uk

www.littlebrown.co.uk

To Judith Gurewich

How slowly the time passes here,
encompassed as I am by
frost and snow!

Mary Shelley

Everything is torment, everything is song
I would love to be loved
And belong to someone
Belong to someone

Endre Ady

Prologue

I was made in a small square dish. The temperature was 37 degrees Celsius, like the inside of a human body. Like a womb. The dish had four shallow wells or indentations, and the word NUNC was stamped along one edge. My mother's eggs were placed in the wells, no more than three in each, and then my father's sperm was introduced, the sperm allowed to seek the eggs in a simulacrum of the reproductive process. The ingredients were all scrupulously harvested, meticulously screened. Something of hers, something of his – a precious pinch of each. Pale-blue figures drifted high above, like clouds.

Within a matter of hours I was transferred to a solution or 'culture medium', where I was supposed to 'cleave'. *Medium, cleave* – these are the technical terms. During the next five days I divided into a blastocyst, consisting of approximately sixty cells. My progress was monitored by the figures dressed in blue. Sometimes they reached down and removed embryos that were judged to be non-viable. Not me, though. I remained untouched. This happened on the fourth floor of a west London hospital, in the Assisted Conception Unit.

Though I was one of several 'Grade 1' embryos – clear cells, tight junctions, no evidence of fragmentation or 'blebbing' – the technicians did not select me for immediate implantation. I was preserved instead.

Freezing me took an hour and a half.

Afterwards, I was stored in a squat steel barrel, vacuum-lined like a Thermos flask, and filled with liquid nitrogen. They put me in a microscopic transparent straw, with air gaps on either side of me. The straw was slotted into a cane. Both the straw and the cane were labelled with the name and date of birth of the patient – my mother. I was suspended in a bath of cryo-protectant and other assorted nutrients, and exposed to a temperature that was constant and extreme – minus 196.

At that time, in the 1980s, there was some dispute as to how long a frozen embryo was good for. Different governments held different views. In the UK frozen embryos were routinely disposed of when they were ten years old. The belief was that our cells deteriorated, forfeiting the resilience necessary to survive the thawing process. But no one really knew. The science was still in its infancy, and research had yet to produce definitive results. Such a curious notion, to be the defunct or superannuated version of something that hadn't even existed. Like being a ghost, only the wrong way round. A ghost is somebody who has died but will not disappear. Can a ghost also be somebody who has never lived? Are there ghosts at either end of life?

The years went by.

Every now and then, and just for a few seconds, the lid was lifted off the storage tank and a torrent of white light poured down through the swirling mist. A number of embryos would be removed, but I stayed where I was, in my see-through straw. The lid was replaced. Darkness descended once again.

One

Another beautiful September. The sun richer, more tender, the colour of old wedding rings. Rome filling up again, people back at work after the holidays. I ride through the city, over potholes and cobbles, the sky arranged in hard blue blocks above the rooftops. The swallows have returned as well, flashing between the buildings in straight lines as if fired from a gun. I park my Vespa outside the station and walk in through the entrance.

It was spring when I first started noticing the messages. Back then, they were cryptic, teasing. While crossing piazza Farnese, I found a fifty-euro note that had been folded into a triangle. A few days later, at the foot of the Spanish Steps, I found a small grey plastic elephant with a piece of frayed string round its neck. I found countless keys, coins, and playing-cards. None of these objects had anything specific to communicate. They were just testing my alertness. They were nudges. Pokes. Nonetheless, I felt a thrill each time, a rocket-fizzle through the darkness of my body, and I took photos of them all and stored them on my laptop, in a file marked INTELLIGENCE. The weeks passed, and the world began to address me with more precision. In May I stopped for a *macchiato* near the Pantheon. On my table was a scrap of paper

7

with a phone number on it. I recognised the prefix – Bologna
– and called the number. A woman answered, her voice
hectic, a baby crying in the background. I hung up. The scrap
of paper was a message, but not one I needed to pay attention
to. In June I entered a changing cubicle in a shop on via del
Corso. Lying on the floor was a brochure for a French hotel.
'Conveniently located for the A8', the Hôtel Allure offered a
'high standard of accommodation'. I borrowed my friend
Daniela's car on a Friday afternoon and drove for seven hours
straight, past Florence and Genoa, and on around the coast
to Nice. At midnight the hotel's neon sign floated into view,
the black air rich with jasmine and exhaust. I spent most of
the next day by the pool. The hot white sky. The rush of traffic on La Provençale. In the early evening a man pulled into
the car-park in a silver BMW. He stood at the water's edge,
his shirtsleeves rolled back to the elbow. His name was Pascal,
and he worked in telecommunications. When he asked me
out to dinner – when he put that question – I somehow realised he wasn't relevant. If the Hôtel Allure was a mistake,
though, it was a useful one. I've been imagining a journey
ever since.

The station concourse smells of ground coffee beans and
scalded milk. I stare up at the Departures board. *Firenze,
Milano. Parigi.* None of the names stand out, none of them
speak to me. Voices swarm beneath the high sweep of the
roof, footsteps echo on the polished marble, and then a feeling, sudden yet familiar – the feeling that I'm not there. It's
not that I'm dead. I'm simply gone. I never was. Panic opens
inside me, slow and stealthy, like a flower that only blooms at
night. The eight years are still with me, eight years in the
dark, the cold. Waiting. Not knowing.

I deliberately collide with someone who happens to be passing. He's in his early thirties. Black hair, brown leather jacket. He drops his bag. An apple rolls away across the floor.

'I'm so sorry,' I say.

'No, no,' he says. 'My fault.'

The moment he looks at me, my existence comes flooding back. It's as if I'm a pencil sketch, and he's colouring me in. I go and fetch the apple. When I pick it up it fits my palm perfectly. The shape of it, the weight, makes everything that follows feel natural.

I hold it out to him. 'I think it might be bruised.'

He looks at the apple, then smiles. 'This is like a fairy tale. Are you a witch?'

'I just didn't see you,' I say. 'I should be more careful.' I'm breathless with exhilaration. I'm *alive*.

'Are you waiting for someone? Or perhaps you're going somewhere—' He glances at the Departures board.

'I'm not going anywhere,' I say. 'Not yet.'

Something in him seems to align itself with what I'm feeling. We're like two people running side by side, and he has fallen into step with me. Nothing needs to be explained, or even said. It's understood. His eyes are dark and calm.

'Come with me,' he says. 'Do you have time?'

'Yes.'

His fingers curl round mine.

We walk to a small hotel on via Palermo. They have a room on the second floor, at the front of the building. I hear the muted roar of a vacuum cleaner. There's a coolness about the place, a feeling of suspension. A hush. It's that hidden moment in the day, the gap between checking out and checking in.

On the stairs he's behind me, watching me. My hips, my

calves, the small of my back. I can feel my edges, the space I occupy. We reach the door. He steps past me with the key. He smells of wood and pepper. As soon as we're inside he kisses me.

The room has a high ceiling and surprising lilac walls. From the window I can look down into the street. He pushes me back on to the bed. I tell him to wait. Lifting my hips, I pull the apple from my pocket. He smiles again.

We take each other's clothes off carefully. We're not in any hurry. One button, then another. A catch. A zip. The TV watches us from the top corner of the room. The curtains shift.

When he's about to enter me I hand him a condom from my bag.

'You've done this before,' he says.

'No, never,' I say.

He looks down at me. He thinks I'm lying but it doesn't bother him.

'I carry them to stop it happening,' I say. 'It's the opposite of tempting fate.'

'You're superstitious?'

I don't answer.

The noise of the traffic shrinks until it's no louder than the buzz of a fly trapped in a jar. There is only the rustle of the sheets and the sound of our breathing, his and mine, and I think of that place in Brazil where the rivers join, two different kinds of water meeting, two different colours. I think of white clouds colliding in a sky of blue.

I cry out when I come. He comes moments later, quietly. When I turn over, on to my side, he adjusts his body to mine. He lies behind me, fitting himself against me as closely as he can, like a shadow. I feel him soften and then slip out of me. This too is part of the colouring-in.

Afterwards, I follow him downstairs. Out on the street I'm worried he will tell me his name and ask if he can see me again but all he does is put one hand against my cheek and look at me.

'*Mia piccola strega.*' My little witch.

He kisses me and walks away.

Later, I think of the apple we left in the hotel room. Lying among the crumpled bedclothes, its red skin glowing.

The next day I go to an outdoor screening of *The Passenger*, which is one of my father's favourite movies. I've seen it before, at least twice, and it has become a favourite of mine as well. A warm evening, not a breath of wind. Stars glinting weakly in a dull black sky. I'm slumped low in my seat waiting for the movie to begin when I become aware of an English couple sitting in the row in front of me. I can't see their faces, only the backs of their heads. The man is wearing a raspberry-coloured shirt, and his bald spot gleams. The woman has nondescript brown hair. They're talking about a friend of theirs who lives in Berlin. His name is Klaus Frinks. Klaus is upset, the woman says in a high-pitched voice. Terribly, terribly upset.

'Upset?' the man says. 'Why?'

'That girl he was in love with. She left him.'

'I never liked that girl.'

'Didn't you?' The woman turns to look at her companion. Long nose, receding chin.

'I didn't trust her,' the man says.

'She was beautiful.'

The man shrugs but says nothing.

'Poor Klaus.' The woman sounds oddly gratified. 'He really thought she was the one.'

I sit up straighter in my seat.

Klaus, I think, and then I think, *Berlin*.

If Klaus is German, and his surname is pronounced 'Frinks', it's probably spelled with a 'g', as in 'Frings'. If I hadn't studied the language at school I wouldn't have known that. My brain cracks open, floods with light.

Klaus Frings.

The man with the bald spot looks round, curious to see if anyone is listening. He's one of those people who talks loudly in public places because he thinks he's interesting. Well, for once in his life he's right: he *is* interesting – to me, at least. When he notices me, he tugs at his shirt collar as if to loosen it, then looks beyond me, pretending to be checking on the whereabouts of the projectionist. *Tell me more*, I whisper inside my head.

Facing the screen again, the man is silent for a few seconds, then he says, 'Is Klaus still living in the same apartment?'

The woman nods. 'Walter-Benjamin-Platz.'

'Penthouse, wasn't it?'

'That's right. Amazing place. You've been there, haven't you?'

'Once. There was that party—'

The lights dim.

The Passenger intrigues me, as always, but I find that I can't concentrate. I keep thinking about Klaus Frings and his apartment in Berlin. The inexplicable shock of recognition when I heard his name. The sense of being summoned, singled out. The sudden disappearance of my heart, as if it had been sucked into a black hole at the centre of my body. There have been so many dry runs and dress rehearsals but I knew that sooner or later one of the messages would feel right. And now, finally, it does.

When the film is over, I linger in the courtyard outside the cinema. The English couple are standing by the gate. In the same loud self-important voices they are discussing the famous scene in which the director, Antonioni, moves the camera out through the bars on Jack Nicholson's hotel window – how Nicholson is alive when the camera leaves, and dead by the time it returns. The woman is taller than the man. Older too, despite her girlish voice.

She catches me staring at her. 'I'm sorry. Do we know you?'

I laugh. 'No, you don't. I'm grateful to you, though.'

'*Grateful?*'

'It's all right. You've played your part.'

The woman flushes.

'You can go now,' I say.

The man fixes me with small hard eyes, and I remember something my Aunt Lottie told me. *Some men are horrid when they meet you but you shouldn't worry. It's just because they fancy you. It's actually a kind of compliment.* She paused, then said, *I wouldn't get involved, though – not with one of them.* I wonder if the man in the raspberry-coloured shirt is 'one of them'. I wonder if he was horrid to Klaus's girlfriend too.

I set off through Trastevere, making for the Ponte Sisto. I have plans for the evening – a late dinner, then a new club on the outskirts of the city – but I decide not to go. I feel too elated, too giddy. As I cross the river I replay the conversation I overheard. Certain phrases have stayed with me. *Penthouse, wasn't it? She left him.* They're clues to a future I can't as yet imagine, fragments of a narrative in which I'm about to feature as a character.

September 3rd. Alone in our rooftop apartment on via Giulia I stretch out on the sofa with the French windows open. My father's away, as usual. The dome of St Peter's floats above a jumble of palm trees, sloping tiles and TV aerials. It's nearly six o'clock. I yawn, then close my eyes. I hear my mother asking if I would like to go somewhere at the weekend. *We could drive to that forest – the one with the yew trees, remember?* She's dressed in a green T-shirt and a pair of jeans. Her arms are slender, tanned. This would have been in England, at a time when she was well . . . It's dark when I wake up. The snarl of a passing *motorino*, the clatter of plates in the restaurant down-stairs. Rome again.

I reach for my phone. I have messages from Massimo and Luca, moody boys with private incomes and slim brown ankles. They want me to come out. There are openings, they say. There are drinks at a film director's house in Parioli. There's a party. I think about my friend Daniela. I wish I could tell her about the man I slept with. How he took my hand beneath the Departures board, and how he came with-out a sound. How he kissed me on the street, then disappeared. *You didn't!* Dani, sitting at a table outside the Bar San Calisto, a cigarette between her fingers, her nails a cool chalk-blue. I would tell her what the man said. *My little witch.* We'd look at each other, wide-eyed, expressionless, then burst out laugh-ing. But Dani's in Puglia with hardly any coverage and she won't be back for days.

I shower, then stand in front of the bathroom mirror, brown all over except for a single blinding strip of white.

Tilting my head one way then the other, I run a brush through my wet hair. The ends come to level with my hip-bones. I really ought to have it cut but I can't be bothered to make an appointment, let alone sit in a chair for hours and listen to all the gossip. I remember the time I wound my hair round Adefemi's wrists. *You're my prisoner*, I said. He always liked me to keep it long.

My phone rings in the living-room. I put the brush down and lean close to the mirror. My face stares at me, unblinking. I look like someone who's about to meet her fate. *Are you superstitious?* I smile, then lower my eyes. The good thing about September is, you still have a tan. Lipstick and perfume: that's all you need.

Once dressed – short skirt, leather jacket, sandals – I check my phone. Four missed calls, three of them from Massimo. *Kit? Kit! Where are you? Call me!* By midnight my arms are round his waist as we race through the warm brown streets, the throaty roar of his Ducati bouncing off the facades of buildings. I rest my chin on his left shoulder and watch the city rush towards me. Massimo's a prince. Rome's full of princes. We cut through the Jewish quarter. A man in a white vest sits on a wooden chair. A cigarette in the corner of his mouth, he's peeling an orange. The smoke unwinds into the air. The opal glitter of a fountain.

Massimo pulls up outside a club in Testaccio. Two revs of the engine then he switches it off. Deep bass notes take over. I can already see the dance loor, a crush of sweat-soaked bodies, jittery strobe lighting. Massimo watches me remove my helmet and shake out my hair. 'You seem different.'

A cigarette arcs down from the terrace and lands on the cobbles in a shower of red sparks.

Later, in the club, we run into people we know, or half-know – Maurizio, Livia, Salvatore. None of us can quite believe the summer's over; there's a sense of nostalgia, an undercurrent of despair. Livia thinks we should spend a few days at her mother's house on Stromboli. Salvatore says Morocco would be warmer. Massimo is already complaining about Milan, where he will soon be studying. *Imagine what the weather will be like up there.* I tell him he won't even notice. He'll be too busy going out with models.

'It's you I want,' he mutters.

'I've only just split up with Adefemi,' I say. 'And anyway, we're supposed to be friends, aren't we?'

'*Adefemi.*' Massimo treads on a transparent plastic cup, which cracks loudly beneath his boot.

'I'll be off as well before too long,' I say.

He nods. 'Oxford.'

I've won a scholarship to Worcester College to study Italian and French but that's not what I'm talking about.

'No,' I say, 'not Oxford.'

'Where, then?'

I don't answer.

'You're impossible.' He lights a cigarette and blows out a thin blade of smoke that blunts itself against the night.

I move to the railing at the far end of the terrace. The air smells of spinach and wet fur. In June a group of us went dancing not far from here. I remember stone steps vanishing into the river, and a boat moored against the bank, and the water, green and milky. 90s techno, dry ice. Ketamine. Then I remember a place Adefemi showed me, on a bridge that links Testaccio and Trastevere. If you stop halfway across and lean over the parapet, a draught reaches up to cool your face,

16

even on a stifling August day. I think about all the people in bars and clubs and restaurants, and how I will soon be gone, and how none of it will change. That's the thing about Rome. Nothing changes. When you're somewhere else you can always imagine exactly what's happening.

Later still, Massimo takes me back to his apartment, which occupies one entire floor of a *palazzo* near piazza Venezia. Massimo has a Thai manservant who wears immaculate white gloves. Every morning he wakes Massimo with a *cappuccino* and a copy of *La Repubblica*. Massimo's living room is the size of a tennis court, with floor-to-ceiling windows and a brown-and-white marble floor. He used to have a brown-and-white fox terrier. Whenever the dog lay down, it disappeared.

Massimo offers me cocaine. I shake my head. He tosses the see-through plastic packet on the coffee table. Some of the white powder spills. He doesn't care. He pours me a cognac, then puts on *Kind of Blue* by Miles Davis. We lie at ninety degrees to each other, on matching cream sofas. I sip my drink; my stomach glows. It's a last night of sorts and I'm only sorry I can't tell him. The sound of the trumpet is clear as glass, some notes so fragile it's a wonder they don't shatter.

'Is your father in town?' he says.

'No, he's away.'

'Where is he?'

'I don't know. Some war-zone or other.'

Massimo smiles. He has always liked the idea of my father. He thinks being a reporter is romantic.

Sitting up, he runs a hand through his hair, then changes the music. This time it's Suicide's *Ghost Rider*. I finish my cognac and slip out of my shoes. We dance back to back on the cool marble floor, our arms lifting dreamily into the air above our heads like a snake-charmer's snakes.

At three in the morning I tell him I'm going home. He starts to cry. 'What if I never see you again?'

'Don't be so dramatic.' I push the hair out of his eyes and kiss him on the forehead. 'You're tired. You should go to bed.'

Outside, as I bend over to unlock my Vespa, a car races down the street, boys leaning from the window, a maroon-and-yellow flag rippling and snapping in their hands. One of them shouts at me. The only word I hear is *culo*. I'm still thinking about the things Massimo said. *You seem different. What if I never see you again?* Sometimes he's so in tune with me that he can read my thoughts even as they're forming. Not that I know what lies ahead. All I can say for sure is that a space will open up between us and the temperature will drop. Perhaps he was right to feel sad.

I ride down to Lungotevere then follow the river. As I pass the Isola Tiburina there is the smell of golden syrup. It's like a memory from another country, a different time. I pull over to the side of the road. The smell's still there, but I can't account for it. There's no factory, no shop. I accelerate away again.

Tonight the city smells like England.

Though it's late I don't know if I'll be able to sleep. It's almost as if I had the coke he offered me. My body feels wound up like a clockwork toy. I need to be set down, let loose.

Goodbye, I whisper as I turn away from the river.

Goodbye, goodbye.

When my father calls on September 6th everything's in place and it's only two days until I act. He's in the Middle East, he

says. In Syria. He's sorry he's been elusive recently. I tell him
I understand. The line swoops and crackles beneath our
words. Sometimes it sounds hollow, as if we're talking in a
cave. Other times, the connection cuts out altogether and
there's an absence that makes me feel queasy, like the numb-
ness you get in your arm when you rest your head on it and
fall asleep.

I ask him how he is.

He's fine, he says. He's not in any danger. Most of the shells
are landing in rebel-held suburbs. I say I'm fine too. Rome is
relatively peaceful at the moment, I tell him, despite a night
of heavy fighting.

'Have there been demonstrations?' He sounds surprised,
annoyed with himself. If there's one thing he can't stand, it's
missing out on breaking news.

'Dad,' I say. 'It was a joke.'

Silence.

At last he says, 'Only a month to go.' Until I start at university, he means. 'You must be excited.'

I say I am. It's easier if I agree.

'You're so lucky,' he says. 'I wish—'

I know what he wishes. He wishes he could be in my position, with everything ahead of him. He has no idea what he's
wishing for. He doesn't have a clue.

I ask him when he's coming home.

'In about a week,' he says, then he appears to hesitate. 'It's
not confirmed. The situation's volatile.'

It's ten years since we moved to Italy but when I hear my
father on the phone it always makes me think of London. I
see our house in Tufnell Park. The peaked, slightly Gothic
roof, the red-brick walls. The hollyhocks by the front door.

Green trees, grey sky. I can almost smell the rain. My father would often be abroad, working on a story. It was just me and my mother, for weeks at a time. She wasn't ill yet but she wasn't quite right either. I would come home from school and find her lying on the sofa in the front room with her forearm over her eyes, or sometimes she would be asleep in bed. In our last year in the city she was always tired.

'Kit?'

'I'm still here.'

'You'll need an umbrella. It's not like Rome, you know.'

He's trying to be light and humorous but I sense him turning away, losing interest, even though his mobile's still pressed against his ear. When filing his reports he tends to stand at an angle to the camera, alert to what is happening behind him, in the unstable darkness of a foreign night. *This is David Carlyle. CNN. Benghazi.*

Or Damascus.

Or Kabul.

When the phone call's over I realise he didn't ask me how I was. He never does. He thinks it's a meaningless convention, a waste of breath. But I always tell him anyway.

Seconds later, Dani calls from Puglia. It's a relief to hear her voice, but when I tell her about the man I slept with her response surprises me. She thinks I was reckless. I laugh and say we used a condom but that isn't what she meant.

'He could have been anyone,' she says. Then she pauses and says, 'Sometimes you frighten me.'

'Dani,' I say, 'I wouldn't have chosen *anyone*—' though even as I speak I realise there was something completely arbitrary and instantaneous about the decision. It was as if I'd been drinking. Not for a moment did it occur to me to think of consequences.

That afternoon I go out and buy an umbrella.

Two days later, on September 8th, I flag down a taxi on corso Vittorio Emanuele II. I have a suitcase with me, and my new umbrella. Draped over my right arm is the cashmere coat my father gave me when I turned eighteen. I'm carrying my passport, several credit cards, and a print-out of my boarding pass. Round my neck is my most valuable possession – a small silver heart-shaped locket containing two pieces of my mother's hair, one blonde and wavy, the other a glinting dark-brown, almost metallic. The blonde hair is what fell out when she first had chemotherapy. The brown is what grew back. I have closed my deposit account and withdrawn my savings. The money my mother left me. My inheritance. It's enough to keep me going for a while.

A few hours earlier, at dawn, I walked to the Ponte Mazzini, my phone in my hand. The city sticky-eyed, hung-over. Still half asleep. I stopped next to a lamp-post in the middle of the bridge. White mist drifting above the river, a blurred pink sun. Leaning on the parapet, I held my phone out over the water and then let go. I thought I heard it ringing as it fell. Who would be calling so early? Massimo? Dani? I would never know. In Rome people ring you all the time and mostly it's not about anything in particular. Back in the apartment I downloaded Eraser and cleaned my hard drive, not just deleting my files but overwriting them so as to make retrieval more or less impossible. I left my laptop under the arch on via Giulia with a note that said FREE COMPUTER. If I'm to pay proper attention, if this is to work, there's no option but to disconnect, to simplify. From now on, life will register directly, like a tap on the shoulder or a kiss on the lips. It will be *felt*.

Entering the station, I have an image of myself a week ago, standing beneath the Departures board, my presence implausible, unreal, as though my lungs were drained of oxygen and my veins were empty. How things have turned around since then! On the train to the airport everything we pass seems highlighted or in relief. The bleached papyrus grass that grows next to the railway line, the waste-ground where gypsies often camp. The big blue signs on station platforms. VILLA BONELLI, MAGLIANA. MURATELLA. Strange how a journey that is only just beginning can feel so final.

At Fiumicino, while queueing for Security, I let out a cry. The old man in front of me turns round and asks if something's wrong. His face is kind, concerned.

'It's my umbrella,' I say. 'I must have left it on the train.'

'You can buy another one.' He chuckles. 'It's not the last umbrella in the world.'

'But my father gave it to me—'

I look at the floor. Why am I lying?

'Your father will forgive you,' the old man says. 'I know he will.'

Two

Rain slants across the window as the plane drops out of the belly of the cloud. Flat wet fields appear below, and rows of trees with yellow leaves. Cars slide along a road that looks silver-plated. Germany. I feel my insides twist, a tightness in my throat. A kind of homesickness. I realise I'm missing my mother and the years when there were three of us. That time's gone for ever, though. My home's gone too. The past is what I'm homesick for.

The plane shudders when it hits the runway, lurching right then left, as if seeking a way out. Mist gathers behind the wheels. A faint burst of applause from the back, the airy roar of brakes.

Before I flew, I Googled 'Berlin accommodation' and found several cheap hotels in and around Kluckstrasse. There's talk online of a red-light area nearby but that doesn't bother me and Kluckstrasse has the great advantage of being central. Walter-Benjamin-Platz is only four stops away on the U-Bahn.

Outside the terminal I climb into a taxi.

'Kluckstrasse, please,' I say.

The driver gives me a look in the rear-view mirror. His glasses have caramel-coloured lenses that make his eyes difficult to see.

I say it again. 'Kluckstrasse.'

At last, and reluctantly – or so it seems to me – he pulls away. It's my clothes perhaps. My luggage. He equated me with somewhere more upmarket.

I stare through the window. Berlin is grey – a gritty, grainy grey. There's no warmth, no beauty; I've left all that behind. I wonder if my father has been to Germany. He probably has. His job has taken him all over the world. His absences used to be a mystery to me but I became accustomed to him being gone. It seemed normal, almost comforting. When he reappeared, after weeks away, I would throw myself into his arms and he would have a spicy smoky smell that I always thought of as his 'work' – the smell of train stations, airport lounges, rented cars – and he would give me a T-shirt or a key-ring, proof of where he'd been.

We pass an Argentinian steak house, then a restaurant called Villa Fellini. The Mercedes smells of deodorant and stale cigarettes. The radio is turned down low. From time to time the driver takes his right hand off the wheel to rub his chin or scratch an ear. With his greased-back hair and his 70s sunglasses he looks as if he might once have been a singer in a seedy cabaret – or on a cruise ship, like Berlusconi.

'This is Kluckstrasse,' he says at last.

There isn't a hotel in sight so I ask him to keep going. A car behind us honks then overtakes. I tell him to turn right. I'm just guessing but as we round a corner I see a two-storey building painted a garish blue. A small sign says HOTEL.

'Stop here,' I say.

Once he has pulled over and switched off the meter I hand him the fare. He turns in his seat and looks straight at me for the first time.

'How old are you?' he asks.

I tell him I'm twenty, though actually I'm still nineteen.

He looks away, then murmurs something.

'I'm sorry?' I say. 'I didn't understand.'

As he passes me my change I lean forwards but he keeps his eyes fixed on the windscreen. There's a thin red line near his ear. He must have cut himself shaving.

I try again. 'What did you say?'

He adjusts his glasses, then gets out, opens the boot and carries my suitcase to the kerb. By the time I'm standing on the pavement he's already back behind the wheel. His indicator flashes and he drives away.

The sky is the colour of an oyster and has a clamminess as well, a glossy, slightly swollen quality. I bring my eyes back down. Opposite the hotel is a squat purple building with no windows. Next to the purple building is a pair of wrought-iron gates painted gold and then a green wall with a sticking-out sign that says AUTO-GLASEREI. Beyond that is a railway bridge. The gutters are clogged with wet leaves. It's quiet, just the murmur of traffic and the distant scream of logs or metal being cut.

I move towards the hotel entrance. The lobby is the size of a doctor's waiting-room with a pre-fab look to it as though, like a film set, it's only temporary and could be dismantled at a moment's notice. The woman on reception has a sallow unlined face, her eyebrows plucked into thin black arcs. I can't tell where she's from. Iran perhaps. Or Lebanon. A room with a shower will cost me fifty euros. If I share a bathroom it's only forty. Her voice is casual, musical, and she makes no attempt to sell the place.

I ask if I can see a forty-euro room. She hands me a key

attached to an oblong piece of wood by a metal ring. The room is on the ground floor at the end of a narrow passageway. Between the two beds is a night-table with an ashtray and a lamp. I move to the window and part the net curtains. On the far side of the alley that runs past the back of the hotel is a streetlight and a wall of blackened bricks. The cool, faintly alcoholic air of Berlin drifts through a crack in the window-frame. The smells are all unnatural – creosote, petrol, methylated spirits. I put my face close to the glass. Out there, somewhere, is Klaus Frings, with his penthouse apartment and his wounded heart . . .

I return to reception.

'Well?' the woman says.

'It's perfect.'

Her eyebrows lift but she says nothing.

That night, after eating in a pizzeria on Potsdamerstrasse, I lie awake for hours. Though the curtains are closed, the room floods with yellow light from the streetlamp outside the window. When I think of Klaus Frings I see a man who is a few years older than me and only an inch or two taller. I suppose I'm being influenced by the sound of his name. Those two pert monosyllables, which seem to invite a limerick, suggest someone with a brittle distracted air. He might even shiver a little, but like a greyhound this would be a sign of good breeding, not nervousness or feeling cold. His clothes seem anachronistic, as if he belongs to another period in history. A figured waistcoat, a cane with a carved head. He doesn't resemble anyone I know. He's like a fictional character, a person I've made up. As I turn on to my side rhymes begin to pop into my head: *drinks, winks, stinks, kinks, sphynx.* The limerick's writing itself.

In the middle of the night I'm woken by a tapping on the window.

'*Was gibt's?*' I call out. What is it?

Nobody answers. My room is no longer yellow. The street-light must have been switched off.

Later I hear bedsprings creaking overhead. A door opens, then closes. A toilet flushes. Someone laughs and then the creaking starts again.

In the morning, after breakfast, I approach the woman on reception and ask who occupies the room above mine. She says she can't give out that kind of information.

I nod. 'It's important to be—' But I can't remember the German for 'discreet' so I say, 'It's important not to tell everything.'

She stares at me.

'No, really,' I say. 'I mean it.'

I walk round to the back of the hotel. The bulb in the streetlamp outside my room is broken, and glass fragments glitter on the cobbles. The window above mine is closed. Hot-pink blinds are lowered almost to the sill.

My first full day disappoints me with sunlight and clear skies, but at least I know it can't go on. Berlin is one of the coldest cities in Europe. Last winter was severe, with heavy snowfalls as late as March. The papers talked of 'Arctic air systems' and temperatures that were 'Siberian'. Out on the street there's something brisk and combative in people's gestures and expressions, even in the language they use. How lazy Rome seems by comparison! A city of lotus-eaters.

It takes forty minutes to reach Walter-Benjamin-Platz. Open at both ends, with tall utilitarian arcades running along its northern and southern sides and a paved area in between, the square feels like a civic monument, built to commemorate a loss or a catastrophe. Since I don't have Klaus Frings's exact address I start at the south-east corner of the square and move slowly westwards, checking the name-plates on every door. When I reach Leibnitzstrasse without having found him I cross to the north-west corner and work my way east. Halfway along I begin to panic. What if he has moved? Approaching the penultimate door, I scan the names on the upright rectangle of tarnished metal: *Nowaczyk, Lutz König, Dr Popp, Hauff-Buschmann, Wimpary, Frau C Alvarez, Frings*—

Frings!

Once again I admire the clipped, almost porcelain ring of that single, simple monosyllable. I touch the buzzer next to his name. Round and satisfyingly concave, it seems to be have been constructed with my fingertip in mind. I step back. Now what? Should I make contact with him? If so, how? I feel ahead of myself, out of sync, like a detective trying to solve a crime that has yet to be committed. The name 'Klaus Frings' is all I have, but what is it exactly that I want? I need to think.

I turn away.

Built into an arch in the corner of nearby Savignyplatz is a café with dark wood tables and red chairs. As I walk in, the radio is playing a Dinah Washington song. My father has always had a thing about Dinah Washington. He used to sing along sometimes when we were in the car. *What a Difference a Day Makes* or *September in the Rain*. His voice wasn't bad but my mother would grin at me and shake her head despairingly, blonde hair covering one eye. An S-Bahn train thunders overhead, blotting out the music. The whole café shudders, but the man behind the bar doesn't react. His

thinning hair is the colour of mahogany. I order a hot chocolate, then sit by the window.

When he brings my drink I say, '*Mille grazie.*'

'You're Italian?'

'Sorry. I forgot where I was.'

I'm English, I tell him, though I've lived in Rome since I
was nine. He's from the north, he says. A small town near
Brescia. But he has been in Berlin for fifteen years. The door
opens and a woman enters. He excuses himself.

I look around. Standing at the counter is a man in his fifties,
dressed in a black suit and a black polo-neck. Another,
younger man is sitting at a table, silver headphones over his
ears. A third man is reading a magazine, a bag of cat litter at
his feet. Is one of them Klaus Frings? It's possible. Anything's
possible. Another train rumbles past, the reflected carriages
flowing right to left across the upstairs windows of the building opposite and crumpling as they cross the glass. I sit there
for an hour. When I finally go up to the bar to pay, the owner
says he hopes to see me again before I fly back to Italy. I nod
and smile and say I hope so too.

For the rest of the day I pretend to be the tourist he took
me for, spending the afternoon at a gallery. Later, in the
shop, I buy a notebook with unlined pages and several
Gerhard Richter postcards. His blurred portraits seem a
comment on my own existence, all the unimportant details
stripped away.

By five-thirty I'm back in Walter-Benjamin-Platz. This
time I notice the hexagonal green kiosk at the east end of
the square. As I approach Klaus Frings's building a man of
about seventy steps out, his white hair gathered in a ponytail. I slip past him, into the lobby. Behind a desk of blonde

wood is a man in a grey uniform, his newspaper open at the sports pages.

'Good evening,' I say. 'Is Herr Frings at home?'

The porter looks up. 'He's not back yet.'

I glance at my watch.

'He should be here in half an hour or so.' The porter's gaze drops to my breasts. 'Would you like to wait?'

I shake my head. 'Thanks all the same.'

Out in the square again I lean against the kiosk. The sky has clouded over and a damp wind is blowing. It's beginning to get dark. During the next thirty minutes only two people enter the building. The first is a middle-aged woman cradling a pug in the crook of her arm. The second is the man with the ponytail.

At ten past six a tall figure turns out of Wielandstrasse and into the square, passing within an arm's length of me. He wears a fawn overcoat and is carrying a leather briefcase. Instinctively I know it's Frings, even though he looks nothing like the person I imagined. I wait until he's about to open the door to his building, then I call his name. He jerks to a halt, then turns slowly. Standing between two of the pillars that form the arcade, he peers out into the dark.

'*Hallo?*' he says.

My heart somersaults. He responded to the name.

'Valentina?'

Valentina. She must be the girl who left him. But would she really wait in the dark for him to come home from work? Surely not – especially if she was the one who ended the relationship. It's more likely that he is upset at having been rejected and can't stop thinking about her.

'Valentina? Is that you?'

I flatten myself against the kiosk and keep quiet. Since he only heard his name called once, I'm hoping he will think he imagined it. A sound carried on the wind, a voice inside his head . . . He looks right and left, then swings round and vanishes into the building. I pray the porter doesn't mention me. The last thing I want is for Klaus to learn that a foreign-sounding girl has been asking for him. I need to come from nowhere, like an apparition. Like a gift.

Like a reward.

The next morning I'm in Walter-Benjamin-Platz at half-past six. I have no idea when Klaus leaves for work and I don't want to miss him. It's still dark and the air has a bitter, coppery smell that is faintly sulphurous, like burnt matches. The layout of the square proves useful. I take up a position on the south side, behind a pillar. Once in a while I walk out on to Wielandstrasse, but never so far that I lose sight of the glass front door and its upright rectangle of yellow light.

I have been waiting for about an hour when Klaus appears, his head lowered, his face illuminated by the small screen of his phone. He turns right, towards Leibnitzstrasse. He's dressed in the same fawn coat and carrying the same leather briefcase. I can't help smiling. It's as if he understands what is required of him – that he needs to be immediately recognisable – and is cooperating.

He has long legs and he walks fast. Every now and then I have to break into a run, otherwise I might be left behind. He stops at a kiosk to buy a paper. I hang back, feigning interest in a shop window. The air is fuzzy, pixellated, like a kind of interference. A row of cars trembles at the lights.

On Giesebrechtstrasse he hurries across the road and

disappears into a *café-konditorei*. From the pavement I watch him talking to the waitress. They seem to know each other. Her dark hair is piled messily on top of her head, and the top three buttons of her black cardigan are undone, showing off her cleavage. She has a sloppy, sensual look about her, as if she just got out of bed. Does Klaus find her attractive? I push the door open. The waitress looks round. Her instant, natural smile surprises me. I took her for one of those women who reserve all their seductive energy for men.

I sit by the wall and order a coffee and a croissant, then I take out my notebook and my pen. Klaus has chosen a table in the middle of the café, and is partially obscured by a woman eating a slice of cake with a fork. Klaus shakes his paper open. This is the closest we have ever been, and once again I wonder what I want from him. Absorbed in the *Frankfurter Allgemeine*, Klaus remains quite unaware of me.

I make a quick sketch of his head. His eyes are too small for his face, and his lips have a plumpness that could seem either generous or sulky, depending on his mood. His hair, which is wavy and light-brown, starts high up on his forehead. Afterwards, I jot down a few simple observations. His hands are large and workmanlike, not elegant at all, though he takes good care of his nails, which are filed straight across and show no sign of being bitten. His glasses, which he removes whenever the waitress speaks to him, have turquoise frames. They look expensive. He wears a watch, but no rings. I estimate his height at one metre ninety, his weight in the region of eighty-five kilos. If I had to guess his age I would say mid- to late-thirties.

I sip my coffee. Something about his appearance disturbs

me. It's true that he in no way resembles the Klaus Frings of my imagination, but that's not it. No, what I find unsettling is that, even though I have now set eyes on him, he still feels like a made-up character. When I first heard his name – in another city, fifteen hundred kilometres away! – I saw him not as a real person but as an opportunity, a trigger. That feeling persists. To be in the same room as him, to have narrowed the distance so dramatically – to have discovered that he *actually exists*: it's hard to believe I've managed it. But somehow there's a gap between the idea of Klaus Frings and the man himself.

The clock ticks heavily, sumptuously. Though Klaus Frings has left the café I can't seem to move. I see my father lying on his back in an air-conditioned hotel room, hands linked behind his head. His eyes are open. His flak jacket, his dusty desert boots . . .

I whisper in his ear. *I've gone.*

If people love you enough, can they hear you?

He has been up all night, travelling with an aid convoy. Endless checkpoints, everyone on edge. Young boys with semi-automatics. His room is tinted with the first lurid flush of dawn. Through the sealed window comes the metallic wail of the muezzin. He's so tired that he can't sleep.

I'm not here any more. I've gone.

In front of the window is a round table and two chairs with low backs. On the table is a half-empty bottle of brandy and two water-glasses. One of the glasses has a smudge of lipstick near the rim. Once, a few hours after my father returned from covering a story in Eritrea, I heard him arguing with my mother. She was accusing him of having an affair. He was denying it.

35

He sits up, puts his feet on the floor and rubs his face with both hands, then he reaches for the phone and dials my number. The screen on my phone lights up. Rocks and sludge. A few tin cans, a bicycle wheel. A woman's shoe. What happens when you call a phone that is lying at the bottom of a river? Does it sound as if it has been switched off? Does it sound dead?

My father calls, and I don't answer. He thinks nothing of it. I'm busy or else I'm talking to a friend. Or maybe I lost my charger. But what if he tries again tomorrow, and I'm still not answering? And then again, the day after? What will he think when he keeps failing to get hold of me? How long before it occurs to him that something might have happened?

Walking east along the Ku'damm, I come across the Kaufhaus des Westens, one of the most famous department stores in Europe. Unthinkingly, I step inside. I wander aimlessly among the perfume counters and champagne promotions until, all of a sudden, I remember the umbrella I left on the train. I take an escalator to the third floor where I choose a dark green model that is small enough to fit into my case. As I turn to leave, the woman serving me asks if I have visited the food hall. I shake my head. Oh, but you must, she says. *Es ist fabelhaft.* It's wonderful. She's so insistent that I promise I will have a look.

Half an hour later, while standing by a gloomy green tank, watching lobsters clamber over one another in exaggerated, almost theatrical slow-motion, I hear a fierce abbreviated hiss, like air escaping from a tyre. Behind the meat counter is a young man in a crisp white jacket, a black bow tie and a long white apron. He has the pallid soggy face of somebody who doesn't get much sun. He glances left and right, then beckons me over.

'What's your name?' he says in German.

I tell him.

He frowns. 'You're a student?'

'I'm a tourist.'

'OK.' His eyes are a dull greenish-brown, like olives. 'Can I trust you?'

I stare at him, and he repeats the question.

'That depends,' I say. But the suggestion of a mission sends the blood tumbling through my veins.

'Take this.' He passes a KaDeWe plastic bag over the counter. His face has become sober, professional. 'When you leave the store, go to Zoologischer Garten and put the bag in one of the lockers.'

'I don't know,' I say.

But then I remind myself that in these strange circumstances, in this new life, it's hard to predict what might be relevant or beneficial. There's really only one rule. Keep an open mind. Nothing that is offered should be rejected out of hand.

'Please.' The young man's olive-coloured eyes shine briefly, as if they've just been dipped in oil.

I take the bag, which is heavier than I expected. Inside is a package wrapped in the thick white paper butchers use.

'Zoo,' he says. 'The station. You can find it?'

'Yes.'

'It's not far from here.' Once again, he sends rapid glances right and left. 'Meet me in Witternbergplatz at five o'clock.' He talks out of the side of his mouth, like a gangster, his eyes slanting back along the counter. 'There's an *Imbiss* there. You know what an *Imbiss* is?'

'No.'

'It's like a kiosk. You can buy coffee, or a hot dog, or—' He hesitates as the metal door behind him opens a fraction, then closes again. 'Or *pommes-frites*.' He gives me directions. 'Meet me there,' he says. 'There are red umbrellas, with Coca-Cola logos on them. You'll have the key to the locker, yes?'

'Yes,' I say. 'All right.'

'Here's something for you. You look hungry.' He passes me another, smaller package, wrapped in the same white paper.

I drop the second package into the plastic bag.

A woman in the same jacket, apron and bow-tie appears at the far end of the counter. She walks with her elbows lifted away from her sides as if she's up to her waist in water.

'Your change,' the man says in a loud voice, handing me some coins.

As I travel back to the ground floor I realise that the man at the meat counter is living with an intensity and purpose that mirrors my own. Did he recognise those qualities in me, or did I simply show up at the right moment, when he wasn't being monitored? And what exactly has he given me? Am I breaking the law? What if I'm stopped?

No one stops me.

Out on the pavement I keep walking, my body moving automatically, my mind quite empty, and I arrive at Zoologischer Garten a few minutes later without having consulted a map or even having paid much attention to where I was going. I find the lockers in a draughty corridor lined with yellow tiles. The locker doors are a grubby cream colour with numbers stencilled along the top in black. Station announcements echo off the walls.

I remove the smaller of the two packages, then place the

bag in a locker and follow the instructions on the door. *1: insert the correct money. 2: turn the key. 3: check the door is locked.* I pay for the locker with the change the man at the meat counter gave me. At the time I thought what he was doing was for the benefit of that burly woman who may or may not have been his supervisor – he was simulating the last stage in a transaction that never actually took place – but now it occurs to me that he might also have been thinking ahead, handing me the coins I would need if I was to carry out the mission he was entrusting me with. Impressed by his ability to operate on two levels at once, I pocket the key and leave the station.

On my way out I pass a photo booth, its curtain drawn aside. The light issuing from the interior is white but hazy – a science fiction glow. I sit on the seat and feed some coins into the slot. The flash goes off four times, then I wait outside. A strip of photographic paper drops into a silver metal cage. My eyes are shut in every picture. A smile smoulders on my lips. I could be asleep and in the middle of a beautiful dream. I could be dead and happy to be dead.

I walk east. The sun comes and goes. When I reach the Tiergarten, a path unspools in front of me. A gold statue of a winged woman stands on a high column, storm-clouds massing behind her. A cyclist hisses past on wheels as thin as hoops. I find a bench and take out the package. Inside are two crusty rolls stuffed with smoked ham. I pick up a roll and take a bite. Food has never tasted better.

At five past five I'm standing by the kiosk in Witternbergplatz watching two teenage girls dip chips in mayonnaise when the man from the meat counter appears. He has changed into a black shirt, a black leather jacket and a pair of jeans, but he has the same eager pasty look he had in the shop. He asks if I have the key.

'You should eat,' I say, 'or it'll look suspicious.'

'Suspicious?'

'Like we're doing a drug deal or something.'

He stares at me. His throat is flushed as if he's got a rash. 'Right,' he says. 'OK.'

Stepping beneath the awning, he orders a *Currywurst* and lays a crumpled five-euro note on the counter.

'Thanks for the ham rolls,' I say.

'They were good?'

'Very good.'

He nods. 'The meat's high quality, I have to say.' He sounds so earnest that I can't help smiling, but he doesn't notice. A paper plate balanced on one hand, he spears a chunk of sausage with a white plastic fork and pokes it into his mouth. 'Any problems?'

'No. I put the bag in a locker, just like you asked me to.'

'Thanks.' He licks curry sauce off his thumb, then looks away, towards Tauentzienstrasse.

I remove the key from my pocket and feel its weight transfer from me to him a moment before I hand it over.

'You already know my name,' I say. 'What's yours?'

'Oswald Überkopf.' The look he gives me tells me he has been teased, or even bullied.

'Oswald? You don't hear that too often.'

The wind whips his hair across his eyes. He tips his plate and fork into the bin then reaches up with both hands. As he scrapes his hair back behind his ears, the sleeves of his leather jacket ride up, revealing a tattooed inscription on the inside of his left forearm. The letters have a Gothic look, but I don't see them for long enough to decipher them.

The sun has dropped below the level of the rooftops and the square is plunged in chilly shadow. A shiver of familiarity goes through me. A sense of eternity, and the abyss. Tomorrow, at the café on Giesebrechtstrasse, I will sit near Klaus Frings again, and this time I will talk to him.

'Are you free tomorrow night?' Oswald is eyeing me, head cocked, thumbs stuck in the belt-hooks of his jeans.

'I don't know,' I say. 'I'm involved in some negotiations at the moment.'

'I thought you were a tourist—'

'And anyway, I can't constantly be doing you favours.'

'It's not a favour.' He scuffs the ground with the side of his shoe. 'I'd like to show you something. I think you might be interested.'

I ask for his number. The fact that I don't have a mobile surprises him – *everyone* has mobiles – but I choose not to explain. He scribbles his contact details on a piece of paper. I'll call, I tell him, though I don't say when.

As I turn away he says my name. I glance over my shoulder. With his flushed neck and his wrinkled black shirt he looks scorched, as if he just escaped from a burning building.

'You haven't asked me what was in the bag,' he says.

'That's true,' I say. 'I haven't.'

'Aren't you curious?'

Other people's mysteries – I've got no time for them. I've got too many of my own.

'It's your business, isn't it,' I say.

Then I walk on.

* * *

41

When I approach my hotel an hour later, a white car with a green stripe down the side is parked out the front. POLIZEI, it says. Police. My mouth is dry suddenly and I pause beneath a tree. Surely it can't be me they're looking for. Not so soon. I take a breath and push through the glass door. In reception two officers are questioning the woman who runs the place. She hands my key over and I move on down the corridor. A silence expands behind me and I sense the policemen watching me but they don't call out for me to stop.

Back in my room I turn the TV on. My German isn't bad – with Oswald I remembered the word for 'negotiations' – but I need to become more fluent. On the news they discuss Angela Merkel's chances of winning a third term in office. Later, there are bulletins about preparations for the Oktoberfest and about pollution in rivers. I think of all the e-mails, tweets and text messages piling up inside my phone, or circling in the infinite expanses of the web, unable to reach their destination, like planes kept in a holding pattern above an airport. My father likes to talk about travelling in the 70s and 80s, and how you would lose all contact with those you left behind. You might write postcards, he says, or letters, but you never used the phone, not unless it was a real emergency. When you were gone, you were *really gone*. It's different for you, he says. You were born into a world where people communicate non-stop. It's not a choice. It's a habit – a necessity. Like breathing.

At eleven o'clock I switch the TV off. Outside, a heavy rain is coming down. I leave my room again. When I pass reception I ask the woman what the police wanted. They were looking for illegal immigrants, she says.

On the pavement I look up into the sky. The rain turns

copper-coloured as it drops through the light of a streetlamp. I open my umbrella. People are queueing on the other side of the road, and I can hear the thud of a bassline, fast and muffled, dull. The purple building seems to shake.

'Hey.'

A scrawny man peers into my face, his eyes hard and shiny, like ball bearings, a crooked fence of teeth. I move away, towards the railway bridge. He shouts after me, words I don't understand. The bass notes fade. A train screeches in the dark.

I walk for an hour. The rain has driven most people indoors. At a T-junction near Potsdamerstrasse a woman leans against a wall, thigh-high patent-leather boots, gold handbag dangling from one shoulder. A car idles by the kerb. I turn the corner. In the next street a balloon that says HAPPY BIRTHDAY is caught in the upper branches of a tree. When I think about how I came into the world, my body starts to throb. It's like toothache, but all over. After eight years in a storage tank I was finally lifted into blinding daylight, a foretaste of the birth that was to come. They moved me from one thawing solution to another – T1, T2, T3, T4 – then put me in an incubator. I had been there before, of course. This was the place where I divided. *Cleaved.* But everything was different this time round. I was being prepared for implantation. I experienced a gradual loss of control, a delicious incontinence. I was unfurling, expanding. Taking shape. A sudden, hectic tumble into life. My cells were yellow – a healthy yellow – and the heat coursing through me triggered urgency and purpose. It wasn't my decision to feel hopeful. Hope happened to me. And then the warm red darkness of my mother's womb . . .

Later that night, as I lie in bed with the lights off, I hear distant yelling.

The scrawny man picking a fight.

Police arresting immigrants.

When I enter the café on Giesebrechtstrasse the following morning, Klaus Frings is already there, sitting at the same table as before. I take the table next to him and order a double espresso. Klaus leafs through his paper, seemingly oblivious to everybody else. Though his overcoat and reading-glasses look expensive I don't see him as a businessman. He could be an architect, I'm thinking, or the curator of a small museum. I'm so focused on him, and speculating so intently, that I'm surprised he doesn't sense my presence, but his eyes don't leave the page, not even when he reaches for his coffee.

My espresso arrives. It's time I made contact and I choose an obvious opening, the one least likely to arouse suspicion.

'Could you pass the sugar?'

He looks at me over the top of his glasses, his eyes wary, almost hostile, and I remember that this is a man who has recently been jilted. He might be feeling resentful towards women at the moment. He might have it in for all of us. Or perhaps it's simply that he dislikes being interrupted.

'The sugar?' I say again, more gently.

'Of course.' He hands me the bowl.

Thanking him, I select two brown sugar-lumps, drop them into my coffee and pass the bowl back to him. 'I'm sorry,' I say. 'My German's hopeless.'

'Not at all.' The angle of his head alters. 'You were here yesterday.'

I smile but say nothing.

'What are you doing in Berlin?' He puts his paper down. 'Are you a student?'

'Not exactly.' I lower my eyes, looking at my coffee. I imagine the sugar-lumps dissolving – a thin layer of crystals on the bottom, and the hot bitter darkness overhead. 'No one knows I'm here. In Berlin, I mean.'

'You've run away?'

'I'm nineteen. Nearly twenty.'

He looks past me, towards the door. 'I didn't mean—'

'It doesn't matter. I can't really go into detail, though. Let's just say that I'm experimenting with coincidence.'

'Is that what this is – a coincidence?'

I give him a quick look. Has the English woman been on the phone to him? *We ran into this girl the other day – at the cinema . . .* But no, why would she mention me? Above all, why would she mention me *to him?* I didn't even hint that I might be interested in her friend, Klaus Frings – and besides, it's clear from his expression that he's teasing me.

'So where do you live when you're not—' and he pauses – 'experimenting?'

'Rome.'

'Ah. That explains the tan.' He appears to think for a moment, leaning back in his chair, one hand massaging the back of his neck. 'Are you staying in the neighbourhood?'

'No.' I mention the hotel where I have spent the last two nights. He hasn't heard of it, which is hardly a surprise. I tell him where it is. His frown returns.

'That's not a good area. At night it can be—' He doesn't want to say it. The word *dangerous*.

'It's not so bad.'

'How long do you plan to stay there?'

'I'm not sure.' Once again, I look down into my coffee cup.

His gaze lingers on me – I can feel it, like heat – then he glances at his watch. 'I must go.' He stands up. 'Will you be here tomorrow?'

'Probably.'

He extends a hand. 'Klaus Frings.'

I know.

'I'm Katherine Carlyle,' I tell him. 'Most people call me Kit.'

'Kit.' He nods, then turns away.

Through the window I watch him run across the road. I don't think it's because he's in a hurry. I think it's because he knows I'm watching and he wants to look active, young.

By the time I leave the café it's after nine. I move through the city with no destination, no agenda, following whichever street takes my fancy. Unlike Rome, Berlin doesn't seem to have any hills. The sky, though cloudy, feels immense. At midday I catch a bus going west and spend the afternoon walking in the Grünewald. As I circle the Teufelssee, a small lake hemmed in by pines and birches, a woman appears on the path ahead of me. She's wearing a one-piece bathing-suit. Her feet are bare. She puts a hand out to steady herself, steps down into the lake and then stands still. The water cuts her off at the knees. Her bathing-suit and the water are both black, which makes her white limbs look detached, dismembered. At last she bends down and pushes forwards, her freestyle neat and confident, almost hydraulic. The lake peels back behind her, and suddenly my head is empty but for a single thrilling intuition. The world will part before me. I'm on a smooth sweet path to everything that matters.

* * *

Towards the end of the afternoon, on Heerstrasse, I hail a taxi and ask the driver to take me to Café Einstein. We labour east, through heavy traffic. Mist hides the tops of buildings and blurs the brightly-lit shop windows.

I passed the Einstein on my first morning, noting the name on the liver-coloured canopies above each window, and the inside of the café is just as ornate as the exterior. The rooms have high moulded ceilings and dark wood panelling, and the décor is old-world, all pale custard, clotted cream, and eau-de-nil. The waitresses wear starched white aprons that reach down to their ankles at the front, and the coffee is served in cups whose rounded rims are encircled with a band of gold. Sitting at a marble-topped table I look sideways. Infinite versions of myself curve off into the still green depths of a mirror.

I remember the time my father took me to a restaurant in Chinatown. This was during the winter when our house in Tufnell Park was up for sale. I would have been eight or nine. My father ordered Peking duck and chicken noodles. Afterwards, he bought me a gold cat with a paw that moved up and down in the air. He told me it would bring good fortune and I pretended to believe him, though I knew he had no time for lucky charms and wasn't even remotely superstitious. I can still see the cat's gold paw glinting and the red lanterns with their tasselled fringes swaying above the street. I can still remember the feeling of my hand in his. On our way home, as we stood on the lower deck of the bus, a man got on, his eyes so dark around the edges they looked burnt. He pointed a long trembling finger at us and said, *You're terminated.* I looked at my father and we both began to laugh. Later, my father told me he thought the man was ill – he had got on at a bus-stop outside a hospital – but it became our catchphrase. Until my mother heard it, that is. She had already been diagnosed with cancer by then, and she didn't see the funny side. *Turn around three times and spit. Both of you.*

The waitress who takes my order has tawny hair that is pinned up in a chignon. Her features look chiselled but when she smiles her face lights up and softens. Strapped to her hip is a chunky leather wallet that bounces like a holstered pistol as she strides about. When she returns with my coffee I feel the urge to speak to her, though I can't think of anything that isn't superficial or mundane.

'I really like this place,' I say.

'It's a strange place,' she says. 'It has a history.' She tells me the villa was once the home of Goebbels's mistress, a silent movie star, and also an illegal gambling den for SS officers.

I glance around but nothing of the past remains. 'Despite all that, there's something – I don't know – relaxing about it.'

'Not if you work here.' The waitress smiles with her eyes. 'Is this your first time?'

'Yes.'

'Did you see the garden?'

'No, not yet.'

'It's at the back. It's very nice to sit out there, especially in the summer.'

'I don't think I'll be here then.'

'That's a shame.' She looks at me, her eyes seeming to narrow a little, as before. 'Maybe you should come back – when the weather's warmer.'

'I'd like to,' I say, 'but it's not so easy.'

'Oh.' Glancing down, she smoothes her apron over her hips. 'Well, anyway. Enjoy your stay.'

* * *

'I've been thinking,' Klaus says as he approaches my table.

It's my fourth day in Berlin. The tree outside the café quivers in the wind, and a man hurries past, one hand pressed to the crown of his hat. Klaus is wearing a different overcoat, charcoal grey with black trim on the pockets and the collar, but his briefcase is the same, and judging by its ancient polished look I would guess it's a family heirloom, since he doesn't seem the type to go to flea-markets. I ask him if he would like to join me.

He sets his briefcase on the floor and sits down. All his actions are deliberate, precise. I'm beginning to be able to imagine his apartment. It will be ordered, spartan. Meticulously clean.

'I'm glad you came.' He sounds faintly disgruntled, as if there's an aspect of meeting me that he finds difficult.

'I like it here,' I say. 'The other place I like is Café Einstein.'

'Ah yes. The Einstein is very well known. An institution, really. I haven't been there for years.'

'Perhaps if you live here . . .'

'Yes, perhaps.'

The waitress brings his coffee. He glances up and thanks her. She's dressed more discreetly today, in a black ribbed sweater with a high neck.

He turns back to me. 'Where you're staying, it's not a good area.'

'I know. You told me that yesterday.'

He sighs.

'There's a nightclub,' I say.

'And prostitutes. There are also prostitutes.'

I remember the idling car and the woman in her shiny boots. I remember the laughter in the middle of the night. The creaking. The hot-pink blinds.

'It's not safe,' Klaus says. 'For a woman.'

As I watch him over the rim of my coffee cup, both my elbows propped on the table, something lifts inside me. I think I know where this is going.

'The thing is, I have a big apartment—' He pauses, then plunges on. 'You would have privacy.'

'I think you might have missed a sentence out.'

'I'm sorry?'

'Are you offering me a place to stay?'

'Oh, I see. Yes. That's what I wanted to say.'

'Do you live alone?'

'Yes.'

'Do you have a girlfriend?'

He hesitates.

A voluptuous woman in a dark-green dress stands smouldering beside him, one hand on his shoulder. *Valentina*. The expression on her face is privileged, dismissive. In her eyes I'm just another girl who is on the make. I may have high cheekbones and good legs but my breasts are small. I'm not a threat to her. I'm too skinny.

'No,' Klaus says at last. 'No girlfriend.'

I signal to the waitress that I want to pay. When I face Klaus again he looks fearful, almost panic-stricken. Perhaps he thinks he has failed to convince me, and that he has blown his chance. The woman in the dark-green dress is gone.

'You can have your own room,' he says quickly. 'For as long as you like.'

'I can't afford to pay much money.'

'I didn't ask for money.'

'You don't know me. I could be anyone.'

'So could I.' He leans back in his chair. For the first time I feel a certain authority or confidence come off him. Once again I wonder what he does.

I finish my coffee. The bill arrives.

'I have an idea,' Klaus says. 'Come and have a drink this evening. Then you can see the apartment for yourself.' He wants to text me his address and phone number, but I tell him I haven't got a phone. 'No phone?' Like Oswald, he doesn't know what to make of this. In the end he jots his details down on the back of my bill. 'The old-fashioned way,' he says, and smiles.

I study the address I have already memorised. 'What time should I come?'

'Seven.'

As I tuck the piece of paper into my bag I think of the dozens of messages I have received in the past few months, only to ignore them. Though this one is obviously for me – I've provoked it, *engineered* it – things haven't got much clearer. I'm reminded of Magritte's famous painting of a man in a bowler hat positioned in front of a mirror. Since the man is painted from behind, all anyone can see is his back. And in the mirror too that's all anyone can see.

Something jerks at the edge of my field of vision. It's the minute hand of the clock above the bar. I look at Klaus again. His eyes, small and steady, are fastened on my face.

'Won't you be late for work?' I say.

When I was twelve and a half my mother took me to a night-club on the coast road not far from Gaèta. We parked with two wheels in a ditch, then walked down a steep path between spiky clumps of aloe vera. The lanterns that hung on thin poles, guiding people to the entrance, swayed and flickered in the warm breeze that blew in off the sea.

'We'll have to pretend you're sixteen.' My mother gave me a sideways glance. 'Can you manage that?'

I wasn't sure.

'Leave it to me,' she said.

Somehow we slipped past the *buttafuori*, with their muscular necks, their headsets and their immaculate tuxedoes, and once we were beyond them my mother hugged me and then stood back.

'We did it,' she said. '*You* did it.'

I wish I had a photo of that moment – her face lit up and full of glee, and only the glittery Neapolitan darkness behind her.

I drank my first ever glass of *prosecco* that night. My mother drank two. Later, we danced. I let the music take me over. My hair grew heavy, spiny with sweat. You could go inside if you wanted, but there were outdoor dance floors too, some cut into the hillside, others down by the water. Steps that were tiled or inlaid with mosaic led from one level to the next. Intense green spotlights made the plants look hyper-real. Far below, white lines expanded sideways in the dark where the waves broke against the rocks.

A man with a shaved head asked my mother if she would dance with him.

'No,' she said. 'I can't.'

He looked puzzled. 'Why not?'

'I'm dying.'

'All the more reason.'

They stood still, staring at each other. Then my mother shook her head and took my hand and led me to the low wall where we had left our drinks.

I liked the man for his directness and his restraint. Round

52

his left bicep was a circular tattoo, an armband made of ink. His shaved head shone. When my mother turned him down he shrugged and moved away and though he continued to watch her from a distance he didn't approach her again. I don't think she wanted anyone to enter the world she had conjured for us. It wouldn't sustain another presence. It was too fragile and too rare, like bone china or gold leaf.

'I'm sorry,' she said later, when we were sitting on a bench next to the sea. 'I don't know why I said that.'

'To frighten him away,' I said.

She looked at me, her face as still and deep as water at the bottom of a well, and I thought I could see myself in it, far away and small and slightly blurred. She drew me close and kissed my hair. She told me she was proud of me and would always be proud of me. She said I should never forget that.

At two in the morning we drove north, back to Rome. A dense fog swirled around the car. We were passing through the Pontine Marshes, my mother said. Before Mussolini drained the area, it was a breeding ground for malaria. If the pumps were switched off, she told me, the water level would rise in less than a week. The fog thickened. She had to slow right down. It was as if we were motionless and big pale rags were being thrown at us. The temperature dropped and she turned the heater on. The heater – in July! Once, I peered upwards and saw a patch of dark clear sky loaded with stars, then the fog closed round the car again.

'We're very late,' my mother said. 'Your father's going to be worried.' She sighed. 'It wears me out.'

I didn't know what to say.

'He hates me for being ill,' she said. 'He thinks I've let him down.'

'He loves you too,' I said.

She reached across and squeezed my hand. 'I know, angel. I'm sorry. You probably think I'm talking nonsense.'

'I think you're beautiful.'

She began to cry and the trunk of a tree leapt towards us. She swerved just in time. 'Oh God.' The car bumped up on to the verge. She put the handbrake on and wiped her eyes. 'Fuck.' Now we were still, bits of fog drifted through the headlights like a flock of ghostly sheep.

'Are you all right?' I said.

I saw her gather herself, all the bravery and sparkle.

'You'll have a wonderful life,' she said, 'I know you will. You'll sleep in palaces, and dance with presidents, and—'

I must have given her a funny look because she broke off and started laughing.

'You'll see,' she said.

Then she shifted into gear and drove on.

I dozed with my forehead against the window and when I woke we were passing the Colosseum. In the moonlight it looked like a big piece of bone picked clean by vultures.

My mother looked across at me. 'Say what you used to say. You remember? When you were small?'

I smiled because I knew exactly what she meant.

'Go on,' she said. 'Please.'

I took a breath and turned to her.

'Are we there yet?'

'I love this painting.' Klaus stands next to the canvas, arms folded. 'It cost half my annual salary. What do you think?'

The painting in question, which is enormous, glossy, and

uniformly grey, hangs on the back wall of his living room, next to the arch that leads out to the hall.

'Very atmospheric,' I say.

'Atmospheric.' Klaus laughs. 'That's good.'

'I studied art history. At school.'

'Did you?' Still chuckling, he turns away. He runs his fingertips along the spines of a row of hardback books, then he lifts the corner of a kilim that is draped over the back of a chair and stares at it with unfeigned admiration. He seems constantly astonished by his environment, even though he's the person who is responsible for it.

I too step back from the painting. The woman in the cinema described Klaus's apartment as 'amazing', and it's easy to see why. When he first moved into the building he had four rooms, he told me earlier, but then he learned that his neighbour was returning to Hamburg. He bought her out and had the two apartments knocked into one. His living room is fifteen metres long, with huge plate glass windows that gaze out over the city.

'I must show you the roof terrace,' he says.

I follow him up a flight of stairs and out through a glass door. Dusk is descending fast and the sky has turned a shade of turquoise that makes the nearby rooftiles look magenta. A high-rise with the logo BHW on top lifts clear of all the other buildings. In the fading light it appears oddly insubstantial, almost transparent, like a portal. I swing round slowly, the breath shallow in my lungs. To the north-west, on the horizon, there is evidence of industry, smoke trailing from three tall chimneys.

'A wonderful view, no?' Klaus is standing at the edge of the roof, his hands in his trouser pockets, his weight on his heels.

'Yes,' I say. 'It's wonderful.'

I bring my eyes back down. With its minimalist vine-covered pergola, its wooden decking, and its glazed pots containing stands of pale-green bamboo, the terrace has an oriental feel.

'Have you lived in the Far East?' I ask.

Klaus laughs again. 'No, never.' He gestures at the table and the two glass bowls designed to shield candles from the wind. 'I sometimes entertain up here – if the weather's fine . . .'

We return to the living room. What is the connection between the prickly English couple and this curious, self-regarding German? I'd like to find out how they know each other, but it's the one question I can't ask.

Klaus leads me into the kitchen. In the middle of the room is a rectangular breakfast bar topped with black granite. A poster advertising a Rothko exhibition hangs on one wall, a framed black-and-white photograph on another. The photograph is by Su-Mei Tse, he tells me. He pours two glasses of chilled Sancerre, then opens a packet of unsalted cashew nuts and trickles them into a dish. I ask him what he does for a living.

'I'm an orthodontist.'

'An orthodontist?' My mind goes blank.

'I correct irregularities. In teeth.' He thinks I haven't understood the word.

'There must be a lot of irregularities around,' I say.

He looks at me uncertainly, his glass halfway to his lips.

I indicate the granite breakfast bar, the art, the wine. 'You seem to be doing pretty well.'

'Ah, I see. Yes. Well, there aren't many of us, so there is

plenty of work – and the procedures are quite costly.' He ushers me back into the living room, with its white leather sofa, its chairs upholstered in ethnic fabrics, its scatter rugs made from the skins of exotic animals. 'So you like the place?'

'I like it very much,' I say. 'I'm very happy.' Perhaps the wine is going to my head. I have eaten nothing since breakfast.

Klaus beams at me from the sofa. 'Would you like to stay?'

'Yes. If that's all right.'

'Of course. You can move in tonight. Your room is ready.'

'But I already paid for a room – at my hotel.'

'You'd be more comfortable here, no?'

'That's true.' I hesitate. 'I won't be here for long. I'm only passing through.'

'Don't talk about that now.' He gets to his feet. 'I have a car downstairs. Shall we collect your things?'

That night I dream about Adefemi. I wake in the dark, my body slick with sweat. I push the covers back. The images inside my head are real as memories, but jumbled, illogical. We're sitting in a bar, drinking beer out of brown bottles. He's telling me about a place he wants to take me to. His fingers, long and elegant, form all kinds of shapes in the air. First crowns, then fans. There's a beach of fine white sand, he says. And palm trees. And there are elephants clothed in red and gold. Elephants? I laugh. But I can see it all – the beach, the elephants, the sunlight splashing down on everything . . .

We need to pack. Our possessions are in storage, though. We hurry to the warehouse. We'll take the minimum, we say. Forget the rest. But there's much more than we remembered. Adefemi climbs to the top of a huge tottering pile of stuff and levers the lid off a box. Things start spilling out. I tell him it's getting late but he doesn't listen. Leaving him to sort through the boxes I enter another warehouse. The lighting is poor. I find myself in a wide central aisle with large cages on either side of me. In the cages, barely visible, are hundreds of people. They stare through the bars, their eyes unblinking, hollow. No one speaks or moves. At the far end of the warehouse, where the daylight is, I can see the place Adefemi has been describing – it's some distance away and far below, over land that is hilly, lush and green – and I know that if I want to see the palm trees and the elephants I will have to walk through the warehouse, from one end to the other, and I know I will never be able to do that . . .

My body has cooled down. A shiver shakes me.

Where am I?

I'm staying with Klaus Frings, in his apartment in Berlin. My heart thuds once, then dives deep. I leave the bed and move across the room. The moon is full and round on one side, worn on the other, the shape of a sucked sweet. I open the window. Cold air floods in.

I think of where Adefemi lives, two rooms and a kitchen on the ground floor of a building in Trastevere. His next-door neighbour is a Brazilian woman who is always laughing, especially when she's on the phone. Adefemi thinks she's a benign spirit; her laughter makes him happy. I remember telling him that it would drive me up the wall. He lowered his eyes. *Kit*, he said reproachfully. This was in the summer of 2012. We were sitting at his green table with the front door open. A view of parked motorbikes and a wire-mesh fence. Overhanging trees. I talked about my mother that night – the IVF, the cancer, the long slow death. I talked about my father too. *He never says he blames me but I'm sure he does. If they hadn't tried to have a child, she wouldn't have died. It was the IVF that gave her cancer. It was all my fault.* Adefemi watched me as I cried. Sometimes his tongue clicked against the roof of his mouth, a sound that meant he disagreed with me, and sometimes he held my hand, but he didn't tell me I was being hard on myself or self-indulgent or that none of it was true. He knew that would only make me angry. I was often astonished by how intuitive he was. How gentle. *He would do anything to get her back. He'd trade me for her, I know he would. He doesn't have any time for me. He can't even bring himself to look at me.* I was exaggerating, but I needed to exaggerate. I had to paint the darkest picture. Seizing a pair of scissors off the table, I snipped at the flesh at the base of my thumb. The pain was like a flash; it made me gasp. I dropped to my knees on the tiled floor, two kinds of tears in my eyes. The blood slid down my wrist with real purpose. Sometimes I have to prove that I exist. That I'm vibrant on the inside. Colourful. That I'm not a freak, an experiment. A shell. Adefemi looked frightened when I cut myself, but he watched me do it all the same, as though he knew it to be necessary. He seemed to realise that it was the mildest form of something that had to be undergone.

At four in the morning, when I finally stopped crying, Adefemi reached out and took off my T-shirt. I lifted my arms above my head to make it easier. I was wearing nothing underneath. I remember the feeling of my hair falling against my spine, my ribs, the small of my back. It was always cool in his apartment, even at the height of summer. The temperature dropped as soon as you walked in through the door. His bedroom smelled of cement, as if it had only recently been built. He kissed my bare shoulders and then unzipped my jeans and pulled them off. He kissed me on the mouth. His breath tasted clean but sour, like vinegar.

To start with, it was tender as the light of the new day pushing through the shutters, and it stayed tender for a long time, but then I wanted it to change. By the end it was fast and hard, relentless. The bed turned through forty-five degrees. Moved halfway across the room. The cries that came out of me were like bright paint flicked against a wall.

'I love the sounds you make,' he told me afterwards. 'It reminds me of those birds that hover so high up that you can't see them. But you can hear them. That's how you know they're there.'

'Skylarks,' I said.

My hand on his ribcage, his heart punching underneath. And the question I had then is the same as the one I have now.

Will anything be that good again?

A light clicks on in the apartment opposite, and a shadowy figure crosses behind a white translucent blind. Someone else who can't sleep. I climb back into bed and lie down on my stomach with my head turned sideways on the pillow and my legs out straight.

When I wake, the window is open and there's a puddle on the floor. It must have rained during the night. I mop up the water, using tissues from beside the bed. I'm about to go and shower when Klaus knocks on the door and asks if I'd like coffee.

I sit at the breakfast bar in a fluffy white bathrobe, finishing the *café-au-lait* Klaus made for me before he left for work. On the bread-board is a paper bag of croissants but I'm not hungry yet. When the hum of the fridge cuts out I can hear the murmur of traffic. Otherwise it's quiet. I put on another pot of coffee, then I read yesterday's paper and the latest edition of *Der Spiegel*. Later, I walk to the window and stare out over the pale-yellow gables of the houses opposite. On the roof of an office-block a huge Mercedes sign revolves. It's strange how distant Rome seems, and how irrelevant; I thought I would miss it more. I picture the apartment on via Giulia – the shelves of books on war and politics, the golden sofa with its lilac and burnt-orange cushions, the autumn sunlight spilling across the parquet floor . . . What will my father think when he returns? Will he put his bags down in the hall and call my name? Will the atmosphere strike him as unusual? Will the rooms look warm and lived-in, or abandoned, bereft, forlorn? First my mother left. Now me.

I turn back to the breakfast bar and pick up the scrap of paper Oswald gave me. I scrutinise his handwriting, which isn't spidery, as I imagined it would be, but forthright, bold. I study the creases in the paper, the perforated edges. I'm so used to looking for signs and clues; there's nothing that can't tell me *something*. When I hold the piece of paper to my nose I smell cured meat. I fetch Klaus's phone and call the number.

Oswald answers almost immediately. I tell him it's the girl who took the package to the station.

'I know,' he says. 'I recognise your voice.'

I don't say anything.

'I wasn't expecting you to call,' he goes on. 'I thought you'd lose my number.' He pauses. 'How did the negotiations go?'

I smile. 'Really well.'

'I'm glad.'

'What are you doing?'

'Right now? I'm walking the dog. It's my day off.'

'You have a dog?'

He laughs. 'Is that so strange?'

I smell the piece of paper again. Perhaps it isn't meat after all. Perhaps it's dog.

'You wanted to show me something,' I say.

'That's right.'

Since he is working long hours for the next three days he suggests we meet on Tuesday, in the evening, at a fast-food place on the Ku'damm.

'You can't miss it,' he says. 'There's a neon sign. Three red sausages with white flames underneath.'

I imagine Oswald walking in a drab windswept park, his eyes glistening like olives in brine, his black shirt flattened against his raw pale body. He throws a stick, which cartwheels through the sky. His dog runs off in the opposite direction.

That afternoon I visit Schloss Charlottenburg. The gardens are shrouded in a clammy mist. Statues stare at me with blurred blank faces, and tree-lined avenues end in nothingness. Though I don't see any other people I have the feeling someone is following me, or about to make contact. Why now, though? I have only been gone a few days, and I'm not due in Oxford until the first week of October. So who am I expecting? Massimo? He would be hopeless in Berlin. I can almost hear the piteous voice he puts on when he thinks he's coming down with something. *Mi sento fiaco. Penso di avere un po' di febbre.* I don't feel good. I think I might be a bit feverish. What about Daniela? I see her in skinny jeans and a parka with a fur-trimmed hood. When we hug each other, her body begins to tremble and I realise she's crying. *Sometimes you frighten me.* I hold her tight. *It's all right, Dani. It's fine. Everything's fine.* But Dani isn't likely to appear. She's still at her parents' house in Puglia. Is there anyone who might be able to track me down? The airline database will show that I boarded a flight to Berlin on September 8th, but after that? What are the chances of somebody tracing the taxi-driver who took me to the blue hotel? Slender, to say the least – and anyway, I checked out after just four nights. And nothing connects me to Klaus Frings, nothing at all. My disappearance is like a crime without a motive, and they're notoriously difficult to solve, aren't they?

I have been staying at Walter-Benjamin-Platz for no more than a couple of days when Klaus asks if I would like to go to a concert with him. Two symphonies are being performed, he says. Tchaikovsky and Prokofiev. I know nothing about classical music, I tell him. I'm worried the ticket might be wasted on me. He seems fascinated and appalled by this gap in my education. *She knows nothing about classical music,* I hear him murmur as he moves across the kitchen, shaking his big head.

On Saturday night we take a taxi to the Konzerthaus in the Gendarmenmarkt. Under my coat I'm wearing a clingy black shirt with mother-of-pearl buttons, a denim mini-skirt, black tights and black ankle-boots with high heels. Earlier in the evening, when I emerged from my room, I asked Klaus if I was appropriately dressed. He smiled, then looked away, ruffling his hair. At the time I wasn't sure how to interpret his response, but as we mingle in the lobby with other concert-goers – tuxedoes, jewels, furs – I understand that I do in fact look inappropriate, and that it pleases him. I'm flouting convention and since he's escorting me this means

that he too is flouting convention but in the only way he can
– at one remove.

Upstairs in the bar Klaus introduces me to a man with
slicked-back hair and a damp handshake. His eyes are damp
too. When he looks at me they seem to leave a deposit, as
snails do, and I have to resist the urge to reach up and wipe
my face. His name is Horst Breitner. Klaus, Horst – German
names are truncated, harsh, almost greedy, like bites taken
out of something crisp. For a split-second I glimpse the apple
on the bed in the hotel on via Palermo.

When Klaus goes off to buy a programme, Horst insinuates
himself into the space in front of me, blocking my view of the
ornate, high-ceilinged room. He holds his champagne flute
below his chin and speaks over the rim, in English. 'You have
known Klaus long?'

'I met him a few days ago.'

'Ah, so this is – how do you say? – *fresh.*'

Horst has an air of urgency, as if he is required to extract
certain information from me before Klaus returns. As if he
has specific goals or targets. The effect is flattering, but
vaguely repellent. I could pretend not to notice, of course.
Frustrate him. For some reason, though, I decide to lead
him on.

'We met in a café,' I tell him.

'Really?'

'He was sitting at the next table. I asked for the sugar—'

Horst lets out a brief breathy laugh of disbelief.

'We started talking,' I say.

'In a café.' Horst's eyebrows lift and he turns through ninety
degrees. Standing sideways on to me, he looks away across
the bar. He raises his glass to his lips, then tilts it quickly,

swallowing a mouthful that is economical, precise. 'And now you live with him, in his apartment . . .'

'Yes.'

'I'm surprised,' he says. 'Really.'

I shrug, then I too look away, scanning the people to see if they have anything to impart. That's what life is like now. I hold myself in a constant state of readiness. Every occasion – every moment – trembles with a sense of opportunity. I have no idea where the next communication will come from, but I know that one will come – perhaps even from the unwholesome, insidious man who is still standing beside me.

Klaus returns with two glasses of champagne and a programme.

'Quite a crowd,' he says.

'Tchaikovsky's *Pathétique*.' Horst twists his lips. 'Always popular.'

Klaus looks wounded.

'You're here too,' I say to Horst.

'I have a complimentary ticket,' he says. 'I do not pay.'

Soon afterwards he moves away. He approaches a woman in a small close-fitting hat of orange feathers and begins an animated whispered conversation, his mouth only inches from her ear.

'How do you know him?' I ask Klaus.

'We were at school together. I don't see him often.' Klaus finishes his drink. 'He runs a gallery.'

I'm still watching Horst. He notices, and allows himself a quick sardonic smile.

Once we are in our seats I consult the programme notes. Written shortly after World War Two, Prokofiev's 6th

Symphony addresses dark themes of loss and damage – 'wounds that can't be healed'. As I lift my head, the conductor raises his arms, and the audience goes still. Loud blasts burst from the brass section, then the strings come in, giddy, out of kilter, somewhat unhinged. I feel as if I missed the beginning but I know I didn't. The turbulence dies down, and the music becomes melancholic, questing. A gradual awakening, a sense of possibility. Then more bombardment from the horns and trumpets. It's like trying to listen to several people talking at once, but maybe that's the whole idea. The lack of a single lucid voice, the absence of a solution. *Wounds that can't be healed.*

I glance at Klaus, who sits upright with his hands flat on his thighs and his eyes fixed on the orchestra. My mind drifts. I find myself thinking about *The Passenger.* There is a scene where Jack Nicholson's wife tracks him down to a small Spanish town and he makes a getaway in a white convertible with his new lover, Maria Schneider. Filmed from behind, the convertible speeds into a tunnel while the car carrying the camera pulls over and stops. For a few daring, hypnotic seconds of screen-time Antonioni allows the main action of the film to disappear from the film itself. I've never known exactly what to make of his decision. I used to think he was drawing attention to Nicholson's predicament: in taking on a new identity, a *stranger's* identity, Nicholson has shrugged off his old life, left it all behind. Now, though, with my own thoughts wandering, I see the scene from another angle. What if Antonioni's parking of the camera is mischievous, or mocking? *The Passenger* is a difficult film, and he might be playing with his viewers, predicting or preempting a lack of concentration. He's looking away before they do . . . Just then, the Prokofiev becomes unexpectedly tuneful, almost sweet. Is it me, or does the symphony seem to have turned into a movie soundtrack? Klaus has not reacted. He remains transfixed, lips slightly parted, as if in awe.

Returning to *The Passenger*, I once again see Nicholson and Schneider disappear into the dark mouth of the tunnel. I see the road's cracked surface, the dusty verge, the weeds. Of course it's always possible that Antonioni is conjuring a sense of apprehension. He can't bring himself to follow his characters. He's fearful of witnessing what's going to happen. *He doesn't want to know...* Or perhaps it's about validity. Perspective. That ordinary stretch of Spanish highway has just as much significance as anything else. Next to the tunnel is a sign that says *GRACIAS POR SU VISITA*. It's ironic. Or naïve—

The curtain falls suddenly, to rapturous applause.

'The interval,' Klaus says.

People rise from their seats. Some have been soothed by the music in a cryptic, almost celestial way. They look benign, incapable of cruelty or violence. Others seem thoughtful, as if they have been set a puzzle or conundrum. And there are those who have a narcissistic air that reminds me of the English couple in the cinema. They have achieved importance simply by attending.

Back in the bar I notice Horst Breitner in the crowd. His eyes rest on me, moist and slightly sticky, then slide away again. Klaus returns with two glasses of white wine. His forehead gleams, as if listening to music is a form of physical exertion.

'Are you enjoying it?' he says.

'Very much,' I say. 'But I think I've had enough for now.'

'You don't want to hear the Tchaikovsky?'

'This is a new experience. I'm a bit overwhelmed.'

He stares miserably down into his glass. 'Would you like me to take you home?'

'No, no. You go back in. I'll wait for you.'

'But there's another hour—'

'That's fine. I'll wait.'

When people surge back into the auditorium Klaus is carried along with them. At the doorway he looks over his shoulder. I wave at him. I wonder if he thinks I'm saying goodbye – that I'll be gone when he comes out, and that he'll never see me again. It's not my intention. These days, though, when I leave a room, I often have the sense that I might not return. Steps can't always be retraced; the path through the forest closes behind me as though it was never there. The repetition that used to characterise my life has gone and I'm left with a trajectory that feels muscular, linear. No day is like another day, no moment like the next.

I buy another drink and sit at a table in the corner. Opening my notebook, I begin to describe my move to the apartment on Walter-Benjamin-Platz, and how I have become separated from what might commonly be perceived as the main action of my life. How I have cut loose. How I'm operating with a kind of freedom I never imagined. Sometimes, as I write, I'm aware of the Tchaikovsky, swelling and fading beyond the closed doors, but mostly it's blotted out by the chatter of the bar staff and the clink of glasses. I glance down at the page. My handwriting looks unfamiliar to me.

I finish my wine and go outside. Wrapping my coat around me, I sit on the top step and look out over the Gendarmenmarkt. Floodlit churches on either side, the low cloud cover glowing orange. I'm about to open my notebook again when a man approaches. He starts up the steps, but stops when he sees me.

'How are you doing?' His voice has grit and gravel in it. His accent is American.

'Fine,' I say. 'You?'

He stands three steps below me, hands in his trouser pockets. The traffic on the east side of the square is on a level with his face. Cars seem to go in one ear and out the other.

'What's so funny?' he says.

I shake my head. 'Nothing.' He's wearing a grey plastic raincoat and a pair of tennis shoes. One of the laces is undone. 'You're not going to ask me for money, are you?'

'Money?' He looks south, towards the cathedral. 'I've got more money than I know what to do with.' He takes out a twenty-euro note, holds it between finger and thumb and sets fire to one corner with a lighter. His thumb and finger open. The burning banknote floats away into the darkness like a vivid ragged moth.

'Beautiful,' I say.

He laughs. It wasn't the reaction he was expecting.

'Don't you like Tchaikovsky?' he says.

'Maybe. I don't know. One symphony's enough.'

He nods, then gazes up into the sky. I close my notebook but leave it resting on my knees.

'What were you writing?' he asks.

'None of your business.' To anyone else this would be rude. With this man, though, it seems natural, appropriate.

'You were recording your impressions of the city,' he says. 'Or your dreams. You always dream when you go somewhere new.'

'You don't look rich,' I say.

He laughs again, then looks at me askance, across one cheek. 'You know what they say about appearances.'

His face is blunt and dented as a boxer's and his hair is thinning, wild. He's probably about my father's age but he has lived a very different life.

'I want to show you something,' he says.

First Oswald, now this stranger in a plastic coat. Everybody wants to show me something.

I hesitate. 'But my friend—'

'He's still inside?'

'Yes.'

'You'll be back in five minutes. Ten at the most.' Mock-gallant, he places his hand on his heart. 'I give you my word.'

We cross the Gendarmenmarkt. Turning right, then left, we emerge into another spacious paved area, bordered on the east side by the Staatsoper. According to the American, the opera house is closed for renovation work. In front of us, fifty metres away, a ghostly fan of light rises from the ground, reminding me of the photo booth in Hauptbahnhof Zoo. Portraits of me with my eyes closed, as if asleep or dead.

'That's where we're going,' he says.

Set in the middle of the square and flush with the paving-stones is a thick glass pane. I stop at the edge. Beneath the pane is a brightly-lit white room, its walls lined with shelves that are pristine, empty.

'This marks the place where the Nazis burned the books,' the man tells me. 'One of the places, anyway. Forty thousand people gathered here to watch.'

The crackle of a fire. Pages lift, then shrivel.

The man looks away into the sky again. 'In those days, the square was called Opernplatz, after the opera house. Now it's named after August Bebel, one of the writers whose work was thrown into the flames.'

I stare down into the empty room. 'If you keep looking you start to see a library.'

He nods. 'Maybe that's the whole idea.'

As he walks me back to the Gendarmenmarkt I ask what line of work he's in.

'Import export,' he says.

'I don't know what that means.'

'I thought you knew everything.'

I give him a look. We're acting as if we know each other, as if we've known each other for years, but he only walked out of the darkness half an hour ago.

'It's an umbrella term,' he says. 'Right now, I'm working with a bunch of Russians.' Outside the Konzerthaus, he turns to face me. 'The city's full of Russians.'

I sense a stirring inside me as if my body is a room with all its windows open and a breeze has just blown in. At that moment people come spilling down the steps. The concert is over. The man stands his ground, forcing the crowd to flow round him. Klaus appears, his mobile pressed to his ear.

'I've been looking for you everywhere,' he says.

'Did you think I'd gone?'

He puts his phone away. 'No. I don't know.'

'I came outside. I needed air.'

'You didn't get cold?'

'No.'

The man gives Klaus a look that is challenging and oddly resolute, but Klaus doesn't notice. Either that, or he chooses to ignore it. Somehow it doesn't feel right to introduce the two men to each other. I hardly know them myself.

'I called a taxi,' Klaus says.

As he turns away to scan the street, the man in the raincoat hands me a small white card. Putting his thumb to his ear and his forefinger to his cheek, he signals that I should call him, then he winks at me and walks away.

'Who was that man?' Klaus asks later, as we pass the Hotel Adlon.

I tilt the card so the streetlights play over it. 'J. Halderman Cheadle,' I say, 'apparently.'

'You met him tonight?'

I nod. 'He's some kind of messenger, I think.'

'Messenger?'

'He's got something to tell me. That's why he was there.' I look out of the window as the taxi accelerates past the Gedächtniskirche and on into the Ku'damm. 'The weird thing was, he seemed to know it. They don't usually know.'

'The way you talk.' Klaus gives a little exasperated waggle of his head. 'You sound like a spy.'

I lean back, green and yellow neon streaming through the inside of the car. 'So how was the Tchaikovsky?'

I meet Oswald on Tuesday evening, as planned, under the sign with the frankfurters and the flames. He tells me it's a famous *Treffpunkt* – a meeting-place – especially after hours. If you come at three in the morning you see millionaires, porn stars, criminals. He indicates the menu on the back wall. That should give me some idea, he says. Though the place functions as a fast-food outlet, offering the usual *Currywurst* and *pommes-frites*, I notice that Russian vodka is available, and Scotch, and even, at a price, Dom Perignon. All very interesting, but I have to remind Oswald, after a while, that I only agreed to meet him because he had something to show me. Unless, of course, this is it.

'No, no.' He laughs, then motions to me, and we walk to the nearest S-Bahn station, at Savignyplatz.

Once we're on the train, I ask him where he's from. He grew up in the south, he tells me. Near Stuttgart. His parents are still there. They're really old. His father's eighty-one. Even his mother's seventy. I ask how old he is. Twenty-eight, he says, then nods firmly, as if he just split into two different people, one who reveals information, another who confirms its authenticity. It's an irritating habit. I ask if he has any brothers and sisters. Three brothers, he says. They're much older – more like uncles. His parents weren't expecting him. He was an accident. His mouth twists awkwardly. He's attempting a grin, but his feelings are too complex and it comes out wrong.

Rush hour is over and we're alone in the carriage. Every time the train slows for a station, the brakes squeal and grate. Sometimes the overhead power lines give off a bright mauve-silver flash. I put my face close to the window. There are no buildings any more, only mile after mile of scrubby heath or parkland.

'They didn't know what to do with me,' Oswald says. 'I always felt guilty you know, for turning up like that.'

'I was a miracle,' I say, startling myself.

'How do you mean?'

As we rattle through the darkness I tell him I was conceived by IVF, then frozen as an embryo.

Oswald is silent for a moment, looking at his hands. 'At least your parents wanted you.'

'That's true,' I say. 'Up to a point.'

He doesn't understand, and I choose not to explain. Just then there's a whiplash crackle from the power lines and he peers through the window. 'This is our stop.'

The sign on the platform says GREIBNITZSEE.

We hurry down a flight of stairs, then through a damp draughty tunnel. Outside the station is a parked truck with a bottle of Pilsner on the side.

Oswald beckons and we begin to walk. We pass a row of silver birches, metallic in the moonlight, and mansions with locked gates and darkened windows. The air is pungent with turned soil and fallen leaves.

'It smells like the country,' I say.

'There are lakes out here,' he tells me. 'There are beaches. In the summer you can swim—'

A cock crows in the distance. So far, I have gone along with his idea, despite the fact that it has involved a journey to the very limits of the city. But now, finally, I'm growing impatient. This whole thing feels like a waste of time.

'Where are you taking me?'

'Don't worry. We're almost there.'

The houses become more modest – cut logs stacked against a garage wall, a rowing boat covered with a mouldy tarpaulin. We pass a gate, its upright metal staves shaped like feathers. The wind lifts. I can smell pine resin and something makes me think of winter. A tingle goes through me, behind my pubic bone.

'Will it snow soon?' I ask.

'Not yet,' he says. 'Not until November.'

I doubt I can wait that long.

He stops at last on a stretch of road that seems utterly unremarkable. This was the only way into an enclave of houses known as Steinstücken, he tells me. The Berlin Wall ran down both sides of the road. He walks to the grass verge and begins to poke about. No trace of the wall remains, but he shows me where it used to be. Here, he says, and here. We move on. Before the wall came down, Steinstücken was a magical place, he says. Though it belonged to West Berlin it was completely surrounded by the DDR. It was like an island, with just one strip of tarmac – a causeway, really – to link it to the rest of the world. His brother, Friedl, rented a house in Steinstücken, and he – Oswald – would often visit. Friedl was twenty years older, more like an uncle than a brother.

'You already told me that,' I say. 'So why are we here?'

Once, Oswald says, when he was staying at the house, he was suddenly hoisted on to Friedl's shoulders and carried outside into the dark. He remembers cheering, and flashing torch-beams, and people wielding sledgehammers, pick-axes and bits of pipe. That night he found a piece of concrete lying on the ground, among the grown-ups' feet. He plunges a hand into his pocket and takes out a chunk of grey stuff about the size of a tennis ball. He stares down at it, his eyes distant, dreamy. It seemed really heavy at the time, he says. He was only four.

'That's it?' I say. 'That's part of the Berlin Wall?'

He nods.

'And this is where it came from?'

'Yes.'

'So you brought me all this way to show me something that isn't here?'

He hesitates.

'OK,' I say. 'That's great. Can we go now?'

His face widens in disbelief.

'Look, I'm sure this is important to you,' I go on, 'but none of it's much use to me.'

'This isn't about what's important to me,' he says. 'It's the past. It's *history*. I'm trying to show you something.'

'I don't care. I'm not interested.'

'You're not *interested*?' He's staring at me, horrified.

'No, not really.' I look around. 'You're just someone I happened to run into in a supermarket. You talked to me. I did you a favour. That's it. That's all.'

'A department store,' he says.

'Sorry?'

'I work in a department store.'

'Whatever.'

'You're harsh, you know that?'

'Oswald, you're not listening to me. I don't have time for this. I've got stuff of my own to deal with.'

'How do you know this isn't part of it?'

This is clever of him and it brings me up short, but only for a second. 'I just know.'

'You're lost, you are. You're—'

'Fuck you.'

He flinches, then moves away from me, into the road. When he speaks again his voice is so subdued that he could be talking to himself. 'If you're not careful you'll get hurt.'

Light explodes inside my head, as if I've tapped into the S-Bahn's power lines, and suddenly I'm so close to Oswald that I can't even take in his whole face. Just a chin, half a mouth. The meagre iron filings of his stubble. My eyes feel white-hot. It's a wonder he doesn't start to smoulder.

'You're an idiot,' I shout, switching to English for the first time all evening. 'You're a fucking fool. Don't you see *anything*?'

A figure looms in a nearby driveway.

'Get lost,' a man's voice says, 'or I'm calling the police.'

Oswald steps in front of me.

'My brother used to live here,' he says. 'He used to live in your house.'

A security light clicks on. The man's face is in shadow.

'Piss off, both of you.'

Oswald glances at the piece of concrete he is holding. His hand tightens round it, then his arm unwinds into the air. There's a bright jangling noise, and a black star appears in a downstairs window. The man lets out a string of curses and lurches towards us, light from the house silvering one raised fist.

Oswald says, 'Run.'

We turn and race along the road, back the way we came. I glance at Oswald but he doesn't look at me.

'Keep going,' he says.

Somewhere behind us a car starts up.

We run for perhaps a kilometre. My throat burns and I taste blood. Near the station we scale a wall and scramble down a railway embankment. A siren wails. We hide under a bridge, among gourmet salami wrappers and empty yoghurt cartons.

'I think we lost him,' Oswald gasps.

A train flashes past. I feel as if someone stabbed me in the ribs.

Oswald leans over, hands braced on his knees, and spits into the grass. 'Do you think he saw us?'

I tell him I don't know.

The siren fades. I can't hear any voices, only the low hoarse barking of a dog.

'I can't believe you did that,' I say.

'I was angry.'

'But your piece of concrete – your special piece of concrete . . .'

He nods, then looks as if he might be sick.

'Maybe you had it for long enough.' I'm trying to make him feel better.

'I don't know. Maybe.'

'In any case, it was a great throw.'

Smiling bleakly, he glances at his watch and then stares off down the track. 'I think that was the last train.'

We have no choice but to walk. Near Wannsee, the hard shoulder almost disappears and trucks slam past, dangerously close. After that, we opt for smaller, more residential streets. Wind in the trees, the far-off rattle of a train. The flicker of a TV in an otherwise lightless house. Once, I hear a couple making love, the woman's cries louder than the man's. Oswald speeds up, careful to avoid my eyes.

On a street in Steglitz a new noise seems to detach itself from the silence – a high ethereal humming.

'What's that?' I say.

Oswald stops and listens.

The sound is coming from behind us. We turn slowly, apprehensively. High above the treetops, at the end of the street, is a spaceship. Lit from the inside, it emits a steady whirring as if powered by a single engine. It has a rounded top and a skirt around the base, like a saucer. A flying saucer.

'It can't be,' I say, 'can it?'

Oswald says, 'No.'

But we both keep staring, and the spaceship goes on being a spaceship. What should we do?

Then, by small degrees, its shape begins to alter. I realise it must be turning. As it swings round, it becomes more elongated, and the word SIEMENS appears on the side. This gradual transformation happens with such complacency and confidence that it's like the punchline to some convoluted joke. I look at Oswald, and we both begin to laugh.

'I thought it was a spaceship,' I say. 'I mean, it really looked like one – for a while.'

Oswald's nodding. 'I thought it was aliens. I thought they might transport us to another planet. Do experiments on us.'

'You should have taken photographs.'

'I didn't think of it. I was too busy being amazed.'

Suddenly we have more energy. We walk faster, keeping to the middle of the street. We seem to know each other better. We talk non-stop. Fifteen minutes later a U-Bahn station appears. Next to the ticket machine is a photo booth, and I suggest we have our picture taken, to mark the occasion.

When the photos drop into the slot, Oswald makes to pocket them, but I grab hold of his arm. I should have them, I tell him. As a souvenir. After all, I'm the tourist. What's more, it was my idea.

'I paid for them,' he says.

'All right.' I let go of him. 'They're yours.'

My sudden indifference unnerves him. He folds the strip, then tears it in half. 'Two for you,' he says, 'and two for me.'

Towards dawn we collapse on to a park bench in Wilmersdorf. The sky is a marbled grey, like the endpapers in an old rare book. My legs ache and my stomach feels hollow. I haven't eaten anything for eighteen hours. Oswald leans over, studying his pictures. Our faces have a radiance that makes us both look famous.

'When I first saw you,' he says, 'my heart felt really strange.' He darts a look at me. 'Like it was too big for my body.'

When I first saw you . . . I let out a sigh. It's not that it's not nice to hear, not that I'm spoilt, or arrogant, or vain. It's just that people keep saying things and then expecting something in return, as if their compliments are a password or a payment, as if they are themselves ingenious, and brave, and deserve to be rewarded, and maybe they are, maybe they do, but I'm tired of it. I'm beginning to think that what I might be looking for is a place where things are no longer being said, where people don't talk at all – or if they do, not in a language I understand. My body twitches, as it often does when I'm on the brink of sleep.

'What is it?' Oswald asks.

'Nothing,' I say.

He has just given me an idea.

By the time I let myself into the apartment on Walter-Benjamin-Platz Klaus has already left for work. I find a note propped on the breakfast bar – *Are you all right? Call me. Klaus* – but there's another call I have to make first, a call that is more pressing. I open my wallet and lift Cheadle's card towards my nose. The earthy mushroom odour of an old man's trouser pocket. I dial his number.

'Who's this?' Behind Cheadle's voice is a rushing sound, like taps running. His German accent is dreadful.

'It's the girl from the Konzerthaus,' I say in English.

'How are you doing, Misty?'

Misty? I'm about to correct him when I realise that being called something different might be useful. Misty isn't a name I would have chosen, or even thought of, but at least it has no personal associations for me.

'Misty?' he says.

'I'm still here.' That watery sound again. 'Are you in the bath?'

'I'm under a flyover, in Spandau.'

I picture him with a mobile clamped to the side of his boxer's head, the grey plastic raincoat flapping round his knees. On the margins – that's where he belongs. He's like a character from a painting by Edward Hopper. Or George Grosz.

'So what can I do for you?' he says.

'I'd like to meet some Russians.'

'That could be arranged.' His voice swirls, breaks up and then returns. 'Call me tomorrow.'

I turn his card on the black granite surface of the breakfast bar. 'What's the "J" stand for?'

'The J?'

'In your name.'

'Jeremiah.'

'Sounds kind of biblical.'

'The prophet Jeremiah. Much maligned.' Cheadle clears his throat. 'We'll talk tomorrow.'

I end the call.

Misty. Now I think about it I'm surprised I didn't choose an alias myself, before I landed in Berlin. It's not just the way it rubber-stamps my break with the past. It's the sense of release that comes with it. In *The Passenger* Jack Nicholson is David Locke, a reporter, but his real journey begins when he appropriates a dead man's identity, an arms dealer known as Robertson. A new name will force me to recreate myself. It might also make me harder to follow, harder to find.

I Google 'Jeremiah' on Klaus's home computer. Jeremiah was a prophet, just as Cheadle said. He warned the Israelites that unless they changed their ways they would face destruction and exile. They didn't listen. Driven to extremes, Jeremiah walked the street with a yoke around his neck. He was thrown into a pit to die. In the end he was proved right.

Jeremiah, I think. Then I think, *Misty*.

I erase the history of my searches and click *Sleep*.

That evening, while exploring Klaus's shelves, I come across a book called *Farewell to an Idea*. The title speaks to me directly, as songs often do. The book is about Modernism – Cézanne, Picasso, Jackson Pollock – and its title is taken from a poem by Wallace Stevens. *Farewell to an idea . . . The cancellings / The negations are never final. The father sits / In space, wherever he sits, of bleak regard . . .* My throat constricts. Like the title, the poem seems to exist especially for me.

I have only been reading for a few minutes when I hear a key turn in the lock. I have been living with Klaus for nearly a week and he always comes home at roughly the same time – certainly never later than seven-thirty. I glance at my watch. It's five past ten.

Removing his coat, he throws it over the back of his chrome-and-leather Barcelona chair, then walks into the kitchen and opens the fridge. He has been to a *vernissage*, he says. In Prenzlauerberg.

'Perhaps I should have invited you. I wasn't thinking. I'm sorry.' He waves a bottle in my direction. 'Some wine?'

'No, thank you.'

'You're sure?' He pours himself a glass and takes a gulp. 'Not even to keep me company?' Shoulders hunched, arms held away from his sides as if his armpits are wet, it's obvious that he has been drinking.

I ask him if he has eaten.

He looks at the floor, ruffling his hair. 'Only crisps.'

We decide on a takeaway.

He rings a Thai restaurant and orders. When the call is over he asks me whether I have ever been to Thailand. 'I know nothing about you,' he says, not waiting for the answer. 'Nothing.' His face opens in wonder. He seems to find his ignorance exhilarating.

'I'm nineteen,' I tell him. 'There isn't much to know.'

'Nineteen? I forgot. I was thinking you were older.' He drinks more wine, emptying his glass. 'All the same. I'm sure things have happened.'

It's Adefemi who I see just then, on a wet night in May. We're sitting side by side on his faded pink sofa, my hands in his. I'm telling him how much I love him. But he's my first, and I'm still young, and so I have to leave. I was seventeen when we met – he was four years older – and though I adored him from the first I always knew he couldn't be the only person I ever loved. It's the timing that's all wrong, I tell him, not the feeling. He looks down at my hands. Nods slowly. Rain falling in the courtyard, both of us in tears.

'I've changed my mind about that drink,' I say.

'Good. I'm glad.' Klaus fetches the bottle and a fresh glass. 'How was your day?'

'I slept for most of it. I was tired.'

Klaus fills my glass almost to the brim. 'Were you out all night?'

'Yes. I had to meet someone. I didn't know it would take so long. I thought I'd be home much earlier.'

He notices that I said 'home', and his face glows briefly, but he doesn't realise how little the word means to me. It can be earned in a matter of moments.

I walk to the window with my drink, stopping when I'm

close enough to feel the cold coming off the glass. I can see my own reflection; I'm made of shadows. The living room floats behind me, areas of bright gold suspended in the darkness, like a ghost ship or a distant galaxy. I see Klaus approach. He thinks I haven't noticed. He thinks I'm looking at the view.

'When we met in the café,' he says, 'on Giesebrechtstrasse, you told me that no one knows you're here . . .'

'That's right,' I say, but I don't turn round.

'Is that really true? No one?'

'Yes.'

He moves into the space directly behind me, a second presence, inked in, opaque. He's so close that I can feel the outer edges of his force field. I imagine tentacles or stamens. They are clammy, pulpy – the colour of polenta.

'Have you any idea,' he murmurs, 'how seductive that is?'
Wie verführerisch das ist.

At that moment I experience a sudden craving for Adefemi, like someone running a finger up the middle of me, but on the inside. *I'm sure things have happened.* I face back into the room.

'On that morning in the café,' I say, 'you talked about privacy . . .'

'Did I? Yes, I suppose I did.' He sighs, then turns heavily away and slumps down on the sofa. Switching the TV on, he stares at the screen with a sullen intensity.

'What's seductive,' I say, 'is not the fact that no one knows I'm here. It's the fact that I'm living the way I want to live – or rather, I'm getting closer to the way I want to live.'

'I've no idea what that means.'

'You're part of it. In a way, you're the most important part. You're where it all began.'

He looks up at me. Though he still doesn't understand, he senses the veiled compliment.

The doorbell goes. The takeaway.

'I'll get it,' I say.

Returning, I unpack the cartons.

'More wine?' Klaus appears to have sobered up.

'No, not yet.'

I fetch plates, forks and paper napkins from the kitchen. Even rejected, Klaus remains polite and I'm not sure I don't despise him for it. I'd almost rather he tore my shirt off and pushed me down on to the sofa. At least that would be honest. I picture my buttons skittering across the floor like chips of ice.

He's ignoring me again. He's trying to punish me. It's not easy for him, though. Deep down he's hoping I will change my mind. He keeps channel-hopping, settling at last on a crime drama.

'I love crime,' he says.

I watch with him and find myself enjoying it more than I expected to. Down-at-heel tower blocks, rainswept motorways. Characters with stringy hair and bad complexions. Kitchens, ashtrays. Guns.

Even before the end Klaus is asleep, one arm laid across his upper body, a half-finished green chicken curry next to him. I tidy things away, then stand by the sofa, looking down at him. His chest rises, falls. The air rumbles in and out of him. Without waking, he reaches up and brushes at his face. What's supposed to happen here?

For the rest of that week Klaus is on his best behaviour, as if he knows he went too far and is trying to make amends. On

Friday he asks me out to dinner. He takes me to a restaurant on Schlüterstrasse, a few minutes' walk from his apartment. The girl at the next table has skin that is pale and luminous, and her long neck rises out of a clingy grey wool dress. With her is a man who has rolled up the sleeves of his jacket like an 80s pop star.

I ask Klaus if he finds the girl attractive.

'Not particularly.' He signals to the waiter. 'The man looks Russian,' he says. 'You often get Russians in here.'

I smile. When I called Cheadle on Thursday, as arranged, he told me he was meeting some Russian friends in a Vietnamese restaurant on Saturday, and that I was welcome to come along.

'I have to go out tomorrow evening,' I tell Klaus.

'Is it the same person you saw before,' he says, 'when you were out all night?'

'No. This is a different person.'

'For someone who doesn't know anyone, you know a lot of people.'

I laugh at that.

During the meal I hardly take my eyes off Klaus's face, not because I'm becoming interested in him, but because I'm trying to determine whether or not he has outlived his purpose. A word I noticed in *Farewell to an Idea* shimmers in my head like a neon sign. EXITLESSNESS. In the book it's attributed to the Russian artist Kasimir Malevich, who wrote about 'the exitlessness of life'. This is what I have to guard against. This is the danger. Is it enough, for instance, that in taking me to the Konzerthaus Klaus has inadvertently introduced me to J. Halderman Cheadle? Is that where my future lies, with a shabby, fifty-something American expatriate? Or should I be focusing on Oswald Überkopf? One thing is certain: as comfortable as it is in the penthouse on Walter-Benjamin-Platz I should think about moving on. It's September 20th, and my father will soon be flying back to Rome. Though he has never heard the name 'Klaus Frings', I don't feel I can afford to stay in one place for too long. I need to muddy the scent. And the fact that I have acquired a new name, an identity Klaus knows nothing about, suggests I have already left him behind, and that he is having dinner with a previous incarnation, a discarded chrysalis, a cipher.

Back at the apartment Klaus offers me a Jägermeister then pours himself a tumbler, half of which he knocks back when he thinks I'm not looking. Encouraged by my attentiveness at dinner, he is working up to some kind of declaration. He has an eager clumsy quality that I find touching.

I settle on the sofa, my legs folded under me. 'Why don't you come out and say it?'

Klaus replaces the top on the bottle. 'Say what?'

'You want to go to bed with me.'

He looks over his shoulder, startled. I feel I might have drunk too much but I can't stop.

'You want to sleep with me,' I say. 'You want to fuck me—'

'Don't.'

'Well, don't you?'

'It's too brutal, putting it like that.'

'How would you put it, then?'

Klaus walks over and looks down at me. He seems older than me, but not wiser.

'It's true,' he says.

He takes my hand and pulls me to my feet, then embraces me awkwardly, his face buried in my hair. I see him reflected in the plate glass window, enormous and dark and stooping over me. One person devouring another.

Straightening up again, he leads me past the grey painting, across the hall and down the corridor. I have already seen his bedroom. I explored the entire apartment on my first day, while he was out at work. I have even used his bath, which is round and deep, like a jacuzzi or a well, and covered with tiny turquoise tiles. I know that his sheets and duvet are maroon, and that he keeps his boxer shorts on shelves, in neat ironed piles. He drains his drink in a single hurried gulp as he follows me into the room.

I put my glass down next to a book on Fabergé and lie back on the bed. Sitting at my feet, he removes one boot, then the other. He handles them as if they're objects of great value, like the jewelled eggs he has been reading about. Why am I thinking of sleeping with him? No, wait. That's the wrong way round. If I *don't* sleep with him, there will be a sense of incompleteness. This tenuous, artificial relationship, which I have fabricated out of nothing, seems to require it of me. It's partly my desire to see it through to its conclusion – going to bed with Klaus is an end, not a beginning – and partly the need to clear the way for whatever might come next.

He places his glasses in their case, then closes the case with a crisp snap. At that moment I have the feeling I won't be able to go through with it. He isn't the kind of man I'm used to or have ever thought of sleeping with. When he turns away to hang his jacket on the back of the door I take off my tights and skirt and slide beneath the covers. He strips down to his boxer shorts, his body larger and whiter than I imagined it would be. The maroon sheets don't help.

After it's over, I lie on my back and stare at the ceiling, my pubic bone bruised from where he ground himself against me, trying to force an erection. The fact that he couldn't get it up doesn't bother me. In a way it's a blessing. Since I wasn't excited to start with I'm not left feeling frustrated. I sense possible orgasms, but they glide far below the surface like fish in deep water, incurious, unruffled.

'Sometimes, the first time,' he says in a low voice, 'if a person's very beautiful—'

'It doesn't work?'

'Yes.' He grimaces. 'It doesn't work.'

'I didn't know that.'

'I'm sorry. Maybe tomorrow . . .'

If what he says is true I suppose his failure is a compliment. I wonder if it also happened with Valentina. The first time.

He asks whether he can read to me. I can hardly refuse him. Putting on his glasses, he reaches for a book. 'Do you know Heinrich Heine's work?'

'I don't think so.'

He reads a poem about love being more precious than the pearls in the sea, and another poem about a man cutting his soul into pieces. He reads a poem about a girl with a frozen heart beneath white branches. After fifteen or twenty minutes he looks at me and asks if I'm all right.

'That was lovely,' I say, 'but I think, if you don't mind, I'll go back to my room now.'

'Of course.' All of a sudden he sounds serene, as if I have returned him to ground that is familiar and safe. It occurs to me that he might be relieved. 'Here.' He passes me a black silk kimono.

'Thanks.' It feels cold and slippery, and I shiver as I put it on.

Back in my room I remember reaching between his legs and trying to make him hard, but his penis was small and slack and rubbery like the bit left over when you've tied a knot in a balloon. Even when I took it in my mouth it wouldn't stiffen.

'What would you like me to do?' I asked. 'Is there something special?'

His eyes were closed, and his face twisted in a kind of agony. 'Nothing. It's all right.'

He turned over in the bed and began to run his hands over my body. Though I knew he was attempting to arouse himself I felt, oddly, as if I were being searched. The silence in the room was pointed, critical. We couldn't seem to move beyond the confines of our bodies.

Maybe tomorrow.

Outside, the wind has risen, and I'm conscious of being high up, on the top floor of a building. Only the terrace is above me, Japanese in its simplicity. The empty glass globes gleam on the table; the stems of bamboo stir. To the northwest, on the horizon, are the tall chimneys. Smoke leaks across the sky like ink in water. Like calligraphy. I think of all the people below me – reading, drinking, talking, making love – then I curl up on my side and face the wall. After a few minutes I drift backwards and downwards, sinking into a place that has no colour, no light.

Not long before chemotherapy began my mother cut her hair off with the kitchen scissors. She did it in the living room, in front of the mirror with the varnished frame. I tried to stop her. *You're making mistakes,* I cried. *It doesn't matter,* she told me, laughing. *It's going to fall out anyway.* I didn't understand – I had no idea of what was coming – but she made it easier by turning it into a game. The gold hair on the floor resembled an illustration from a fairy tale.

A few months later I walked into her bedroom and found her lying on her back with her eyes closed. Only her head showed above the covers. It was the middle of the day. The sky in the window was patchy and grey, rain threatening. Rome in the winter, the river breathing its damp vapours into the city. All the old, sad stones. Her hair was gone by then. Her eyebrows too. She looked fragile, ethereal. Half erased. A baby bird, an alien. A ghost. My throat ached at the sight of her. *I love you so much*, I whispered. She wasn't aware of me. She didn't even wake.

There were good times after that, moments of almost hysterical elation, the brightness of forgetting. Then something would catch in me and I would remember what the future held. Like the statue of the winged woman in the Tiergarten, and those clouds gathering behind her, loaded, black . . .

I was with her when she died. It was the evening of May the twelfth. My father was in the kitchen with my mother's sister Lottie who had flown over from England. He had opened a bottle of wine and laid out olives, artichokes, *prosciutto* and fresh bread. To keep our strength up, as he said. I couldn't eat. Instead, I sat by the bed, my mother's hand in mine, the sky above the Vatican warm yellow streaked with red, like the flesh of a peach. The usual sounds rose up from the street – plates being stacked, a church bell tolling, a motorbike. I wasn't conscious of my body, only my hand holding hers. I was walking along a beach. On one side tall grasses fenced me in. Bleached to a pale, sugar-cane yellow, they tapped and clicked in the offshore breeze. Off to the right was a brooding ocean, the waves explosive, the dark blue further out flecked savagely with white. The sand beneath my feet was cool and slightly gritty. I don't know where I thought I was. Puerto Rico, perhaps. Or Nicaragua. No place I had ever been. My mother was drawing breath, with long gaps in between, each intake arduous and harsh. As I walked on that imaginary beach I remained aware of her breathing, regular, relentless – hypnotic. But then the sounds ended and I realised that the last breath I had heard had been her last, though I hadn't known it at the time, having expected to hear another, and then another, having become accustomed to the rhythm, not having been able to accept, or even contemplate, the possibility of silence. It had been like being on a train and watching the telegraph poles flick by, the wires rising and falling, linking one pole to the next. You watch the poles, you're always waiting for the next one, and then, suddenly, they're gone. There's nothing in the foreground, nothing to focus on. The view that was always there is all there is. Gaping. Empty. I stared at the veins on the back of her hand and thought about the blood slowing down. Once it stopped, it would never move again. She would never talk to me, or stroke my hair, or drive me to unexpected places. I buried my head in the duvet, and my body was returned to me, shaking uncontrollably, and cold.

'The way I see it,' Cheadle says, 'you could use some support. Some backing.'

We are sitting at a corner table. It's Saturday, a fortnight since I landed in Berlin. The restaurant walls are yellow and the air smells of lemon grass and coconut. The light is operating-theatre bright.

'Here's the thing.' The American hunches over, his head wedged between his shoulders, no neck apparent. 'How about I adopt you?'

I've heard a few propositions in my time but never anything like this. A devious smile creeps on to his face, not because he's joking but because he knows he has wrong-footed me.

'Adoption of adults,' he says airily, 'it happens all the time. In Japan, for instance. To give the person in question better prospects.'

'Better prospects?' I consider his plastic raincoat, his dented face. His wild, wispy hair.

'We'd have to do it legally. Everything kosher. There'll be forms to fill in. Depositions. Affidavits. Whatever the fuck the word is.'

I look past him, into the restaurant. The other customers are mostly people in their twenties. People leading normal lives. Apartments, jobs. Relationships.

'You only met me twice,' I say.

Cheadle finishes his whisky, then reaches for his beer. 'Sometimes you've got to go with your instincts.'

I could hardly disagree with that.

'Who's the guy you were with the other night?' Cheadle asks.

'That was Klaus.'

'You sleeping with him?'

'Not really.'

'Not really.' Cheadle chuckles.

'He's been very generous,' I say.

'I bet he has.' Cheadle signals for another whisky. 'So anyway, you want to become my daughter?'

'I'm not sure my father would approve.'

'Don't tell him.'

'Isn't that bigamy or something?'

Cheadle laughs so loudly that people at the nearby tables turn and stare at us.

'I don't know,' I say.

'I'd take better care of you than he does.' A prawn cracker explodes between Cheadle's teeth. 'I'd probably leave you more money too. You'd be better off all round.'

'What's in it for you?'

He stops chewing and I realise I've impressed him. Perhaps that's what he likes about me: the quickness, the unpredictability – the cheek.

'Nothing,' he says. 'I'm a philanthropist.'

'In the great American tradition.'

'Right.'

'No small print? No hidden clauses?' I'm thinking of Klaus's promise of privacy. 'No strings attached?'

Cheadle opens his raincoat, like a man about to try and sell me watches. 'No strings.'

'Where are these Russians, anyway?'

'They said they'd be here at ten.'

I glance at my watch. It's twenty past.

'So you'll think about it?' Cheadle says.

When you're young, a lot of older people have a grasping quality, like vampires. They're all over you, even if it's only with their eyes. They used to *be* like you, though you usually can't see it. That's why they need you around. They want to siphon off a bit of what they've lost. Because you've got plenty and you don't even know it – or if you do, you take it for granted. I don't think Cheadle's any different, though he's more adept at disguising it.

A metallic-sounding guitar starts up, bright chords with surf crashing and hissing underneath. Cheadle takes out his phone.

'I spent a lot of time in Santa Cruz,' he says.

He puts the phone to his ear and stares past me at the wall. He says yes and no, and very little else.

When the call's over, he tells me that his Russian friends aren't coming after all. 'Still, Pavlo should be here soon.'

'Who's Pavlo?'

'He runs a gallery on Winterfeldplatz. He sells icons. Beautiful things.' Cheadle pauses. 'Pavlo's from Sebastopol.'

'That's not Russia.'

Cheadle shrugs. 'Close enough.'

Actually, I think, you're wrong. It isn't.

Pavlo is a small muscular man with a closely trimmed grey beard and moustache. His clothes are sober – a black jacket over a black V-necked sweater – but he has a pumped-up, skittish quality, like a thoroughbred before a race. The moment he sits down he tells Cheadle he's in love.

'Who's the lucky girl?' Cheadle asks.

Pavlo ignores the sarcasm. She's twenty-three, he says. From Lithuania. Her name is Katya. She works in the laundromat next to his gallery. For the next hour he talks about nothing else, his eyes welling up when he describes her.

It's not until we order coffee that the conversation turns to icons. Most of the pieces he acquires have a Russian provenance, Pavlo tells me – or sometimes they come from Greece. They tend to date from the eighteenth and nineteenth centuries. It's always been profitable, he says, but he would never have been able to open a gallery if Cheadle hadn't come in as a partner.

'So he really is a rich American,' I say.

'Rich?' Pavlo's mouth turns down. 'I don't know. All I know is, he invested in my business.'

Cheadle reaches into his inside raincoat pocket, takes out a piece of paper and passes it to me. It's a bank statement. The account is in the name of J. H. Cheadle, and the balance is in excess of one million euros.

'Believe me now?' he says.

I'm not sure what to believe, but Cheadle seems to feel that he has proved a point.

Later, when Pavlo has left, Cheadle walks me to the nearest U-Bahn station. We pass a shop that sells electrical equipment. There must be forty or fifty TVs in the window, all tuned to CNN. I come to a standstill, shock waves spreading outwards from my heart. It's a moment before Cheadle notices I have stopped.

'You want a TV? I'll buy you a TV.' He steps back and stares at the sign above the shop. 'I'll buy the whole damn place.' He drank beer and whisky with dinner, and his eyes have a fanatical glitter.

I point at the window. 'That's my father.'

'You're not serious.'

'I am. It's him.'

We stand in the gauzy Berlin drizzle and watch my father talk into a microphone with the earnest controlled enthusiasm so typical of TV journalists, his royal-blue shirt thrown into beautiful relief by the sun-blasted landscape behind him. With his free hand he gestures to lend emphasis to the point he's making. Once or twice he half-turns to incorporate a heap of rubble, a burnt-out car. Reading his lips, I decipher the words 'chemical weapons'.

'You don't look anything like him.' Cheadle sounds disgruntled.

Ordinary everyday reality isn't good enough for my father. He has to appear to me in HD. I turn from the window and walk over to the gutter. Trees line the kerb. Are they maples? Limes? I ought to know.

'He doesn't even know you're here,' Cheadle says.

A dark van races past, its tinted windows closed. From inside comes the thud of hip-hop, as if the van is an animal. As if it has a heart.

Cheadle swivels on the pavement, jaw tilted, truculent. 'I'd be a better father.'

Now the TVs are showing golf.

My collar up, my hands in my coat pockets, I peer down the road. Two sets of traffic lights glow red.

'Where's this U-Bahn station?' I say.

Waiting on a damp platform, I replay the scene outside the TV shop. Not one image of my father. Dozens. So perfect, that. The duplication questions – or even mocks – the idea of an intimate relationship, and then there's the fact that I watched him from outside, on the street, that we were separated by at least two sheets of glass.

I didn't notice if his report was live or not but I feel he must be on his way to Rome by now. Those shock waves round my heart again. I suppose I have been waiting for this moment the way a bullet waits in its chamber, cold and snug, for someone's finger to squeeze the trigger. That sudden burst of speed, a lightning transition from cool oiled darkness to a world that is brilliant and odourless. It won't be long before he notices my absence – if he hasn't already. After all, it's his job to sense when something's not quite right. Who will he call first? Adefemi?

'I haven't seen her, Mr Carlyle, not for months.'

'Really?'

'We broke up.'

'Oh.' My father pauses. 'I'm sorry to hear that.' And he *is* sorry. He likes Adefemi.

'We broke up in May.' It's Adefemi's turn to pause. 'She didn't tell you?'

'No.'

An awkward conversation, which only lasts a minute or two.

A cul-de-sac.

My father will contact my friends and it will rapidly become apparent that none of them knows where I am. They will be disconcerted, bewildered; they might even feel betrayed. Massimo is the only one who might be able to help. Intuitive and oddly transparent, he's always spilling people's secrets, things he doesn't even know he knows. My father might pick up on this tendency in him. If Massimo is still in Rome my father will arrange a meeting – probably at his favourite café, in Campo di Fiore.

Late September. The sunlight a tarnished gold that turns the shadows purple. Cut flowers in buckets. My father sits outside with a black coffee and a paper. He thinks Massimo is lazy and spoilt. *What do you see in him?* he always says. *I don't know what you see in him.*

Massimo is half an hour late.

'Mr Carlyle.' He drops into a chair next to my father and

runs a hand through his unruly dark-brown hair. 'It's good to see you.'

My father, who has been growing impatient, is surprised to find himself disarmed by Massimo's smile.

Massimo orders a *cappuccino*. Someone is playing scales on a piano, the notes spilling from an upstairs window.

'Have you seen Kit?' my father says.

'Not for a while,' Massimo says. 'She hasn't returned any of my calls. I thought she might be in England.'

'She doesn't seem to have been in our apartment – at least, not recently – and she's not in Oxford either.' My father hesitates. 'You don't know anything?'

Massimo toys with a sachet of sugar. He wants to do right by my father – he probably wants to impress him – but he doesn't respond well to questioning or pressure. He might be wondering if I've gone off with someone. He knows I'm capable of that. Little jagged shafts of jealousy might be going through him. *It's you I want.*

'When did you last see her?' my father asks.

Massimo starts talking about the night we went to the club in Testaccio.

My father interrupts. 'What date was this?'

'What date?' Massimo frowns. 'It was a Wednesday. About three weeks ago.'

'What happened?'

'The usual things. We talked – and danced. There were a few of us. Then she came back to my place. I don't remember too much after that. I was a bit wasted.'

'What about Kit? Was she "wasted" too?' My father's tone is acidic but Massimo doesn't notice.

'No,' he says, 'not really.'

'How do you know?'

'She rode home.' Massimo thinks back, then remembers. 'I offered her some coke. She didn't want it.'

My father gives him a look.

Massimo gazes off into the distance. Once again it's possible that he doesn't register my father's disapproval – or if he does, he might murmur, 'Yes, I know. I really should stop.'

He has no intention of stopping, of course.

'I had a feeling that night,' he goes on.

My father leans forward. 'Tell me.'

'She seemed – I don't know – different . . .'

'Can you be more specific?'

'Not really. It was just a feeling.' Massimo smiles complacently.

My father sits back. Though inwardly infuriated by how calmly Massimo is taking the news that I've gone missing, he senses that Massimo knows something. What he needs to do is tease that knowledge out of him. It shouldn't be a problem. He has done it hundreds of times, all over the world.

Then Massimo jerks upright in his chair. 'I just remembered.'

'What?'

'She talked about going away, and I said, "You mean, to Oxford?" And she said, "No."' Massimo looks at my father. Massimo's eyes have filled with tears. 'You don't think she's—'

He doesn't finish the sentence. He can't.

Back at the apartment on Walter-Benjamin-Platz Klaus is perched on a high stool at the breakfast bar, working his way through a plate of profiteroles. His two mobiles and his reading glasses lie nearby. I watch him from the kitchen door-way, my arms folded, the TV muttering behind me.

'Is that supper?' I ask.

'It's just something I found in the fridge,' he says. 'How was your evening?'

'Good. How about you?'

'I stayed in. I was tired.' He rests his spoon on his plate. 'Are you hungry?'

'No, I've eaten.'

Ever since our attempt at sleeping together, he's had a guilty, embarrassed look. It's not easy being on the end of it. And there's another thing. My time with him was always going to be limited – I told him so at the beginning – but he has consistently refused to acknowledge the fact. There's a stubborn wounded weight to much of his behaviour, an insis-tence that won't go away. He's like someone who hammers at a door and goes on hammering, even though he knows it's locked and nobody's inside.

I stifle a yawn. 'I'm tired too. I think I'll go to bed.'

He looks at me for a moment longer and I feel I ought to give him another chance but I just can't face it.

He spoons up the last profiterole.

'Sleep well,' he says.

On Monday morning the sky is dark. The air crackles, and my scalp seems to have tightened round my skull. Though I sense a storm is coming I decide to walk to Winterfeldplatz. When I asked Pavlo about icons at dinner on Saturday he was too distracted to tell me much. I want to find out more.

On entering the square it's the laundromat I notice first. I look through the window. A young woman is loading wet clothes into a dryer. Her dirty-blonde hair is tied back in a ponytail, and her breasts push against a pink T-shirt that is a size too small. Grey sweat-pants hang low on her hips. This must be Pavlo's dream girl, Katya.

I move next door and ring the bell. After a few moments the Ukrainian emerges from a back room. He's dressed in a white T-shirt and dark-blue jeans. The clothes look brand-new, as if he only bought them a few hours ago and has just put them on for the first time.

'Ah, Cheadle's friend,' he says.

The gallery has plain white walls and spotlights in the ceiling, and there are about half a dozen icons on display. Behind it, through a narrow archway, is Pavlo's office, as cluttered as the gallery is bare, with out-of-date computers, a dusty plant, and piles of unopened junk mail. Four mismatched chairs crowd round his desk, and several hands of cards lie face-down in a cleared space at one end, together with a couple of shot glasses and a full ashtray, smoke twisting upwards from a half-extinguished cigarette.

'Did I interrupt?' I say.

'Some friends were here.' Pavlo's eyes drift past me to the open door at the back of the office and the cramped court-yard beyond.

Later, as I sip treacly Turkish coffee, he tells me that when he first started out he used to treat icons as simple merchandise. He just bought and sold. Did deals. Icons were known as 'wooden dollars'. He chuckles. It was only recently that he began to look into their significance. I recall something he said at dinner about icons not functioning as paintings do, and ask him to elaborate. Icons are conduits, he tells me. Aids to contemplation. The person who truly 'reads' an icon is able to pass beyond it and achieve a kind of spiritual communion with the prototype. For that reason people often refer to them as 'windows on heaven'. For that reason, also, the names of icon painters are never mentioned, and are not to be found on the icons themselves. Painters are seen as servants of God. Mere vessels.

'There's another aspect.' He ushers me back into the gallery and points at a Virgin Mary hanging a few feet away. 'That Virgin, for example. Her gaze moves beyond you, into another world. *Her* world. It rebounds off reality, turns inwards. It's like she's looking in a mirror.' He steps closer. 'You see the hand, how it seems to gesture? The Greek for it is "hodegetria" – "that which points the way".'

I remember the outdoor screening in Rome, and how a random conversation between two strangers reflected me back into myself, revealing the path I needed to take.

A loud whirring starts up as a washing machine clicks into its spin cycle, and Pavlo's eyes veer towards the wall his shop shares with the laundromat.

'Did you see her?' he asks.

'She's very pretty.'

'You think I have a chance?'

'No harm in trying.'

'How old would you say I am?' He stands up straighter, his chest swelling beneath his crisp white T-shirt.

'I don't know. Forty-two?'

'Fifty-six!'

'You're in good shape,' I tell him.

Eyebrows raised, he glances at his mobile, pretending my compliment is neither here nor there, but I see him carry it off to a place deep inside himself. He will pore over it later, in private.

I open my notebook. While I make a drawing of the Virgin's hand, Pavlo tells me about the wanton destruction that took place during the years of the Red Terror. He once saw a piece of film footage in which Soviet officials emerge from a church with armfuls of icons, tear off the silver covers and throw the actual icons on to a fire. He talks on. He's a good talker, Pavlo. I imagine it comes in useful in his line of work. It might even be indispensable.

The gleam of gold leaf, the steady hum of the machine next door. The rain streaming down into the square.

Pavlo asks if I would like more coffee.

'No thanks,' I say. 'I'm good.'

When I walk into Klaus's apartment that evening I sense that he's already home and that he has been waiting for me. The place fizzles with impatience; the air itself is on edge. Sitting in an armchair, he appears to be reading, but I'm sure he only opened the book when he heard my key turn in the lock and his eyes aren't even focused on the page.

'You've been very kind to me, Klaus—'

In an attempt to avoid a gaze I know will be reproachful I move beyond him, to the window. The lights are on in the yellow gabled house across the street, but the rooms look empty.

'The time has come for me to leave,' I say.

'Where will you go?'

'Friedrichshain. I met someone who's got an apartment there.'

'Who is he?'

'I didn't say it was a he.'

'It is, though, isn't it.'

'He's like a father – or an uncle. He's older.'

'Ah, so that was the problem. I wasn't old enough.' Klaus laughs bitterly. 'All this time you made me wait. You let me hope. Why didn't you say something?'

I turn to face him. 'How could I? I didn't know.'

'Oh, you knew.'

'You've been lying to yourself,' I say. 'You weren't helping me or being generous. You were just out for what you could get.'

There's an ominous silence during which he gathers himself. 'If we're telling the truth now, perhaps you'd be so good as to explain yourself.'

'Explain myself?'

He rises to his feet in stilted, loosely assembled sections, like a film of a dynamited chimney run backwards, then stands in front of me, swaying slightly, as if the film might start running forwards again, as if he might collapse. 'Explain what's been happening here,' he says.

'I don't know what you mean.'

He grips my upper arm. 'You and your games.'

I didn't imagine he could be like this. My eyes drop to his hand but he doesn't let go. If anything, his grip tightens.

'Does it excite you, being violent?' I say.

He releases my arm, then swings away, one hand reaching into his hair. When he speaks again, he has his back to me. 'Did you honestly think I wouldn't notice?'

All of a sudden he has a calm authority. This must be the voice his patients hear, when they're undergoing those costly procedures.

'Notice what?' I say.

'Don't act so innocent. I saw you follow me.'

I had no idea that he knew – that he has known all along. He kept it cleverly concealed. Perhaps he wanted to see what my intentions were. Or perhaps he felt empowered – emboldened – by the knowledge. My deception gave him licence: any advantage he took would be justified, forgivable. What to say in my defence, though? I can't tell him that he is merely a starting point. He will hardly want to hear about his relative insignificance, his disposability.

Before I can find an answer, he whirls round again. 'Did *she* put you up to this?'

'Who?'

'Valentina.'

'I don't know anyone called Valentina.' I push him away but he weighs almost twice as much as I do and he doesn't move more than a step. 'Who's Valentina? Your girlfriend?'

Something in him seems to sour or curdle and he looks at the floor.

'You told me you were single,' I say.

'I could have you right now.' His voice has thickened. 'I'd be within my rights—'

I stare at him.

'And afterwards I could kill you,' he says. 'Do away with you. No one would know.'

You can never guess what lies behind the face a man presents you with, but it doesn't surprise me and I'm not frightened. This is part of what I signed up for when I bought a ticket to Berlin. I don't dare laugh at Klaus, though I'm tempted to. I still have to extricate myself. I need to think of an explanation, one that will make sense to him. No one does things for no reason.

I slap him so hard that his whole head jars. His cheek reddens, and blood blooms on his bottom lip.

'I'm sorry,' I say.

He leans over, cupping a hand below his chin, as if he expects a deluge. I leave the room, returning moments later with some kitchen roll.

'Thank you,' he says.

He's docile, repentant. He seems to accept the fact that he was in the wrong.

'If I told you the story you wouldn't believe it,' I say. 'By this time tomorrow I'll be gone. You won't see me again.'

He sighs, then disappears into the kitchen, where he rinses his mouth with cold water. When he comes back, I'm sitting down.

'You don't have to leave,' he says.

'OK, it's true,' I tell him. 'I followed you.'

'So I was right.'

'I thought you looked interesting, but I didn't think I'd talk to you.' I consider him dispassionately, as if trying to rediscover that initial urge, the first tingle of curiosity. 'I suppose I wanted to find out what kind of person you were. Sometimes you see people – in a café, or on the street – and you start wondering what they do, where they live, what their lives are like . . .'

'You don't usually follow them.' His voice is gentler, and more understanding. There's even the suggestion of a rueful smile on his face. He believes me.

I push my hair back behind my shoulder but don't say anything. I simply let the new conciliatory mood establish itself.

'You thought I looked interesting,' he says quietly, after a long silence.

'Is that so strange?'

He gazes at me steadily and I know what's going through his mind. *And now? What about now? Do you still think I look interesting?*

'How old are you?' I ask.

'Thirty-seven.' His large face lurches away from me. 'Age doesn't matter.'

My eye falls on the painting that cost him half his annual salary, and in that moment I think I understand what makes it good. Although I'm aware that the artist built the picture up slowly, layer by layer – Klaus told me as much – there isn't a trace of effort or persistence in the finished product. It appears to have come into being in a finger-snap. Glossy, smooth, and two-dimensional, its subject is the surface – the power of the superficial – but at the same time it's an exercise in concealment, inscrutability.

Ostkreuz. Apartment buildings line both sides of the narrow street. Five or six storeys high, their scabby greyish-brown facades are busy with graffiti. In the distance a red cross flashes on and off. APOTHEKE. I pass beneath a railway bridge. A train curves out of the east. Windows slide past, filled with brooding sky, and the stench of burnt rubber and electrics stings my nostrils. It's hardly the kind of area where you'd expect to find a rich American.

Cheadle's apartment is on the ground floor of one of the more run-down buildings. I press the buzzer several times. At last, the outer door snaps open.

'Misty?'

His voice comes from the gloom beyond the metal lift-cage. I drag my suitcase down the hall, over broken brown-and-yellow tiles. Cheadle stands in a doorway in his raincoat, like a man expecting a storm. His eyes look muddy, and he smells of beer and tobacco.

'I haven't been to bed,' he says.

'Is it all right,' I say, 'me turning up like this?'

What I like about Cheadle is the fact that there's no longing in his eyes when he sees me. My looks are an irrelevance. He treats me as if I'm as hard-bitten and disillusioned as he is.

'I'll give you a tour,' he says.

He shows me into a vast bare room with steel-roll doors at the far end. Rusting tools and faded girlie calendars hang on the brick walls. The lumpy armchairs and couches were probably salvaged from the street. The concrete floor is stained with oil.

'This place used to be a garage,' Cheadle tells me. 'It's great for parties.' He indicates the deep trench in the middle of the room where mechanics would once have worked on the undersides of cars. 'We call it "The Grave". People dance down there.'

He guides me along down a corridor lit by a single white fluorescent tube. One side is piled high with cardboard boxes. There are laptops, toasters, scanners, shredders, vacuum cleaners, kitchen blenders.

'Import export,' I say, half to myself.

Cheadle points to a door painted to resemble camouflage. 'Tanzi's asleep in there. She works nights.'

'Tanzi?'

'My girlfriend.'

We reach two large rooms, one painted green, the other white.

'I just made coffee,' he says.

I sit at the formica table and he pours me a cup from a battered metal pot. I help myself to sugar. He lights a thin cigar. Running along the back wall at head-height is a horizontal panel of frosted glass. The weak sun that filters through turns his cigar smoke blue.

'So,' he says at last. 'Had enough of the concert guy, did we?'

'He was a stepping stone.'

Cheadle rolls the tip of his cigar against the edge of the ashtray. 'And I'm not?'

I don't know how to answer that.

'It's all right,' he says. 'I don't give a jack.'

I sip my coffee. 'This is good.'

After about half an hour, the street door buzzes. Cheadle heaves a sigh, then goes to answer it. He returns with a tall spindly man who has a zigzag of lightning tattooed below one ear. A second tattoo – the English word OUTSIDER – shows just above his T-shirt, at the base of his neck. He has a pinched face, rockabilly hair.

'Echo, this is Misty,' Cheadle says by way of introduction.

Echo grunts, then leans his shoulderblades against the kitchen wall, legs crossed at the ankles. His black leather jacket creaks. There's dirt under his fingernails.

Cheadle opens a storage jar and takes out a packet wrapped in silver foil. Echo gives Cheadle two crumpled twenty-euro notes. Cheadle hands him the packet.

Echo glances to his right, up the corridor.

'Not here,' Cheadle says.

When Echo has gone, Cheadle leans back in his chair and tucks the money into his trouser pocket. 'You disapprove?' he says.

'I didn't say anything.'

'I saw your face.'

I should be more like Klaus's expensive painting, a smooth exterior, the truth buried layers deep.

'It's no concern of mine,' I say. 'Is there any coffee left?'

Cheadle pushes the dented pot across the table.

'Echo,' I say. 'What kind of name is that?'

Cheadle roots in a drawer and gives me keys to the apartment. My room is the one next to the bathroom. It's mine for as long as I want. I begin to thank him but he interrupts. Don't thank me until you've seen it, he tells me. Then he says he's going to get some sleep. If he hasn't appeared by six, would I wake him?

When Cheadle's gone, I open the door to my room. It's dark inside. I feel for the light-switch. A white fluorescent tube on the ceiling pings, then flickers on. It hangs at a precarious angle, on two thin wires. There's nothing in the room except for a single bed, a metal ladder, and two car tyres, which are propped against the wall. The only window, which is high up, looks out on to the corridor. It feels like a tool-room or a bunker. I strip the bed and cram the dirty linen into a plastic bag, then I leave the apartment.

In a laundromat on Warschauerstrasse I pay for a service wash, and the Turkish woman who runs the place tells me to come back at five. I cross a bridge into Kreuzberg. To the west, the last of the sun gold-plates the TV tower in Alexanderplatz. From time to time, as in the gardens at Charlottenburg, I sense I am being followed. Someone has started looking for me, or asking questions, and I'm feeling the ripples of that. I imagine a discreet cough. *Miss Carlyle?* When I turn round, a shifty balding man is standing on the pavement, the collar of his jacket raised. The whites of his eyes are foggy, jellied. He obviously has a problem with alcohol –

No, wait. My father wouldn't hire an alcoholic. The detective would be an ex-policeman. Decent, innocuous. Hardworking. His suit would be off-the-peg, his shoes clean and sturdy. He would have a civil servant's respectability.

Is there somewhere we can talk?

We sit on a bench like spies in a movie. He wants to know what my intentions are. My answers make no sense to him. But then, why would they? I can't tell him the truth. It's too overwhelming, and too fragile. He tries doggedly to persuade me to 'come home'. Those are the words he uses, freighted as they are with so much raw emotion . . .

But when I glance over my shoulder no one ducks into a doorway, or takes a sudden feigned interest in the contents of a shop window. No one stares down into his phone like a daredevil about to dive into a small pool from a great height. The people on the street aren't even aware of me. They brush past me, step round me. Leave me where I am, quite motionless. This isn't a detective story. Do I want it to be?

Under a railway viaduct is a greengrocer's, with wooden crates of clementines on the pavement outside. I buy three and watch the shopkeeper drop them, glowing, into a plastic bag. I peel one as I walk on. The segments are so cold they hurt my teeth. So far, I have been approached by Oswald Überkopf and J. Halderman Cheadle, complete strangers who don't know me and have never heard of me, and I'm beginning to think that's all I should expect or hope for.

Maybe it's even the whole point.

* * *

On my way back to Cheadle's place with my clean laundry I pass a middle-aged man and a young girl. She skips along beside him, pigtails bouncing, her small hand in his. Will my father look for me? Will anyone? That feeling of being watched, or followed – those faint, urgent ripples . . . There are moments when I panic. I've been careless, I've left a trail of clues. What if, by some miracle, my laptop is recovered? I have heard of people who can analyse the magnetic fields or charges in files that have been overwritten. If they retrieve the file I called INTELLIGENCE, my last entry will be there for everyone to see: *Klaus Frings – Walter-Benjamin-Platz – Berlin*. The chances of that happening are minimal, of course. Even so, I'm glad I left Klaus's apartment. In moving to the no man's land between Friedrichshain and Lichtenberg I've put myself below the radar. I'm lost to view now – surely. At one remove from the unknown.

Back in the apartment it's quiet except for canned laughter coming through the wall. I find a broom in the kitchen and sweep my room, then I mop the floor and make the bed. At six, I knock on Cheadle's door. There's no response. I knock again. Still nothing. I open the door a crack. Absolute darkness and a dense musky smell. Unwashed skin and stale breath. Gradually, my eyes adjust. In the spill of grey light from the corridor I see a king-size bed and clothes dumped on the floor in jumbled heaps. Cheadle is lying on his side, with his back to me. He's naked. Beyond him is a black woman, also naked. She's lying face-down, one arm circling her pillow.

'Cheadle,' I whisper. 'It's six o'clock.'

But it's the black woman who lifts her head. She stares at me blankly.

'He asked me to wake him,' I tell her.

She pushes roughly at Cheadle's shoulder.

Cheadle rolls over. 'Fuck.'

I shut the door.

Later that night he opens a litre bottle of red wine and we sit at the kitchen table drinking out of jam jars. They had some people over, he explains. The glasses all got broken.

I ask when I can meet his Russian friends.

'It's all you ever talk about.' He lights the stub of a cigar. 'You're using me.'

I smile but keep quiet.

'What is it with you and Russians?' he says.

I'm about to answer – or avoid answering – when the toilet flushes and the woman from Cheadle's bedroom appears in a purple halter-neck and pink hot-pants.

'Well, this is cosy.' She reaches for Cheadle's jar and swallows half his wine.

Cheadle introduces us.

'He found me on the street,' Tanzi says.

'Me too,' I say.

'Not sleeping with you as well, is he?'

I shake my head. 'Too old.'

Tanzi lets out a raucous laugh. 'Damn. You've got a tongue on you, girl.'

We're talking about Cheadle as if he isn't there and he seems to be enjoying it. Cigar between his teeth, he's leaning back in his chair with a grin on his face, his fingers interlocked behind his head.

Tanzi is curious about my age.

I tell her.

'Nineteen,' she says dreamily, like you might say 'diamonds' or 'caviar'.

Cheadle stubs out his cigar. 'The thing is, when you're young, you're always adding to yourself. Accumulating. Even negative experiences contribute to the sum of who you are. When you're older, it's different.'

'What happens then?' I ask.

'You're like a battery that's going flat. You've got less energy, and you can't be recharged as easily. The day will come when you can't be recharged at all. You just go dead. In the meantime there's a dwindling. Everything's trying to get away from you.'

'You're not flat yet, right?' Tanzi gives him a cheeky look, then finishes his wine.

Old people often think they know more than young people, simply because they've been around for longer, but it's not necessarily the case. They can be as wrong about things as anybody else. Once in a while, though, Cheadle comes out with a line that switches a light on in my head, and whenever that happens I know without a shadow of a doubt that I'm in the right place.

Even negative experiences contribute to the sum of who you are.

If I'm really staying, Cheadle says – if, as he puts it, I'm going to become 'one of the family' – I will be expected to do chores and given that he hasn't asked for any rent that seems reasonable enough. On my second morning, as I'm heating milk for his coffee, he places a BlackBerry on the work surface in front of me.

'A gift,' he says.

I tell him I don't need it. I tell him what I did with my last phone.

'But that was your old life,' he says.

He has a point.

I accept the BlackBerry as a symbol of all the changes I have made. I have a new number – a Berlin number! – and only one contact: J. Halderman Cheadle.

That afternoon I add two more: Klaus Frings and Oswald Überkopf.

A couple of days later I'm in my room, looking at recent entries in my notebook – the quote from *Farewell to an Idea*, my drawing of Pavlo's icon – when my phone rings for the first time. Cheadle's name appears on the screen. He tells me he has organised a dinner with his Russian friends for nine o'clock that night. The restaurant is on Schlüterstrasse. I fall silent. It's only a week since Klaus took me to a restaurant on Schlüterstrasse, which is just round the corner from his apartment. What if he walks in while we're there?

'Misty?'

'Yes?'

'Happy now?'

When I arrive that evening Cheadle is sitting at the back of the restaurant with a drink in front of him. He's alone. I take a seat beside him, facing out into the room. The walls are the colour of wet sand, and a vase filled with red gerberas stands on the bar. It's not the restaurant Klaus took me to.

Cheadle glances at his phone. 'They're on their way.'

'What,' I say, 'like last time?'

He grins, then swirls the whisky in his glass. 'Drink?'

I order sparkling water. I want to stay sharp.

My eyes swerve towards the door every time it opens. My left leg is jiggling under the table. To distract myself, I go to the Ladies. As I walk back across the restaurant, Cheadle looks past me.

'Here they are,' he says.

A man and a woman join us. We all shake hands. The woman looks about forty. She has short reddish hair, which may or may not be dyed, and very white, slightly greasy skin. Her full lips conceal small uneven teeth. Her name is Anna. The man – Oleg – is younger. He is wearing a designer black leather jacket with an open-necked white shirt, and his round head is covered with close-cropped hair of an indeterminate colour, like bean sprouts or Tupperware. Anna chooses the seat opposite mine and studies the menu. Oleg brushes at the tablecloth with the backs of his fingers, even though it's spot-less, immaculate. No one speaks. It's as if we're about to play a game so esoteric that it doesn't require any pieces.

For the first half hour talk revolves around business. Delivery dates are mentioned – the fifteenth, the twenty-fourth. Place names too. Kiev, Piraeus. Minsk. There's a lengthy debate about Pavlo, and mention of somebody called Raul. Anna's English is fluent, though heavily accented, and she tends to be the one who answers Cheadle's questions. Sometimes they switch to Russian, and Cheadle's under-standing of the language surprises me. Oleg seems distracted throughout. He tilts his beer in its glass, and his vague, violent eyes keep drifting round the room.

Eventually – and abruptly – the conversation stops, and a busy silence ensues, as if everybody at the table is thinking different but interconnected thoughts.

'It's Misty's first time in Berlin,' Cheadle says at last. 'She arrived two weeks ago.'

I hear a faint click as Anna's lips part on her teeth. It's the stealthiest of smiles.

'How do you like the city?' she asks.

'I like it very much,' I say.

Oleg is watching me, but nothing shows in his face. Neither curiosity nor interest. He doesn't even convey indifference.

'You like to travel?' Anna says.

'I like new places.'

I didn't know it was possible for a conversation to be both mundane and tense, but that is how it feels. Though I requested the meeting, the Russians suddenly seem to have more invested in it than I do, and more to lose. Oleg is looking at my mouth rather than my eyes. He looks so intently that I imagine he can see my words emerging, one by one, like plastic ducks in a fairground rifle-range. Cheadle gazes into his glass. He is smiling to himself. For some reason, I have the feeling he's proud of me.

'And when you leave Berlin,' Anna says, 'you will go back to Rome?'

'Oh no. No, I don't think so.'

She looks at me steadily, her voice quiet but insistent. 'Where will you go?'

'Somewhere else. I haven't decided yet.'

'Somewhere you have never been?'

The question lacks rigour – the future I imagine is intensely foreign, and yet familiar as grass or water – but I try to answer truthfully. 'I'm looking for a place where I'll feel at home.'

'You're not at home in Italy?'

'Not really.'

'And in Berlin?'

'No.'

The conversation has arrived at a crucial point more quickly than I envisaged. If you're speaking a language that isn't your own, perhaps you become less subtle, more direct. Or it might be a Russian characteristic. Anna glances at Oleg, then back at me. Is it my imagination or did one corner of Oleg's mouth curl upwards just a fraction?

'You have money?' Anna asks.

'Enough for now.'

'And when it runs out?'

'I'll earn some more.'

'What can you do,' Anna asks, 'to earn money?'

'I'm not sure. Something will turn up.'

'Turn up?' For the first time Anna's English lets her down.

'Something will happen,' I say.

Oleg mutters a few words in Russian.

'You're very confident,' Anna says, 'for someone who is so young – or perhaps it's *because* you're young.'

Cheadle lifts his head. 'More drinks?'

'Vodka,' Oleg says.

'Also for me.' Anna smiles at Cheadle. Her front teeth are white, but the teeth further back in her mouth are a dark rotten yellow.

Cheadle orders two large vodkas, a sparkling water for me, and another whisky for himself. When the waiter has gone I ask Anna where she's from.

'I live in Moscow,' she says, 'but I was born in Cherepovets. It's north of Moscow, about an hour by plane.'

'And your friend?'

'He's from further north – from Arkhangel'sk. Or you would say Archangel.'

A sweet shaft of anticipation cuts through me, and I stare at the tablecloth in an attempt to disguise what I'm feeling. I can't allow myself to think *Cherepovets* or *Arkhangel'sk*. I think *glass* instead. I think *plate* and *spoon*. Even so, I sense Anna's interest growing, as if I'm a safe to which she now, quite unexpectedly, has the combination.

'I'd like to visit the north.' I turn to Cheadle. 'Do you think your friends could help with that?'

'The north?' He makes a face. 'What do you want to go there for?'

'I'd like to see it.'

'It can be dangerous,' Anna says.

'Also in Moscow,' Oleg says, addressing no one in particular, 'it can be dangerous.'

'And it's cold,' Anna says. 'Extremely cold.'

'Yes,' I say in a low voice, almost a whisper. 'Do you think it can be arranged?'

'Do you have a visa?' Anna asks.

'No.'

'It's not so easy to get a visa,' she says. 'You need a letter of invitation or support. You need to book hotels in advance. You need –' and she turns to Cheadle. 'What do you call it – the list of destinations?'

Cheadle smothers a yawn. 'Itinerary.'

'Yes,' she says. 'You must tell the authorities where you are going, and when.'

I look down into my glass.

'Maybe we could help,' Anna says after a few moments.

'Really?'

Anna glances at Oleg again. 'Yes. We have a contact. At the embassy.'

The drinks arrive, and I excuse myself.

Alone in the Ladies I look at myself in the mirror. Suddenly, I'm so excited that my arms are in the air above my head and

I'm dancing – crazy dancing, like I'm at a rave. It occurs to me – too late – that I might be caught on a security camera. I stop what I'm doing. Begin to wash my hands.

When I return to the table, the bill is already paid. Anna tells me she needs my passport. I hesitate. She can't get me a visa, she says patiently, if she doesn't have my passport. I reach into my bag and hand it over. She will also need a scan of my credit card, front and back. She'll be in touch, she says. Through Cheadle.

Out on the street Oleg hails a taxi, and the two Russians climb in. I wait until the car has turned the corner, then I thank Cheadle for the dinner and kiss him on the cheek.

'I don't think you should go,' he says.

'That's what you're *supposed* to say,' I tell him. 'That's what *everybody* says.'

He's shaking his head.

'I mean, I can't stay *here*.' I look up Schlüterstrasse, towards Savignyplatz, then swing round and look the other way. The Ku'damm with its clogged traffic, its splashy neon. 'This isn't what I had in mind, not even *remotely*.'

'What's wrong with it?'

'You don't understand. You never will.' I open my arms wide and spin slowly on the pavement, my face on a level with the murky sky. 'This is only the beginning.'

'Maybe,' Cheadle says, 'just maybe, you're the one who doesn't understand.'

It's two days later, and I'm drinking beer and vodka with Oswald in his two-room apartment in Neukölln. He lives alone, with his dog Josef. We're sitting in the kitchen, which is a bright, sickly green, like the algae on canals. The heating has broken down, and we have kept our coats on. Our breath shows as we talk.

Oswald faces me across the table, his left hand flat on the zinc surface, his fingers spread, as if he's about to do that trick where you pick up a knife and stab the gaps as fast as you can. He has drunk more than I have and his eyes look fierce, bleached.

I ask to see his tattoo. He pushes his sleeve back to the elbow. Running up the inside of his forearm in Gothic script are the words *Religion ist eine Lüge*. Religion is a lie.

'*Umstritten*,' I say. Controversial.

He pushes the sleeve down. 'I'm going to tell you something – something no one knows.'

I steady myself. We have reached a certain point in the night. He's going to try and impress me or confide in me and then I'm supposed to sleep with him. I've no intention of sleeping with him, though. If I imagine him naked, his body looks raw and urgent, like an animal that has just been skinned. I shudder, then feel guilty.

'Jesus wasn't really Jesus.' He sits back, pleased with himself.

'You know something?' I say. 'That would make a good tattoo. You could put it on your other arm.'

'I'm serious.' Without taking his eyes off me, he adjusts his position on his chair, staying within the frame of my gaze but moving inside it, as though testing its limits.

I finish my vodka. 'Who was he then?'

'You remember the Slaughter of the Innocents, right?' Oswald leans forward. 'Everyone thinks Jesus escaped – but he didn't. He got put to death, along with all the rest. He *died*.'

'So who did all the miracles?'

'That's what I'm saying. That's the thing no one knows.'

'Except you.'

My words have a sarcastic edge, but he doesn't waver, or even seem to notice. 'Except me,' he says, as if it's true, and obvious, and can't be disproved.

I finally ask the question he has been longing for me to ask. 'If Jesus wasn't really Jesus, who was he?'

'Herod's baby.' He nods slowly, agreeing with himself, a habit of his that still annoys me, then he reaches for his cigarette papers and his Ziploc bag of grass. 'Herod had Jesus killed and had his own son placed in the manger and Joseph and Mary were sworn to secrecy, under pain of death, and then the Wise Men came with all their gifts—

'The *Wise* Men.' He lets out a derisive snort. 'Joseph and Mary fled into Egypt,' he goes on, '*pretending* they had got away with the Messiah, but *actually*—'

What Oswald is telling me is giving me a glassy feeling, and I'm worried I might black out on his sticky lino floor. I wish he would shut up, but he's on a roll with his Jesus-wasn't-Jesus theory. I light one of his cigarettes, hoping it might straighten me out.

'—everything people believe in,' he's saying, 'everything that comforts them when they feel alone, or when they're in trouble, or when they're dying, it's all a fabrication, all a lie—'

The cigarette is making me feel even dizzier.

'Let's go for a walk,' I say.

Josef hears the word and jumps to his feet, eyes eager, tail whacking the fridge door.

Outside, on the pavement, the night smells of ash and salt. The sky looks brown. We hurry across Karl-Marx-Allee, which is wide and bleak, like some urban prairie. There are almost no cars. I wonder what Cheadle's up to. He's still determined to adopt me but I keep postponing it. I have discarded one father. Why would I want another?

When I was sixteen I got top grades in all my GCSEs, and shortly after the results came through my father and I flew to London. One night he took me to a restaurant in South Kensington to celebrate. I wore an elegant black dress and pinned my hair up. I was trying to look sophisticated – I wanted him to be proud of me – but the evening proved awkward from the outset. When the waiter took my coat he gave me a sly look, and I knew he thought I was my father's mistress. I couldn't believe my father hadn't noticed. He was a journalist, after all. An *observer*. It would have been so easy to clarify the situation – *My daughter just did brilliantly in her exams* – but he didn't, and my discomfort led me to broach a subject that had always been taboo – for us, at least.

We had nearly finished our starters when I told him that something was bothering me. It had been bothering me for a long time, I said. As long as I could remember. My father chewed slowly, watching me. What I felt, in general terms, I said, was an absence of something, a sense of deprivation. A loneliness. But I had never been able to put it into words. How could I have done? I was too young – only a child. And then my mother died, and the feeling of having been neglected or forgotten became harder to make out, even harder to bring up. My mother's death was so immediate, so shocking. So *recent*. My mother's death had buried it. I looked at my father across the table, hoping he would understand, but we had never talked about the difficult things – there was no history, no precedent – and nothing was coming back. He just seemed puzzled, and slightly apprehensive.

'I'm not describing it very well,' I said.

My father told me to try again.

'OK.' I took a breath and decided to go straight to the heart of it. 'When I was an embryo, why wasn't I injected into my mother right away?'

The waiter, who had been hovering nearby, refilled our water glasses, and then withdrew.

'I'm not sure injected is the right word,' I said, 'but you know what I mean.'

My father leaned forwards, over the table. 'Kit, for heaven's sake. We're in a *restaurant*.'

'You had me frozen and then you left me in the hospital—' My voice was trembling, despite my efforts to control it. 'You left me there for *eight years*.'

My father put down his fork. His face had stiffened. It was obvious he had never expected – or even imagined – anything like this. Also obvious was his fear that I might make a spectacle of myself, and ruin the evening.

A kind of fury surged through me, scalding and bitter. 'Why did you make me wait?' And then, before he could answer, 'I know why. It's because you thought I'd be a monster, didn't you. And maybe that's exactly what I am to you.'

'This is ridiculous,' he said.

'You *abandoned* me . . .' But all the force had gone out of me, and I sounded sulky, a typical teenager, a spoiled child.

'Stop it.'

'I wish my mother was the one who was alive and you were dead. At least I could talk to her—'

I began to cry.

'Is everything all right?' Our waiter had returned and was standing at my father's elbow, one hand cradling the other.

'Everything's fine,' my father said, looking blankly into the middle distance. 'Thank you.'

For the rest of the evening – and the visit – we did our best to avoid each other. I was horrified by what I'd said. I didn't wish him dead. Of course I didn't. At the time, though, I felt he hadn't taken me seriously. He had driven me to it. I'd had to say *something*. To make matters worse, I had embarrassed him in one of his favourite restaurants, something he wouldn't find it easy to forgive. Address one grievance and you create another. It seemed I couldn't win.

Oswald calls out to me. 'This way.'

We cross a bridge. Off to one side and far below are warehouses and lorry parks. A canal glistens like a seam of coal.

'Oswald,' I say suddenly, 'I'm not going to sleep with you.'

He doesn't respond.

When I glance at him, his eyes are lowered, and he has a frown on his face, as if he is trying to solve a problem that involves his shoes. Josef trots along beside him, looking worried.

I repeat the words twenty minutes later, when we're slouched in a booth in the corner of a dimly lit bar.

'I wasn't thinking about that.' He reaches for his beer, then puts it back on the table without drinking. 'I mean, to be honest, I've probably *thought* about it,' he says after a while, 'but I could never do it. I wouldn't be able to. You're too sort of – I don't know – *exotic*.'

I laugh. 'Exotic? You can talk, with a name like Oswald. I didn't think anyone called Oswald still existed. I thought they all died out about a century ago – or maybe longer.'

He watches me with distance in his eyes, as if I'm a

shimmering figure on the horizon, approaching slowly, and he's curious to see who I turn out to be.

'When will you go back to Italy?' he asks.

'That's not on the agenda.'

'Maybe your agenda needs updating.'

'It's being updated right now. I'm just waiting for certain documents to come through.'

'More negotiations?'

'That's one way of putting it.'

'Do you need money?' He studies me for a moment. 'No, probably not.'

'What's that supposed to mean?'

He doesn't answer.

I think of his kitchen – the queasy green walls, the broken central heating. 'You haven't got any money anyway.'

'Someone's looking after you. Someone's paying.'

Since I told him I'm not going to sleep with him he seems to have become stronger. More of a man.

'I've got a free place to stay,' I say, 'if that's what you're driving at.'

'Are you—' He checks himself.

'Am I what?'

'Nothing. it doesn't matter.'

'You're jealous.'

He gives me a look.

'You can't have me,' I say, 'so you want me gone.'

'There could be some truth in that.' He smiles wistfully down into his drink. 'But it wasn't what I was about to say.'

Later, on Britzerdamm, a white stretch limo glides past, tyres trickling on the tarmac. A window opens. A pale hand waves. I'm reminded of the night I last saw Massimo, the boys with their Roma scarves and their loud mouths. Sometimes, when I think of where I am, I shiver, and I'm not sure if it's terror or delight.

'I'm going home,' Oswald says.

It will take me an hour to get back to Cheadle's apartment, and dawn isn't far away. 'Oswald, can I sleep at your place?' I pause. 'Just sleep, I mean.'

After the way I spoke to him earlier he probably can't believe what he's hearing, but when I keep looking at him, too tired to be capable of anything manipulative, let alone flirtatious, his gaze drops to the pavement and he shakes his head.

'Come on, then,' he says.

When I walk into Cheadle's apartment the next day, I find him sitting at the kitchen table with Anna. Dressed in a black coat with a fake-fur collar, she is showing him a series of images on a digital camera. In the daylight she looks even paler, and the pores show on her cheeks and on the sides of her nose.

'Where did you get to last night?' Cheadle says.

'I stayed at a friend's house.'

'The dentist?'

'No.'

Cheadle and Anna exchange a look.

Anna reaches sideways into a bag and takes out an unsealed envelope. 'Your visa,' she says, 'and a letter of invitation.'

My heart leaps. 'That was quick.'

'I told you. We have a contact.'

I open my passport and find the visa, which occupies an entire page. The date of entry is October 10th. The visa expires on November 9th.

'Thirty days,' I say.

Anna nods. 'Yes.'

'And if I stay longer?'

'It's illegal. If the police stop you, you will have big problems. Also when you try to leave the country.'

I turn to the letter. Since it's written in Russian I can't understand a word, but I spot my name in the middle of a paragraph, surrounded by Cyrillic script, like a ship in rough water. I ask Anna what it says. Cheadle answers. The letter is from an acquaintance of Oleg's, who remembers having met my father at a conference in Geneva. He has invited me to stay with him and his family in Arkhangel'sk, and assures me of a warm welcome.

'This man never met your father in Geneva,' Cheadle goes on, 'or anywhere else, for that matter, and there will be no warm welcome. When you get to Arkhangel'sk you'll be on your own.'

I nod, then turn to Anna. 'Perhaps I will also visit your home town.'

Nothing shows in her face, though I sense rapid thoughts beneath the surface, a kind of scurrying, like rats inside a wall.

'You're from Cherepovets,' I say.

'Yes,' she says. 'But it's a steel town. Very industrial. Not so much to see.'

'There's always something. You just have to look.' I glance at my Russian visa. 'I can't thank you enough for this. You've been very kind.'

Anna's eyes glint, as sequins do when they catch the light, and she says something to Cheadle in Russian. Her words have a flat interrogative sound.

'In exchange for the visa,' Cheadle says, 'Anna will require your services.'

In the kitchen no one moves. Even the fridge seems to be holding its breath.

'My services?' I say.

'It won't take up more than a few hours of your time.'

I swallow. 'What's involved?'

'You'll go to a hotel – the Kempinski – where you'll meet a man called Raul. You'll be his companion for the evening.'

Raul. I've heard the name before. In the restaurant on Schlüterstrasse.

'Who is he, this Raul?'

'That's none of your concern,' Cheadle says.

The fridge shudders, then begins to hum.

'What about Tanzi?' I say. 'Wouldn't she be a better choice?'

Cheadle smiles. 'She doesn't have what it takes.'

'I'm sure you understand,' he tells me later, when Anna has left, 'that my Russian friends are not the sort of people who would give you something for nothing.'

'No,' I say. 'I see.'

'If you feel uncomfortable about it or if it seems too high a price to pay you don't have to do it. But your visa will be rescinded.'

I say nothing.

Cheadle picks up a big glossy bag off the floor and hands it to me. 'Something to wear, when the time comes.'

Inside the bag is a gold dress by a designer I have never heard of and a pair of matching high-heeled sandals. I hold up the dress.

'It's beautiful,' I say. 'Where's it from?'

Cheadle shrugs. 'Anna brought it.'

* * *

That evening I sit on my bed and sketch a section of my room – the transom-window, the car tyres, the cracked yellow wall. It's my aunt Lottie who first inspired me to draw. When I was young she showed me her notebooks – she designs costumes for theatre and film – and talked about the importance of recording your ideas and your experiences. Later, I started keeping notebooks of my own. The fluorescent tube light sizzles overhead, its frosted plastic cover filled with dead flies. My door is ajar, and the smell of roasting meat creeps up the corridor and through the gap. Tanzi's cooking.

Putting my notebook down I open the silver heart I carry everywhere with me. The two locks of my mother's hair lie curled into the tiny musty space, one fair, one dark, and I think what I always think: *before and after*.

There was a period of about a year when it seemed she had made a full recovery. Chemotherapy was over, and the operation to remove a tumour from her ovaries had been a success. Her doctors had found no evidence of metastasis. Apart from the scar on her abdomen and the colour of her hair she was the same Stephanie Carlyle. That was how I saw it anyway. But I was only twelve. Looking back, I think she behaved as if her time was limited, the pleasure she took in things disproportionate, nostalgic. Somehow the present was no longer the present; it was already past. She loved Rome as you love a place you're about to leave. She walked the streets with her face tilted towards a sun she no longer took for granted. She sat on the rounded lips of fountains and dangled her bare feet in the cool green water. She touched every plant she saw, as if hoping to leave an imprint of herself, as if prompting them to remember her. Even the air she drew into her lungs was treated as a luxury. Even the simple act of breathing.

Everything was precious all of a sudden, me included. Her love could feel like a weight. *Love me less,* I wanted to say, though I could never have put such a complex feeling into words, not at the time. She was always drawing attention to the world – the beauty of this, the power of that – when all I wanted was to read my books or think my thoughts. She was exhilarating to be around. She was exhausting. Though she was approaching fifty she didn't seem to have an age any more. The gap between living and dying, usually so unimaginably wide, had narrowed to almost nothing. She would not grow any older. The face she woke with every morning was the last face she would ever have.

My poor brave darling.

In her final months she became capricious, and I would sometimes feel she was usurping territory that should have been my own. I was the adolescent, after all. *Let's go shopping,* she might say. Or equally, *Let's go to Venice.* She appeared to have such energy. Only later did it occur to me that it wasn't energy at all but hunger. Only later did I realise how hard-won these seemingly whimsical projects were, and how much they meant to her. We often argued. We weren't always the good friends people took us for.

One Friday afternoon she picked me up from school as usual but instead of taking me home she drove out along via Nomentana, the road narrowing as it moved north-east, the dusty verges lined with pizza places, umbrella pines, petrol stations and washed-out pink apartment blocks. There were stalls stacked high with ripe fruit – apricots, cherries, watermelons – and the jammed cars ahead of us sparkled and vibrated in the heat.

I asked her where we were going.

'Switzerland,' she said.

We crossed the border that same night – my mother loved long drives – and by the afternoon of the next day we were walking along the shore of Lake Zurich, the air drowsy, the partially snow-capped mountains showing through the haze like pieces of white lace. She had been an au pair here once, she told me, before she met my father. This was a time I knew nothing about, and could not imagine.

On Sunday she bought a local paper. There was a cruise, she said, with live country-and-western music.

'A country-and-western cruise – in Switzerland!' She was laughing. 'You couldn't make it up.'

On the boat that evening two women stood out from the Swiss holidaymakers. They were both elderly, in their late sixties or early seventies. One had squeezed herself into a backless leopardskin-print dress. Her hair was a frizz of bright orange candyfloss and she smoked non-stop. Her companion's dress was made from a shiny electric-green material that resembled satin. They looked like extras from *Priscilla Queen of the Desert*. By eavesdropping on their conversation we learned they were from Naples.

While we were eating the 'English-style' meal – grilled meat, baked potato, baked beans – my mother noticed a Swiss couple pointing at the Neapolitan women and sniggering. Her lips tightened. She put down her knife and fork, rose to her feet and walked over to where the Neapolitans were sitting.

She spoke to the woman in the leopardskin outfit. 'I just wanted to tell you. *Stai benissimo.*' You look great.

'*Sì, è vero,*' the woman said. '*Hai ragione.*' Yes, it's true. You're right. She gestured at her friend. '*E lei?*' And her?

'*Anche lei,*' my mother said. She looks great too.

Sitting down again and flushed by her behaviour – she wasn't usually such an extrovert – my mother poured herself more wine.

'To Neapolitans,' she said. 'In fact, to all Italians.'

'Except Berlusconi,' I said.

We clinked glasses.

Clouds veiled the mountains and the water was dense as mercury. White mansions lined the southern shore. Their decks were made of dark wood and the green lawns sloped down to jetties where speedboats were moored.

After dinner three short men in tartan shirts appeared on a low stage. They played famous songs like *Night Train, Me and Bobby McGee* and *California Blue* and everybody had drunk enough by then to sing along. My mother sang too, one hand pressed to her collarbone. The boat seemed to have speeded up. Lights blinked and glittered all along the edges of the lake.

When the cruise was over we lay on a grass bank and stared up at the stars. The warm, almost brackish air lifting off the water. The tiny lazy waves collapsing . . .

My mother's mobile rang. She glanced at the screen and hesitated and then she answered.

'No, we're in Switzerland,' she said.

'*Switzerland?*' I heard my father say, his voice so small and pinched it sounded comical.

My mother stood up and walked a few paces. 'She's not going. She's ill.' She listened again, then said, 'Don't worry. We'll be home tomorrow.'

'You told him I was ill,' I said when the call ended.

'Well, you are,' she said. 'Look at you. You're in a terrible state.'

We both laughed, then she stared out across the lake, into the blackness, and sighed. 'Perhaps we should go back.'

'But you've been drinking.'

'I only had two glasses.'

We drove through the night, stopping at a motorway hotel outside Milan. I went to school on Tuesday. Three months later her cancer returned and this time it proved too strong for her.

Tanzi appears in my doorway, making me jump. 'The chicken's ready. You want to eat with us?'

At the beginning of October the sky lowers over Berlin and an east wind whips dead leaves into vicious spirals. Angela Merkel embarks on her third term in office after victory in the elections. Uncontrolled gypsy migration from Bulgaria and Romania is causing tension, and the last existing stretch of Hitler's motorway network – the A11 – is to be resurfaced. On Paul-Lincke-Ufer a black umbrella leaps from a man's hand and somersaults into the canal. I have a Russian visa but can't use it yet. I feel thin-skinned, irritable. There's the sense that I'm treading water. Marking time.

One afternoon I meet Oswald in Café Einstein. He starts talking about life at KaDeWe, and he's being so outrageous that the waitress with the chestnut hair stops at our table to listen. Oswald's supervisor – the burly woman – has been seen leaving an infamous nightclub in Mitte, but he isn't overly surprised. A day-job handling meat, a nocturnal fixation with leather. It's only to be expected, he says. He has often felt the urge himself. We're all still laughing when my phone vibrates. It's Cheadle and he comes straight to the point. My services will be required that evening.

By the time the call is over the waitress has moved away and Oswald's texting.

'Who was that?' he says.

I stare at the screen. 'No one special.'

'Your mood's changed completely. You're like a different person.' Head cocked, he considers me. 'Your phone *never* rings.'

Back at the apartment I wash my hair and shave my legs. Later, I slip into the clingy gold dress and the high heels. Standing in the hall by the front door I study myself in a dusty full-length mirror.

'You look great.' From where he's sitting, in the kitchen, Cheadle can see all the way down the corridor.

'I look like an escort,' I say.

'High-class, though. Top of the range.' Cheadle rolls the tip of his cigar against the edge of the ashtray and reaches for his beer.

'That's not the kind of thing a father's supposed to say.'

'I'm new to this. I make mistakes.' He brings the cigar up to his lips. 'Anyway, you haven't agreed to be adopted yet.'

His phone beeps twice. It's the taxi firm, he tells me. My car's outside.

Our conversations always go like this. He veers between affection and callousness, and expects me to be able to handle both. There are times when he seems to think I'm too full of myself and wants to see me come unstuck. Like now.

I check myself in the mirror one last time. Thigh-length dress, gold high heels. I'm reminded of the girls I used to see on via Flaminia, or on the dark sticky roads that surround the Stadio Olimpico. I have never looked so unlike myself, and for a moment I feel capable of anything. I put on my cashmere coat and pick up my purse, then I move across the hall to the front door.

'Not out of your depth, are you, baby?' Cheadle says.

I give him a look. 'No one says baby any more.'

He touches two fingers to his forehead in a mock salute. '*Viel Glück.*'

The dim light in the corridor and the upright rectangle of the doorway combine to frame part of the kitchen. A man hunched over a simple wooden table. The blue of cigar smoke, the dull gold of a glass of beer. If it were a painting it would be an Old Master.

Later, in the taxi, my thoughts circle back to the American who keeps asking if he can be my father. There was an uncharacteristic tenderness in the roundness of his shoulders and the attentive angle of his head, and also in those last two words, which he probably didn't mean to say. *Good luck.*

In Potsdamerplatz a man who looks Turkish steps out in front of the taxi. My driver brakes, then swears at him. There are too many bloody foreigners, he says. They're taking all the jobs.

'So there are all these Germans, are there,' I say, 'desperate to clean offices at night?'

'You know what I mean.'

The Kempinski slides into view, its lobby brightly lit, its front steps carpeted in red.

I pay the fare on the meter, then lean close to the grille. 'I know one job they should take.'

'What job's that?'

'Yours.'

Before the taxi driver can respond, a man in a top hat opens the car door for me, his face a mask, revealing nothing. I thank him and set off up the steps. In the lobby of the Kempinski there are shiny wooden pillars ringed with polished metal and sofas the colour of tangerines. The murmur of voices mingles with subdued Peruvian pipe music. The air feels staticky, filled with ions, as if a weather front is moving in.

The moment I enter the Bristol Bar I feel his eyes on me, even though I have yet to work out which of the many men he is. I'm acutely aware of the skin that covers me; it's as if I have goosebumps. Then I see him. He's sitting on a bar stool. Dark-blue suit, white shirt. No tie. I walk towards him. He doesn't look round but watches me indirectly in the mirror where all the bottles are. He's built like a wrestler with wide shoulders and a deep chest. His hair is black.

'Raul,' I say.

He turns to face me. 'Yes.'

'I'm Misty.'

When I shake his hand it feels warm and smooth and oddly padded. I have the sensation that his fingers are stuffed with something other than blood and tissue. Silicone maybe. Or down. I wonder if Raul is his real name. It's possible we're both using false identities.

'There is a car waiting to take us to the restaurant,' Raul says. 'Or perhaps you would like a drink here first.'

His English is flawless. I can't even detect an accent.

I look around. 'This place is a bit depressing.'

He smiles, then makes a call.

As we leave the hotel a dark car draws up outside. Neon slides over the roof, smooth as a hand stroking a cat. The man in the top hat is there again, opening the door for me, and this time I sense something protective rising off him, something almost paternal, though his face doesn't alter in the slightest.

Once in the car Raul addresses the driver in a language I have never heard before. I ask him where he's from. Croatia, he says. Zagreb.

'I don't know Zagreb,' I say.

'No.' He looks straight ahead and smiles, as if I have just stated the obvious.

For three or four minutes neither of us speaks. Now we are in a confined space I'm picking up a sweet charred smell, a little like burnt sugar.

'I'm glad it's you,' he says.

I'm not sure what he means or how to respond. Instead I ask him where we're going. He says a name that begins with 'b'. I stare out of the window. Judging by the route we're taking, the restaurant is in the east. A line comes to me. *But what shall I say of the night? What of the night?* I can't remember where it's from. A book I studied while at school. Something I loved. I feel Raul's eyes move across my face, then down my body. This happens several times during the journey and not always when I'm looking the other way. He doesn't seem to care if I notice. He isn't even faintly self-conscious or embarrassed.

We stop on a tree-lined street near the Gendarmenmarkt. The restaurant is located on the ground floor of a grand stone building that looks as if it might once have been a bank or an insurance company. When we walk in, I gather from the welcome we receive that Raul is a regular customer.

Once seated he orders champagne, then looks around. 'Movie stars come here. And politicians.' He shrugs.

'Do you live in Berlin?' I ask.

'I live in Croatia.'

'But you're often here. For business.'

'Yes.'

He holds my gaze for a moment. His eyes are opaque and lacklustre, like someone who has been watching too much TV. I have the sense that I shouldn't probe too deeply into his life. At the same time it's my job to keep him entertained.

'This is my first time in Berlin,' I say. 'I live in Rome.'

He looks up from the menu. 'You're Italian?'

'No, English. I was born in London.'

'An English girl,' he says slowly and sips his champagne.

The waiter arrives. I ask for the roasted gilthead. Raul orders breast of musk duck with glass noodles.

It occurs to me that I can trust Raul with anything, even the truth, because he doesn't know me and he never will. He's even more of a stranger than Oswald or Klaus Frings or Cheadle. He sits at the table like something built to hold a secret. Like a safe. It also occurs to me that I will have to do most of the talking. Despite his command of the language he's not a man who is profligate with words. For him, words are tools. Words fix things. Get things done.

'I'm nineteen,' I tell him, 'but I'm also twenty-seven.' I reach for my champagne.

He stares at me and his face doesn't change. He has a small scar near the edge of his mouth. His eyes are like wet wood.

'I was born twice,' I say.

He's still watching me.

I tell him about my conception in a London hospital. I was an IVF baby. Does he know what that means? He nods. I tell him I was frozen. I was stored for eight years before I was finally implanted in my mother. I was put together

– formed – but then I had to wait in the cold, with no knowledge of how long that wait was likely to be, or whether it would ever end.

'Like a hostage,' he says.

The analogy catches me off guard and though Raul remains quite still and solid the room appears to liquefy behind him.

'Yes,' I say. 'Exactly.'

'But you don't remember that. It isn't possible.'

'How can you be so sure?'

He doesn't answer.

Although I imagine him to be a man who has no patience with hypotheses and speculation, although his mind is almost certainly practical or even prosaic, he seems prepared to hear me out, and if I can find the right combination of words I might be able to convince him.

'Somewhere inside me,' I say, 'there is a memory of that time. I *carry* it. Not in my brain necessarily – not *consciously* – but in my bones. My marrow.'

'Marrow?'

'It's the fatty substance in our bones. But we also use the word metaphorically, to describe the very centre of our being.'

He nods slowly.

I tear off a piece of bread. Since English isn't his first language I'm having to alter the way I speak and it's giving me an unexpected freedom. I can come at things from a different angle. Make discoveries.

'It's not that I *remember* it,' I go on. 'It's more as if I have a sense of it.' I sip my champagne and the bubbles fizzle against my upper lip. 'You know what it's like to be caught in a thunderstorm? Well, the time I'm talking about is like the quiet before a storm arrives. It's like uneasiness or apprehension. You feel the air begin to change. You feel something electrical –

'Or imagine you're in a foreign city and you go to a movie and you get lost in it. At the end, when you walk out of the cinema, it's not the city from the movie, and it's not the city you're used to either, not the city you know, it's somewhere else.'

Raul is frowning. 'This is how you feel,' he says, 'when you think about this time?'

'Those frozen years, they're still with me. They're imprinted on my cells. On my DNA.' I pause. 'I'm actually *made* out of those years.'

I finish my champagne. A waiter appears and pours me another glass. Sometimes I suspect I haven't quite thawed out yet. My emotions are still frozen, my nerve-endings numb. Sometimes I imagine I have been carved out of ice, like a swan in a medieval banquet, and that my heart is visible inside, a gorgeous scarlet, but motionless, trapped, incapable of beating or feeling.

'I'm living in a different way now,' I say. 'I'm trying a new approach. I think it's working.'

Our food arrives.

Head lowered, Raul inspects his duck.

'I've gone out on a limb.' I watch him as he picks up his knife and fork and starts to eat. 'Do you know that phrase?'

Perhaps I'm talking too much. How much champagne have I drunk? Two glasses? Three? It can be exhausting, having to listen to someone. But I'm supposed to entertain him, aren't I.

'It's when you step on to the branch of a tree,' I say. 'You begin to walk along the branch, cautiously, because you're not sure it will take your weight. But you keep going. At any moment the branch might break. At any moment you might fall. That's going out on a limb.'

'I understand.'

'I thought you would.' I'm smiling. 'Your English is very good.'

He looks at me. 'No. Not really.'

I eat a mouthful of gilthead, which is so soft that it seems to melt on my tongue. A bottle of wine arrives in a large silver bucket. The waiter pours us both a glass.

'How is the fish?' Raul asks.

'Delicious.' I reach for my wine. 'There's something I forgot to say. It's exciting, going out on a limb. No, exciting isn't the right word. It's too small. Too weak. When you go out on a limb you feel alive – in every part of your being. Your whole being sings.' I look at Raul and see him as a man who has taken more risks than I can possibly imagine and so I say, half to myself, 'But perhaps you know that already.'

He pushes his fork into a slice of duck but doesn't lift it towards his mouth. He hasn't touched the noodles.

'You're beautiful,' he says.

His voice is so grave that it makes me laugh. Once again I wonder if I've had too much to drink.

'Thank you,' I say. 'Are you married?'

'Of course.'

'Do you have children?'

'One child. A boy.'

'He's in Zagreb?'

'In the country. Outside.'

I tell Raul about my childhood, and how I associate the

greyness and rain of London with stability and contentment, and how the sunlit years that followed were years of illness, frailty and sorrow.

'We moved to Rome because my mother was diagnosed with cancer,' I say. 'We went because she wanted to. All her life she wanted to live in Italy.'

'Your mother's dead?' Raul says.

'She died six years ago. I scattered her ashes myself. I did it secretly.'

'And your father?'

'He's a journalist.'

Raul pours us both another glass of wine. Black hairs bristle on the backs of his fingers. The symbol on his signet ring is an animal. I can't tell what sort.

'You're not eating,' he says.

'I've been talking too much. Am I boring you?'

'I like to hear you talk. It's relaxing.'

'Relaxing?' I laugh again.

'Did I say something strange?' For the first time I sense that he might be vulnerable, and that the balance of power has shifted in my favour. But it doesn't last. Aware of the lapse he makes immediate internal adjustments.

'You make it sound as if I'm playing an instrument,' I say. 'As if you're listening to music.'

He nods. 'Yes.'

Later, as we speed back to the hotel – he doesn't offer to drop me where I'm staying – all the energy drains out of me. The tyres hiss on the road and everything beyond the window gleams; it must have rained while we were having dinner. The driver has turned up the heating. I can't seem to draw any air into my lungs. The car rocks and sways, and I could easily fall asleep in my seat, but Raul's gaze is on me, just as before, and I dare not close my eyes.

The Kempinski appears. Gold lights bouncing, a blur of tinted glass. As I climb out on to the pavement, Raul takes me by the arm and guides me up the steps and into the lobby. Behind me I hear the car glide off into the night. The sound of the engine fading is like loneliness. Raul's thumb presses into the slender muscle in my upper arm. Everything feels different suddenly. There's an urgency, an undertow – and the way the car raced away the moment the doors were closed, as if fleeing a crime scene . . . But we're on the far side of the lobby, near the black doors of the lifts, before I find my voice.

'What's going on?'

He still has a tight grip on my arm and he is breathing heavily like someone who's been running.

'You come to my room, yes?' His English has deteriorated since leaving the restaurant.

'I should be going home,' I tell him.

'Home?'

'My friend's apartment.' I gesture towards reception, which seems far away, on some horizon. 'He'll be worried.'

'One drink,' Raul says. 'In my room.'

As he alters his grip on my arm he brushes my breast with the back of his hand.

'That wasn't part of the agreement,' I say.

'They didn't tell you?'

'Tell me what?'

He pushes me up against the wall next to the lift, then jabs the call button. 'One hour in my room,' he says. 'You come now.' He has me pinned. I can smell the musk duck on his breath.

An elderly Japanese couple approach, the man in a business suit, the woman in a traditional kimono. The man is holding an umbrella. Water drips off the tip and collects in a pool on the sand-coloured marble floor. Raul pretends to be adjusting the collar of my coat, then he turns to the couple and says good evening. The man's head dips. The woman blinks.

I look straight at them. 'Help me. Please.'

The couple don't seem to have heard. Their faces, curiously unlined, are tilted upwards, fixed on the glowing red numbers above the lift.

'Can't you do something?' I say.

There's a brisk *ping!* as the lift reaches the ground floor. The doors slide open and the couple step inside. We stay where we are. The doors slide shut again.

'Nobody will help you,' Raul says.

A second *ping!* as another lift arrives. Raul bundles me inside and presses the button for his floor.

'Excuse me? Is everything—?'

A bell-hop in a round red hat and a grey jacket has appeared and is asking if I'm all right but the doors close over him before I can answer. Raul is facing away and doesn't notice. As soon as we're alone he puts a hand round my throat and pushes me up against the wall.

The lift soars upwards.

You're not out of your depth, are you, baby?

Raul pulls my coat off my shoulders, then turns me round and forces me into the corner. My arms are pinioned behind my back. I feel him reach beneath my dress.

'Do you know what my name means?' he says.

I try to kick backwards, but he's standing up against me, between my legs. One of his hands is in my knickers.

146

'Wolf,' he says. 'It means wolf.'

I remember a vase in the lobby, huge and glossy and stuffed with tropical flowers and blossoms. I wonder if I'm about to faint.

The lift doors open.

Raul grunts, then lets me go. Two men are waiting by the lift. One of them is bald. He has black eyebrows and wears a sheepskin jacket. The other man is taller, with silver hair. Raul ushers me out of the lift.

'You dropped your coat.' The man with the silver hair picks up my coat and hands it to me.

The other man wants to know if there's a problem.

I lean against the wall next to the lift while Raul addresses the two men in German. I'm too sickened and dizzy to follow what he says. I only know he sounds indignant and threatening and that he scarcely allows the men to speak. But they stand their ground. Raul swears at them and then at me and walks away.

There's a long still moment, then the bald man asks if I'm a guest at the hotel. I shake my head. He offers to escort me back to the lobby. The lift has already gone, and the man with the silver hair steps forward and presses the call button. After what has just happened, though, I don't want to travel in the lift. I try to explain but my German has deserted me. Still, the men seem to understand. In the distance a door slams.

As we walk down the stairs the bald man asks if I want to file a complaint. Should the police be called?

'No,' I say. 'I'm fine. Thank you.' My legs are trembling and it's all I can do to stay upright.

On the ground floor the men guide me to one of the orange sofas. Would I like to sit down? I shake my head again. The man with the silver hair fetches me a glass of water. I drink half of it, then straighten my clothes.

'You're really all right?' he says.

I nod quickly. 'I think so.'

They will see me out, he says, when I feel ready. He tells me I should take my time.

As we cross the lobby a few moments later I keep thinking the Croatian will intervene. He's a man who can impose his will on any given situation and extract exactly what he's after. He's accustomed to being taken seriously, to being obeyed. To being effective. But there's no sign of him. Only the hum of voices, like insect life, and the muzak, which is orchestral – a low lush wash of strings. I seem to see him as if from behind, sitting on the edge of a wide bed, his head lowered, his suit jacket stretched tight across his shoulders. What will he do now? Smash something? Get drunk?

'Let's find you a taxi,' the bald man says. 'Do you have money?'

'Yes. Thank you.' I glance over my shoulder. 'That man, he was dangerous.'

'So are we,' the bald man says.

He looks at his friend, and they both laugh.

I let them walk me down the steps and out on to the pavement where they hail a cab for me. I thank them again and tell them how grateful I am to them for intervening.

'Any time,' the bald man says.

The man with the silver hair gives me a tender, almost wistful smile, then says, '*Pass auf dich auf.*'

Take care.

* * *

148

I hear the music as soon as I step out of the taxi. At first, though, I can't tell where it's coming from. I let myself into Cheadle's building. The door to his apartment is already open and people are leaning against the wall outside, drinking and smoking. Among them is a girl in a T-shirt that says NOTHING TO WRITE HOME ABOUT.

'Good T-shirt,' I tell her.

'Thanks,' she says.

I edge past her, into the room that used to be a garage. Strings of coloured bulbs loop through the darkness and the music is so loud I can't hear what anyone is saying. Smoke hovers in a flat cloud below the ceiling. Tanzi's down in The Grave with three other girls.

Cheadle walks over, raincoat flapping, a cigar stub in the corner of his mouth.

'Come and dance,' he roars.

I tell him I need to change.

'You're fine as you are.' He lurches backwards, then looks me up and down. 'Better than fine.'

'You didn't say you were having a party.'

'I didn't know!'

Tanzi came home with two friends and a duty-free bottle of Malibu, he tells me, then a DJ from the neighbourhood showed up and – Boom – the whole thing just took off. While Cheadle's talking, I scan the room. I'm looking for Anna and Oleg but the dim lighting and the crush of people make it difficult to see. When I refused to go to Raul's room with him did I renege on my agreement? Panic surges through me and I'm sweating suddenly. I don't dare ask Cheadle if he's expecting the Russians. Apart from anything else I don't want him to remember what I was doing earlier. When he turns away from me to accept a spliff from a man in a pork-pie hat, I seize my chance and sink back into the crowd.

In my room I change out of my clothes, then pack my case. It's the work of a few minutes. I leave the gold dress and the sandals on the bed. Taking a last look round, I peel my Richter postcards off the wall and push them into my coat pocket, then I open the door and peer out. The girl in the T-shirt is halfway down the corridor, a cigarette between her fingers, bending into the flame of someone's lighter. There's no sign of Cheadle, or of the Russians. I pick up my bags and make for the front door.

'Going somewhere?' the girl says, smoke emerging from her mouth in little chopped-up clouds.

I smile but don't stop.

Outside, a fine drizzle veils the buildings. The streetlamps look soft and fuzzy, like dandelion flowers, a whole row of them reaching in a long diminishing straight line, all the way to Ostkreuz. It's the early hours of Tuesday morning. I'm going to have to leave Berlin as soon as possible. In the next two days for sure. In the meantime I need to disappear.

My first instinct is to check into the hotel near Kluckstrasse, but it might be dangerous to retrace my steps. I reject Klaus Frings for the same reason. No backward glances, no unnecessary complications or entanglements. What I crave more than anything is a hot shower. I want to wash away all memory of that Croatian. I think of my father and his weakness for modern hotels with state-of-the-art plumbing. On Warschauerstrasse I flag down a taxi and ask the driver to take me to a Hilton or an InterContinental.

The driver looks at me. 'Which one?'

'Whichever's nearest.'

I climb inside and close the door.

On the morning of October 9th I have breakfast in my room, then I sit at the desk in a white towelling bathrobe and write two letters to my father, both on hotel stationery. In the first letter, which is only a few lines long, I tell him I'm in Berlin, and that I need to talk to him. Could he meet me at midday on the 17th in Café Einstein on Kürfürstenstrasse? I know my request might seem unreasonable and that it might disrupt his schedule but then again how often do I make demands on him? He *is* my father, after all. I hope he can make it, I tell him. It's important to me. I sign the letter – *With love, your daughter, Kit* – then I seal the envelope and address it to the apartment on via Giulia.

The second letter, which is more complex, runs to three sheets of writing-paper and will be delivered by hand. I'm not sure how to address the envelope. In the end I settle for DAVID CARLYLE. I take the short letter down to the lobby and ask the woman on reception if she can post it for me. No problem, she says. It will go today. First class. Her eyes are dark-brown and depthless, like those of a shop mannequin, and seem at odds with her clipped efficient sentences.

'How's Klaus?'

I turn to see Horst Breitner standing at my elbow in a camel coat and a large orange scarf. Horst Breitner, from the Konzerthaus.

'What are you doing here?' I say.

'Breakfast with a client.' His smile is condescending, and only lasts a second. 'You were living with Klaus, I think. Is he well?'

'I don't know. I haven't seen him in a while.'

'So it's over?'

I consider him for a moment. His slicked-back hair, his damp eyes. His lavish clothes. Then I turn back to the woman on reception and ask her to put the postage on my bill.

Horst places his card on the counter in front of me. 'A drink, perhaps – when you are free . . .' Pulling on a pair of fawn leather gloves, he leaves through the revolving doors.

As I watch him go I wonder if it matters that I've been spotted in the lobby of the InterContinental. I examine all the angles and decide it doesn't make the slightest difference.

On the way back to my room I drop Horst's card in the silver rubbish bin next to the lift.

After spending an hour in the hotel's business centre I set off for Berlin Hauptbahnhof where I am hoping to buy a ticket for that evening. In the back of the taxi I take out the longer of the two letters I wrote to my father and read it through again.

Hotel InterContinental
Berlin
October 9th

Dear Dad,

Thanks so much for turning up. Actually, that's a weird way to begin, since I have no idea whether you turned up or not. But I have to assume you're sitting in the Einstein with my letter in your hand, otherwise there's no point writing. It's what I'm imagining and I hope I'm right. By the way, please order anything you like. I left some money with the waitress. She'll take care of the bill.

You'll have noticed by now that I'm not there. It's not because I'm late. It's because I'm not coming. I'm not even in Berlin any more. I left days ago.

I imagine you looking up after reading those last two paragraphs and rubbing the back of your neck like you always do when you're annoyed. I don't blame you for being annoyed. Please don't think it's a wasted trip, though. There are things I need you to hear, and this is the only way I could get your attention.

When I was growing up, you spent a lot of time away from home, and though I missed you I got used to it. Normal's whatever happens – when you're a child, anyway. And you have to live for yourself – we all do – or you risk losing sight of who you are. Isn't it also true you avoided me, though? Or was that only later?

After Mum died, you certainly went missing. You left me with relatives, the parents of my friends, au pairs. They were nice enough, but they weren't you. And even when you were there, you weren't there. I know you were grieving, but still. You seemed to find it hard to be at home. Was that because it reminded you of her? Or was it because I reminded you of her? Maybe you blamed me for the whole thing. Because in a sense I was responsible. If she hadn't had a child, she would still be alive. There'd still be the two of you. I know we never really talked about her death, but sometimes I imagine us having an argument and that's what you always say. Why her? Why not you? Because if you'd had to choose between us I know you wouldn't have chosen me.

In fact, I'm not even sure you wanted me in the first place. Maybe I was her idea. Her dream. As Rome was. And when she got ill you were proved right, and that made you angry. I can imagine you shouting at her. You should have listened to me! If only you'd listened! Yes, you wanted her, not me. But she wanted me. So when

I lost her, I lost everything. Is that unfair? If so, I'm sorry. It's how I feel, that's all. It's how I've always felt. Some things you always thought were solid turn out to be made of fucking tissue paper and rubber bands. It's not until you touch them that you find out. Not until they fall apart in your hands.

I'm not coming home, Dad. I'm going in the opposite direction, returning to something I'm used to. Something that makes sense to me. I don't expect you to understand that.

I'm not even sure you're reading this.

Are you reading this?

Your daughter,

Kit

I don't much care for the letter. It seems confrontational, and the 'fucking' is overly dramatic, but I don't have time to make any alterations. It will have to do. At the last minute I decide to enclose one of the passport photos Oswald gave me. I study the picture before I slip it inside the envelope. My face is joyful, and also fierce, my chin tilted in a suggestion of defiance, which seems in keeping with what I have written. Oswald looks unwholesome, as always, but the exhilaration is visible in both of us. We're giving off a kind of glow, and I'm reminded of the morning I spent in Pavlo's gallery. The light that illuminates an icon is an inner light, he told me. In an icon there are no shadows.

When the taxi stops at a set of traffic lights I scribble on the back of the photo: *Me and my friend Oswald, on the night we saw the spaceship.* A bit enigmatic, perhaps, given the tone of the letter, but I'm feeling light-hearted, mischievous. Will my father keep the picture? Will he treasure it?

Or will it end up in the hands of the police?

* * *

I have only been sitting in the Einstein for a couple of minutes when the waitress with the chestnut hair stops at my table.

'Still here, then,' she says. 'How are you?'

My encounter with Raul left me with bruises on my neck, my upper arm and my wrist, but since I'm wearing a sweater and a scarf nothing shows.

'Fine, thanks,' I say. 'You?'

Her eyes narrow. 'I'm surviving.'

Half an hour later, when I have finished my coffee, I call her over and ask whether we can speak in private. There's a subtle alteration in her face, as if it's a computer screen and someone turned the brightness up. She has a word with the woman at the cash till, then motions to me. As I follow her outside she says she only has five minutes.

At the top of the steps that lead down to the street she turns to look at me. I wonder what she thinks I'm going to say. Ever since I first saw her I have found her intriguing. She's aloof but also provocative; I'm fairly certain she's bisexual. Freckles are sprinkled across her nose like grains of demerara.

I ask if she's working on the 17th.

'The 17th . . .' She looks past me, thinking. 'Yes,' she says eventually. 'Yes, I am.'

'Would you do me a favour?'

Her eyes, which are the colour of autumn, a blend of yellow, brown and gold, widen a fraction.

'It's not difficult,' I say.

On October 17th, I tell her, at midday, a man will walk into the Einstein. He will be looking for me but I won't be there. I produce the letter.

'I'd like you to give him this.'

She looks at the envelope and reads my father's name

out loud. She has trouble with 'Carlyle'. I correct her pronunciation.

'It's very important that he receives the letter,' I tell her. 'It couldn't be more important.'

'What does he look like?'

I think of my father as I last saw him, on TV, in the window of that shop in Mitte. He's in his early fifties, I tell her. Tall, with dark-brown hair and dark eyes. He's English.

'He sounds attractive,' she says. 'Is he your lover?'

'He's my father.'

'Oh.' She's about to apologise but then she sees me laughing. She starts laughing too.

I give her fifty euros. I want her to pay for anything my father orders, I tell her. If there's any change she should keep it.

'And if he doesn't appear?' she says.

Though I have addressed this possibility – obliquely in the short letter, more frankly in the longer one – I haven't really wanted to envisage it. The idea that the letter might lie unopened until such time as someone decides to dispose of it isn't easy to bear, or even think about.

'You get to keep the money,' I say.

'And the letter?'

I shrug.

I thank her for helping me, then start down the steps. As I reach the pavement I turn and smile at her.

'Will you be coming here again?' she calls out.

'I'm afraid not.'

She looks over my head, into the street. Her face, laid bare by the white light, loses its hardness and becomes much younger suddenly, like that of an anxious child. She runs down the steps and throws her arms round me. There's a staggered feeling, something intense and yet displaced, the emotion and the situation not compatible exactly, but parallel somehow, equivalent. Tears lift through me but don't quite reach my eyes.

She stands back. 'Well,' she says, 'it was nice meeting you.'

'What's your name?' I ask.

'Lydia.'

'It suits you.'

She thanks me with a quaint, almost theatrical dip of the head. 'And you?'

'I'm Kit.'

She repeats my name.

'It's short for Katherine.' I check my watch. 'I have to go.'

'Goodbye, Kit.'

'Goodbye.'

That evening I'm just settling into my seat when I see Oswald below me on the platform. He has Josef with him. Since he can't possibly know I'm there I could easily hide from him but I decide there's no need. I go to the door at the end of the carriage, slide the window down and call his name. His head snaps round. Looking worried, he walks over.

'I was wondering where you'd got to.' He registers the fact that I am on a train. 'What are you doing?'

'I'm leaving.'

He looks back along the platform, checking on my destination. '*Moscow?*'

'I'm glad you're here,' I tell him. 'It means I can say goodbye. It was good to meet you, Oswald. We had a great time, didn't we – though I'm sorry you lost your special piece of concrete.'

'Oh that.' He smiles. 'Well.'

'I feel it was my fault. If I hadn't been shouting at you—'

'No, no.' He looks at his shoes, then up at me again. 'It was worth it.'

'That man, he was so rude. I mean, we weren't doing anything—'

'That's right. We weren't.' A loud blast from the train echoes off the curved glass roof and Oswald's features tighten. 'Will you be coming back?'

The sight of his upturned face, half inquisitive, half hopeful, is so poignant that I'm deceived into thinking I know him much better than I do, and that we've been friends for years, and in that moment I come close to loving him.

'No,' I say gently. 'I don't think so.'

'That's what I thought.'

He looks back along the platform again, partly because he wants to see if the train is about to leave and partly to use up some time. There are only seconds left, and as with all goodbyes there is the pressure to do or say something moving, something unforgettable. Perhaps, also, it's in his nature to squander what is precious to him, and then regret it later.

'Can we keep in touch?' he says. 'Can I call you?'

'Best not.'

He nods. It's the answer he expected.

'In fact, here,' I say, 'take my phone.' I hold out the BlackBerry Cheadle gave me.

Oswald laughs, then shakes his head. 'You can't just give me your phone.'

'I don't need it any more.'

'You don't *need* it?'

'No.'

His hand lifts into the air, then falters.

'Take it,' I say. 'It's probably stolen anyway.'

He reaches out and takes the BlackBerry, then he stares at it as if he has never seen one before.

'Maybe I'll send you a postcard,' I say.

He looks at Josef who is sniffing at a puddle. I don't think he believes me.

'How come you're here?' I ask him. 'I mean, it's late.'

'I like stations.' He pulls Josef away from the wet patch. 'Josef seems to like them too.'

'*Gleich und gleich gesellt sich gern,*' I say. Birds of a feather. It's wittier in English but he still smiles. I lean out of the window. Further up the platform a green light is showing.

'I never told you about the parcel,' Oswald says.

The train jerks, then checks.

'It wasn't anything important,' he goes on, the words tumbling out. 'It was just an excuse to talk to you. We're not allowed to talk to customers, you see – not unless we're serving them.'

I remember the weight of the package. 'So what was inside?'

The train jerks again and starts to move.

Oswald seems calmer suddenly. Even though the train's pulling away from him, even though the distance between us is increasing, he takes his time.

'Bones,' he calls out. 'Bones for the dog.'

A smile cracks his face wide open.

He shouts something else but I can't hear him above the hiss and screech of the departing train. The platform slides past, and his face becomes a pale dot. I watch until he's hidden by a bend in the track, then I close the window and return to my seat. The train picks its way over the points like a drummer trying to find a rhythm. *Bones for the dog.* I'm smiling too.

Three

We arrive in Warsaw just after three-thirty in the morning. I leave my compartment and walk along the platform. The low ceiling traps the scorched smell of trains. At a kiosk run by a woman with peroxide hair I buy a litre bottle of water. Cool and metallic, it has the same taste as the night.

No sooner has the train pulled out of the station than I doze off, only to be woken at dawn by a guard from Belarus who checks my transit visa. Though I have fled Berlin, memories of the Croatian still haunt me. I regret having told him about my mother; it's not something he should know. I try to shut him out but the images keep coming. He hurls a lamp across his room. He opens the fridge and swallows the miniatures one by one – gin, vodka, whisky, rum. He reaches for the phone and dials. Who's he calling? I feel a growing apprehension about what might happen when we cross the border into Russia. What if Cheadle's friends have seen to it that my visa is rescinded? What if I'm turned back?

Along with her will, my mother left a letter asking that her ashes be scattered in the Protestant Cemetery. We would often walk from via Giulia. It was the Roman equivalent of going to the park. In the spring, when the daisies flowered, the grass was a dazzle of white. On summer afternoons the trees stood in deep pools of shade. We used to visit the famous people – Keats, Shelley, Goethe's son – or watch stray cats eating pasta near the Pyramid of Cestius. My mother talked about the contrast between the peace inside the walls and the traffic jams and shouting just beyond. It was a cusp of a place, she said, removed from life yet still a part of it. Her wish made sense – it *sounded* like her – but my father told me that unauthorised scattering was forbidden, and also disrespectful. The urn containing my mother's ashes could be 'interred' in the cemetery wall, he said, but until such time as that could be arranged it would be kept in a drawer in his bedroom.

One weekend, while he was out of the country, I took the urn from his chest of drawers and tipped the ashes into a plastic bag. Coarse and granular, like gravel, there was more than I had imagined there would be. I left the apartment with the bag hidden under my dress. It was an August afternoon. Grey and pale-orange clouds with messily torn edges bumped about in the sky, and my body ran with sweat where the plastic pressed against it. The streets were hot and quiet, everyone at the beach.

I had been worried the gatekeeper might search me, but when his eyes met mine he nodded and let me through. Inside the cemetery I wandered aimlessly, pausing at the place where Shelley's heart is buried. Then I remembered how my mother and I would often settle beneath a certain cypress tree and snack on chocolate or figs. Once I had found the tree I dropped to my knees and trickled the ashes in a circle round the trunk. In daylight they looked obvious, a glaring white. Someone was bound to notice. I was just thinking I would have to cover them with blades of grass when the air shifted. Thunder banged overhead, loud as a dustbin lid. Seconds later, the rain came down. The ashes darkened, and sank into the earth.

My father lost his temper when he found out what I had done but my anger more than equalled his.

'It's what she wanted,' I shouted.

'You broke the law—'

'I don't care. You think she was happy in a *drawer?*'

I put my face close to the train window. Flat fields show through a mist of condensation. There are no primary colours any more, only faded browns and greens, drained yellows, subtle shades of grey. No houses, no people. A kind of wilderness. Out in the corridor I slide a window open. The air smells of parsnips and stainless steel. I whisper the word 'Russia' to myself, and a shiver travels up my spine.

That morning I slip into a trance, scarcely aware of my fellow passengers and oblivious to the landscape we're passing through. I don't talk to anyone, nor do I make a single entry in my notebook. There's a force at work, something I failed to anticipate. Since the place I'm heading for is clear in my mind only as an idea, and isn't therefore, strictly speaking, a destination, I'm beginning to suspect that my eventual surroundings, whatever they might turn out to be, will have little or no relevance. The country I have chosen is hardly incidental, but this is not, at heart, a physical journey. It's more like a journey back in time – or sideways, into another dimension. If the English couple in the cinema were messengers or heralds, pointing the way, then everything that has happened since is the fruit of those few moments – a gathering up, a realignment, a kind of distillation. My life is light and tidy now, like a rucksack that holds nothing but the bare essentials. The letters I wrote may have had their faults but they were as honest as I could make them. There will be no returning – at least, not in the geographical sense. This is a one-way ticket, a permanently ebbing tide.

As the train rattles north-east, through endless, leafless forest, my father floats back into my thoughts. I can visualise the apartment on via Giulia, though the blue sky is becoming harder to believe in, more unreal. There he is, standing on the roof terrace in a shirt and shorts. On his feet are his favourite red leather slippers, which he bought in Morocco. Kit, he mutters. A vertical crease appears between his eyebrows. He is holding my first letter – the short one – and he is clearly vexed. It's quite possible that the meeting I have proposed is inconvenient. He might be working on a story that means he has to be elsewhere, in which case flights, accommodation and interviews will already have been arranged. Should I have given him more notice? A choice of dates? Maybe I'm asking too much of him. Maybe all the letter will do is confirm his current view of me – namely, that I've become demanding and unreasonable, and that I seem determined to disrupt his life.

Still, I think he will travel to Berlin. It's not so much that he loves me or feels responsible for me – or rather, those considerations won't be in the forefront of his mind. No, I have presented him with a mystery, one he won't be able to resist the urge to solve. My letter will back up anything Massimo might have said. What's more, it's brief and to the point, employing the kind of language he's used to. It resembles an assignment, in fact. I have appealed, unwittingly, to the part of him he values most, the part that can be relied on.

Yes, he'll go.

I see him booking himself on to a flight that arrives on the 16th, the day before our rendezvous. At the outset his journey echoes mine – Termini, then Fiumicino. He might even leave his umbrella on the train! During the flight he looks at mainland Europe far below and smiles because he's once again in transit, but then he remembers the reason for the journey, and his mood sours. No, he won't have any 'hot or cold snacks'. No, he doesn't want 'a beverage'. No, he isn't 'interested in purchasing' any cigarettes or fragrances or teddy-bears dressed up as pilots.

Kit, he thinks. What are you playing at?

On landing, he takes a taxi straight to the InterContinental. Since my letters were written on hotel stationery he might assume that I am still a guest, but when he asks for me at reception the woman with the doll's eyes tells him they have no one by that name. He shows her my letter, dated October 9th, and asks her to check her records. The natural emptiness of her gaze adds tension to the twenty-five or thirty seconds she spends scanning her computer screen. Katherine Carlyle stayed for two nights, she says at last, arriving in the early hours of October 8th and departing at midday on the 9th. She takes another look at the letter. She thinks she remembers posting it.

My father leans on reception, inviting a confidence. 'Was she alone?'

'Yes.'

'Did she seem upset?'

The woman considers him.

'Was there anything unusual about her behaviour?' my father says.

'Not that I remember—' She starts. 'Someone spoke to her, just after she gave me the letter.'

'A man?'

'Yes.'

'Was it him?' He shows her the photo of me and Oswald.

'No.'

'Do you know who the man was?'

'No. He gave her a card. She threw it in the bin.' She looks past my father, towards the lift.

Oddly enough, for all his anxiety and irritation, he sleeps well that night.

If he does fly to Berlin it seems inevitable that he will read my second letter. I imagine him at the table where I used to sit, near the mirror with its pond-like glass. The atmosphere, as always, is restrained, bookish, faintly erotic. The second letter is hard for him to stomach, but he reads it twice, from beginning to end, and then looks up. *The opposite direction.* What do I mean by that? Unless he manages to trace either Oswald or Cheadle – and I can't see that happening, not given the entirely coincidental nature of my encounters with the two men – he has no way of finding out where I have gone. The trail will go cold in Berlin – even, possibly, at the Einstein. But wait. What about Lydia? He's a reporter with a keen intuitive sense and decades of experience. He looks at Lydia and wonders what she can tell him.

He looks at Lydia—

The train stops abruptly, jolting me forwards in my seat. We appear to have reached the border with Russia. I take out my passport and my letter of invitation and place them neatly on the table by the window, ready for inspection. The muscles in my stomach have tensed up. My mouth tastes of coins.

When the Russian border guard steps into my compartment I say good evening – *Dobry vyecher* – then I look straight ahead with my hands in my lap. He opens my passport to the page that holds my visa. I can hear his breathing, thick and steady, as if he's asleep. A chill clings to his dark-green uniform; drizzle pearls his grey fur hat. At last he hands my passport back with a brisk nod. Outwardly I remain the same – calm expression, folded hands – but inside I'm bubbling over. *My visa is still valid. He has let me in.*

Even before the train begins to move again I'm back in the Einstein. My father signals to Lydia and she walks over. Her smile is professional, as usual. There's an extra element, though – an intensity or lustre. She knows she's in a story, and that he's part of it. Is he as attractive as she expected him to be? And what does he think of her?

He questions her as she stands beside the table, her left hip only inches from his right shoulder. She answers thoughtfully. He looks up, charmed by the freckles scattered across her nose. There is no way of avoiding the hackneyed line. *What time do you finish work?* When he leaves a few minutes later he insists on paying. She gets to keep my money.

At the end of her shift they meet outside the café. Though they don't know each other at all, and are facing different ways, looking for a taxi, they are connected by something so vibrant that it's almost visible. When I wrote my letter, did I know that it would throw them together?

In less than half an hour they are in his room at the InterContinental, with its wide bed, its floor-to-ceiling window, its soaring view over the Tiergarten. It's all so obvious and effortless. Seamless, really. As the gap between their faces narrows, I turn away. It's as if I'm standing at the window, looking out. Grey clouds swirling, trees stripped of all their leaves.

Later, he reaches across her bare shoulder for my letter. The hairs on his forearm glint in the light from the bedside lamp. The window black, the rush-hour traffic murmuring below. He begins to read. Halfway through, he puts the letter down.

'So you didn't actually *know* my daughter . . .'

Lydia rolls on to her back and looks at him. She's still wondering who he is, this glamorous older man she has allowed into her life. This stranger.

'I saw her three or four times,' she says.

'You think she was staying nearby?'

'It's possible.'

'She didn't mention a hotel?'

'No.'

'What about the last time you saw her, when she gave you the letter? Did she tell you where she was going?'

Lydia thinks back. 'She said she couldn't come to the café again. I had the feeling she was leaving that day. She looked at her watch. She was in a hurry.'

'That was two weeks ago?'

'Not so long. Eight days maybe.' She lifts herself higher on the pillows. 'There was a kind of – I don't know – *Engültigkeit* about the way she talked.'

'*Engültigkeit?*'

'Something final. She seemed to know what she was doing – in the future. It was all decided.'

My father stares at the ceiling, a knotting in his chest, around his heart. I know what he's thinking, but he's wrong. Then a new question occurs to him. 'Was she always by herself?'

'Yes,' Lydia says. 'Except for one time. There was a man with her.'

'What was he like?'

'Pale, quite thin. In his twenties.' She pauses. 'He was German.'

My father reaches for the envelope that held the letter and shows Lydia the photo.

She nods. 'That's him.'

'His name's Oswald.' My father pronounces it the English way, as you would an Anglo-Saxon king.

'You think he's her boyfriend?'

'I don't know.' My father studies the photo. 'What do you think?'

'No,' Lydia says. 'She'd be with someone more good-looking.'

'Because she's good-looking?'

'Yes.'

Despite the circumstances they can't help smiling at each other. In talking about me it seems they have also said something about themselves.

I turn to the window. A wall runs parallel to the railway, its concrete covered with graffiti. The words look squeezed from a tube. In the background is a row of grim apartment blocks.

Moscow.

No snow has fallen in the city but a shiver goes through me as I step down on to the platform. I've been travelling for twenty-seven hours. Before I left Berlin I booked into the Peking Hotel, which is near the station, and though it's after midnight I decide to walk. The weather is cold and overcast. Still, at least it isn't raining.

Once outside the station I make for a tunnel that leads beneath a raised main road. Two mismatched chairs stand by the entrance, against the wall, as if the tunnel usually has guardians who charge a fee. One is a grey office chair with wheels. The other has spindly legs and a plywood seat. A dense yellow glow seeps from the lights in the ceiling.

I'm halfway through the tunnel when a group of figures appears at the far end. One of them is freakishly tall, in a coat that has a patent-leather glint to it, and he holds his arms out in front of him, at right-angles to his body, like a zombie. Another wears a Pussy Riot balaclava and a frothy tutu. Her black calf-length boots bristle with silver studs. A third carries a bottle of vodka and a scythe. They surround me before I can retrace my steps.

'Tourist?' one of them says, in English.

I nod. '*Da, eto pravda.*' Yes, it's true.

The Pussy Riot girl stands in front of me, one hand on her hip. 'You speak Russian?'

'*Nyet.*' No.

That gets a laugh.

'You want to come to a party?' The girl speaks English with a languid American accent. In the yellow light her eyes look bloodshot.

'It's late,' I tell her. 'I need to check into my hotel.'

'We prepare for Halloween,' the zombie says. 'Here in Russia Halloween is – how you say – not legal.'

'We are protestors,' says the boy with the scythe.

'What if the police see you?' I ask.

The Pussy Riot girl shrugs. 'We escape.'

She offers me a cigarette. I shake my head, then watch as she lights up. She sucks the smoke deep into her lungs and holds it there. I look past her at the boy with the scythe, his vest and bare arms spattered with fake blood.

'You look great,' I say. 'I really like the outfits.'

'We look great,' the zombie says.

The Pussy Riot girl asks where I'm staying.

I hesitate. 'The Peking Hotel.'

'Nice,' she says, 'but this is not the way.'

She walks me back to the station, then points across the square to a gap between a bar's yellow neon sign and a slowly pulsing green cross that looks like an all-night chemist. The Peking is down that road, she says. Ten minutes. There's no reason not to believe her. I thank her, then say goodbye.

As I move away, a man's voice floats up into the air behind me. 'Maybe we visit you, in your hotel . . .'

Then only the rush of late-night traffic on the raised main road, and two taxi drivers on the pavement, arguing.

The next day, after breakfast, I approach reception and tell the man on duty – Vladimir – that I need a travel agency. Is there one nearby? As Vladimir consults his computer he makes a curious monotonous humming sound, then writes down a name and address on a sheet of paper. It's two stops on the Metro, he tells me. Or I could walk. He gives me directions. It will take half an hour, he says.

Out on the street the air has a bite to it but the sun is shining and the sky is a vast unexpected blue. I follow Vladimir's advice and set off down Sadovaya, my breath making pale clouds. When I woke, at half past six, I parted the tall bronze curtains in my room and stood at the window, staring out. I thought of my next port of call, Cherepovets, and pictured Anna as a young girl, her hair as yet undyed, her teeth still white. At that moment I somehow understood that Cherepovets was an unnecessary distraction and could be dispensed with. I will head for Arkhangel'sk – preferably by air.

I locate the travel agency, on the first floor of an office building, arriving before it opens. As I take a seat in the hallway, next to an old man in a black leather cap, he doubles over coughing. I offer him some water. He waves a hand, meaning no. He has white hair and thick black eyebrows, and the lines that curve past his mouth are so deep they look carved.

Finally the coughing fit passes and he asks where I am from. I tell him I'm English.

'Yes,' he says. 'That is what I thought.' He touches his cheek with his fingertips. 'The skin.'

He speaks English haltingly, as if the inside of his mouth is sore, but his command of the language impresses me.

'Moscow.' He shakes his head. 'Too many cars. I can't breathe.'

I murmur something sympathetic.

'You're a tourist?' he says.

'Yes.'

He stares straight ahead, his mouth turned down at the corners.

'What about you?' I say. 'Why are you here?'

He tells me he has spent the last three weeks with his mother, and that he's now returning home, to Arkhangel'sk.

'But that's where I'm going!' I say. 'I'm about to try and book a flight.'

'I also need to book a flight.'

'Perhaps we could travel together. It would be much easier for me.'

'If we travel together,' the man says, 'I can practise my

English. I haven't spoken English since I retired ten years ago.'

We introduce ourselves. His name is Yevgeny. When I tell him I'm Misty I feel like a fraud, and also faintly ridiculous, but he doesn't seem to find it strange. He asks what I will do in Arkhangel'sk. I'll be spending a few days with a colleague of my father's, I tell him. I'm studying languages at university, so I'm hoping to pick up a bit of Russian. Yevgeny believes everything I say – but then, why shouldn't he? It sounds plausible enough. All the same, I'm glad he doesn't ask who my father's colleague is. Arkhangel'sk isn't exactly a metropolis. If Yevgeny knows the man, my cover story will collapse.

In the travel agency Yevgeny talks to a woman who gives off an Addams family glamour – long black hair, pale lips, black blouse unbuttoned to reveal a silver crucifix. She answers at some length and he translates for me. There are no direct flights to Arkhangel'sk until Tuesday, he says. We could change planes in St Petersburg but that will be expensive.

He puts his head in his hands and groans. 'Another four days in this terrible place.'

The woman toys with her crucifix, indifferent.

Yevgeny asks about trains. She tells us there's a sleeper from Yaroslavsky station, with seats available tomorrow. It's a long journey – twenty-one hours – but we will be in Arkhangel'sk early on Sunday morning, and it will cost a third of the price.

Yevgeny turns to me, eyebrows raised.

'Let's go by train,' I say, then ask if he could book me an extra night at the Peking Hotel.

Later, out on the street, I thank him for all his help, and we agree to meet at the station, an hour before the train departs.

With Yevgeny gone, I hesitate, unsure how to spend the day. I feel a surge of impatience, then a kind of lethargy, and I'm reminded of the time I drove to the south of France and sat by a pool, waiting for something to happen. One thing's certain: I won't be seeing any sights. Moscow is a staging-post, not an end in itself, and I can't allow it to make too much of an impression.

In the Metro I take the grey line, going north. With their marble hallways and their elaborate chandeliers, the stations astonish me, but I'm content with glimpses. I leave the train at the last stop, Altufevo. There are underground kiosks selling painkillers, warm pies known as *pirozhki*, and woolly bobble-hats. No trace of chandeliers or marble now. I think of Oswald, who took me to the edge of Berlin to show me something that wasn't there. He thought it was worth looking at and he was right. I should send him a postcard, as promised.

I set off up a main road, passing bus-shelters papered over with adverts and flyers. Old women squat on low stools by the kerb. There are jars of pickled vegetables for sale, and tiny cloves of garlic, and pink-bellied river fish laid out on sheets of cardboard. The men are dressed in black leather jackets and jeans. Most of them carry bottles of beer. There are no ordinary houses or shops, only supermarkets and tower-blocks. On the flat grassy areas in between are birch trees, and also trees I don't recognise, with clusters of red berries dangling from their branches.

I stop for a bowl of soup in a café run by a family from

Uzbekistan. Later, I cut through a park. Thin clouds veil the sky; the sun is weakening. Some distance from the footpath an old couple are picnicking on the trunk of a fallen tree, their shoulders touching. Their laughter reaches me. As I walk on, the man lifts a hand and waves. It's only among strangers that I'm seen, only among strangers that I exist.

The following morning I meet Yevgeny at Yaroslavsky station, as agreed. Though he has booked us into separate sleeping compartments – an example of his tact – we sit together for the first leg of the journey, sipping the black tea he buys from a conductor. As Moscow recedes, the outskirts giving way to countryside, I ask Yevgeny about his mother. She's ninety-four, he says, and he has spent the last three weeks trying to persuade her to move house. You should live near me, he tells her. Why? she says. So I can do your washing? He smiles, the lines deepening around his mouth, then he takes off his cap and ruffles his white hair. She's so stubborn, he says. Tough as old shoe leather. During the Second World War she flew with the Russian air force. She was one of a handful of female pilots known as 'night witches' who dropped bombs on the advancing German army. She was shot down twice, but made it through unscathed. She has received numerous medals and decorations from the state, though she lives modestly, in an apartment in the suburbs. He has the feeling she will outlast him. It's possible that she's immortal. He sees the look on my face. He's joking, he says. Then, abruptly, he tells me he would like to rest his eyes. Even talking about her makes him tired.

I take my tea next door, to my compartment. That after-noon, as I sit beside the window, endless birch trees flashing by, I return to the InterContinental. Though two days have passed in my world, only an hour has gone by for my father and Lydia, enough time for them to have made love again and drifted off to sleep.

My father wakes suddenly, one hand grasping at the air. He has had a bad dream. The curtains have yet to be drawn; the windows are black. Light spills from the half-open bathroom door but doesn't reach the corners of the room. Does he know where he is? Not right away. Then he notices the sheet of paper on the floor, my handwriting visible. Of course. Berlin.

And he has a lead.

Oswald.

Lydia stirs beside him and reaches for his hand. 'David? What will you do?'

'I don't know.' Sitting up, he stares at the tall vase of exotic twigs and grasses opposite the bed. 'I really don't know.'

'I should leave,' she says.

She crosses the room in the half dark, pinning her hair up as she goes. He is struck by how at ease with her nakedness she is. His mind jams. She shuts the bathroom door and switches on the shower.

The train jerks, then speeds up. The sky has lowered, and rain streaks diagonally across the window. My imagination keeps racing ahead, and I have to remind myself that the Café Einstein rendezvous is still five days away. My father won't have left Rome yet but he ought to have received my first letter. Though short, it will have been a comfort to him. Scenarios that might have crossed his mind – abduction, murder – can be ruled out. He still has a decision to make, however. What will he do?

A station slides into view. Sheets of water on the platform

reflect its green facade. One of the buildings has a spire with a cross on top. The door swings open, and I glimpse lighted candles and a wall hung with icons.

I see Pavlo briefly, in his immaculate white T-shirt, accompanied by the seductive whir and hum of a spin-drier, then I go back to thinking about my father. Despite myself, I have left clues as to my whereabouts, my movements – the hotel stationery, the photograph of Oswald . . . As my father travels from the airport into the city he studies the photo, trying to memorise the young man's unmemorable face. He needs to be able to recognise Oswald if he comes across him. But what's the likelihood of that?

I remember how Lydia stood by our table and listened to Oswald gossiping about his supervisor at KaDeWe. If Lydia recalls the stories and repeats them to my father he will have no trouble tracking Oswald down – and Oswald has valuable intelligence, for it was he who saw me at the station, on a train bound for Moscow . . .

My father might fly to Russia – or perhaps he will follow my example and take a train, arriving at Byelorusskaya station in the middle of the night. It's October in Moscow. Dressed in an open-necked shirt and a pair of chinos, he has dark smears beneath his eyes, like the stains water leaves on bath enamel. Other travellers give him suspicious glances and push past, intent on journeys of their own. His finishes right there, though, under the mint-green sign that glows on the roof of the main station building. He could go to the police, but Russia, as he knows, is a profoundly bureaucratic country, impenetrable and vast, and I'm just another foreign girl. Though he is accustomed to difficult predicaments, he looks out of place, and his mouth is trembling, uncertain. I would like to be able to walk up to him and give him a hug. I'd like to say, *You've done all you can do, Dad. Stop worrying. Go home.* And he'd say, *Honestly? Is that what you want?* And I'd say, *Yes, it's what I want.* I'd kiss him on the cheek and tell him that I love him. He'd say, *I love you too, Kit. I always have.* He'd pause, and then he'd say it again. *I always have.* He'd be holding me, looking down into my face. I need him to repeat those words. Some things you can't hear enough.

As afternoon shades into evening I drop in on Yevgeny. He orders more black tea, then asks me about university. When I mention Oxford, his face opens in astonishment. He visited the city once, he says, when he was a professor, and then a second time, not long after he retired. In a garden next to Christ Church he saw a tree whose bright-yellow star-shaped leaves were thrown into relief by the dark stone of the wall behind them. He doesn't know what kind of tree it was – it looked oriental somehow – but he has never forgotten the way it stood out against that wall. He also went to a museum filled with weapons, tribal masks and musical instruments. The place was so dimly lit that a curator handed him a special wind-up torch. He could live in Oxford, he says. The air itself seemed educated, busy with knowledge. You could learn things simply by breathing. He laughs and then falls quiet. We rattle across a river. Low in the sky, on the horizon, is an orange vent, the first sun we have seen all day. Then more bare trees, more soggy rumpled land. Yevgeny's reminiscences prompt no regrets in me, no nostalgia for the life I have rejected, only the wish that I could trade in my scholarship and send him to Oxford in my place.

At seven o'clock we pull into a large station with an elaborate red-and-white facade.

'Vologda,' Yevgeny says.

In the corridor Russian men are already dressed for bed, in shorts and flip-flops. I edge past them and jump down on to the platform. Some new passengers are hurrying to climb on board, struggling with heavy bags. Others stand about, talking and smoking. Three army women in green uniforms and fur hats pose for a photo under the harsh lights. Steam lifts from the wheels of the train, and the sides of the carriages are ridged, gleaming and faintly dented, like old-fashioned biscuit tins. The night feels brash, dramatic. Nickel-plated.

I return to Yevgeny's compartment and he holds out a bag of *pirozhki*. As I take one, his gaze falls on my bruised wrist.

'Your arm,' he says.

I pull my sleeve down. 'It's nothing.'

'What happened?'

'It was an accident. I tripped over my suitcase. In my hotel room.'

His eyes drift past me, to the window. He senses that I'm lying. At the same time, I don't imagine he would want to hear the truth. I change the subject by asking about Arkhangel'sk. Relieved perhaps, he responds enthusiastically. The region's earliest inhabitants were hunters and fishermen who lived fourteen thousand years ago, he says. Mysterious legendary tribes such as the white-eyed Chudi. Arkhangel'sk itself was founded by Ivan the Terrible in 1584. A wooden city sprang up within a year and became Russia's first major commercial port. Surrounded by forest, the economy was driven by timber, not just shipbuilding, but paper mills, pulp factories. The university is excellent. He taught engineering there for many years. There's also a medical school. Mikhail Lomonosov, an eighteenth-century scientist and writer, is one of the city's celebrated sons. He discovered the atmosphere of Venus. His fame is such, Yevgeny says with a wry smile, that a local potato is named after him.

At half past nine his cough returns.

'I've talked enough,' he says. 'I think I'll sleep.'

I wish him a restful night.

Back in my own compartment, I suddenly feel hungry and unpack the provisions I brought along – black bread, cured meat, gherkins, vodka. I'm trying to prise the top off the bottle when a train official knocks on my door. She's holding a wicker basket of items for the journey – crackers, tissues, chewing gum. I gesture at the bottle and say the Russian word for 'open'.

'It's forbidden,' she tells me.

'Vodka's forbidden?'

'Yes.'

'But this is Russia . . .'

She smiles. 'It's the regulations,' she says, then moves on down the carriage.

Putting the bottle on the table by the window I unscrew the lid on the jar of gherkins and have just begun to eat when the door to my compartment opens again and two men appear. One of them is huge, with blond hair cut close to his skull and the smooth round face of a baby. He sits opposite me and starts foraging in a sports bag. The other man, who is smaller and darker, climbs up on to one of the top bunks and lies down, facing the wall. The huge man looks at me steadily, his eyes the colour of antifreeze. He goes by the name of Sergei, he says. His friend is Konstantin. Using sign language and basic Russian, I ask Sergei if he would like to share my food. He thanks me and takes a slice of bread and ham. Then he notices the vodka.

'It's forbidden,' I say.

'Yes.' He shrugs.

He twists off the top and pours us half a glass each, then he reaches into his sports bag and lifts out some apples. They come from his garden in Tutayev. Next he produces a jar and unscrews the lid. It seems to be some kind of chutney. Made from tomato and garlic, he says. Excellent with meat. While we eat and drink I ask Sergei what he does for a living. He works in a sheet-metal factory, he tells me, as does his friend. I ask about his family. He has a wife, three children. Though Konstantin has his back to me I sense that he's still awake. I help myself to one of Sergei's apples.

'You travel alone?' he asks.

I think about mentioning Yevgeny but decide against it. After all, we will only be together for the duration of the train journey. 'Yes. I'm alone.'

'You don't have to worry.' Sergei places a massive, scarred hand over his heart. 'We're good people.'

I pour him another vodka.

In the window birch trees flash past, white lines suspended upright in the darkness.

Sergei takes out his mobile phone, an ancient Nokia, and offers to play me some of his songs. I'm worried they'll be terrible, like karaoke, and that I'll have to be diplomatic, but his voice, which is unaccompanied, is haunting and tender.

'This is you?' I say.

'My songs. I wrote them.' He batters at his chest with both palms. 'In your soul you must have the whole world.'

The vodka bottle is almost empty.

I go to the bathroom. On my way back I look in on Yevgeny, thinking to say good night, but he's already lying down with his eyes shut. Returning to my compartment, I tell Sergei that I need to sleep.

'*Kharashó*,' he says. That's fine.

Out of the corner of my eye I see him drain the contents of two glasses, one after the other. Did he finish my drink as well? No, I still have mine. Looking more closely, I realise the second glass is actually a jar. He must have drunk the liquid the gherkins came in.

'*Spakoinai nochi*,' he says. Good night.

I thought the men would sleep in the top two bunks. Instead, Konstantin climbs down, and without speaking again the two men leave the compartment. I switch off the light and stretch out on my bed.

Some time later, when I open my eyes, I make out several round shapes on the table by the window. Sergei forgot his apples.

I'm walking through Trastevere with my parents. They're in their twenties, and in love. Though this is before they had me, I'm there between them, a child of seven or eight. The night is warm. The facades of churches lit up, shop windows glowing. I feel light but anchored, like a balloon on the end of a long string.

We enter a piazza filled with stalls and people. It feels like the *Festa de' Noantri*, which happens in July. We pause by a boxing ring. A man in green trunks slumps against the ropes, his eyes glazed and watery. The other man holds his arms above his head, his gloved hands dark-red and shiny, like giant cherries. My father gazes up into the ring. My mother rests her head against his shoulder. He puts an arm round her, and they walk on. I have to run to catch up.

Later, we eat at a local pizzeria nicknamed *L'Obitorio* – The Morgue – because all its tables are topped with marble slabs. We sit outside, next to the road. Suddenly my father points. *Look!* A truck crawls past in low gear. Dangling from a winch at the back is a naked woman, her hair and body painted gold. Since the cord or wire that holds her isn't visible she appears to be floating in mid-air, halfway between the truck and the overhanging trees.

I wake with a feeling of elation, still in that imaginary, timeless world, the trouble that awaits our family out of sight or even sidestepped altogether, our happiness untouchable.

The rhythmic clatter of the train. I turn in my bed and peer out of the window.

Endless woods, no moon.

A guard flicks on the light and makes an announcement I don't understand. I glance at my watch. Twenty-five past six. Half an hour to Arkhangel'sk. When I part the curtain my breath catches in my throat. The loose stone chippings next to the rails are sprinkled with snow.

A few minutes before we arrive Yevgeny appears in a clean shirt. He asks me how I slept.

'I don't feel I slept at all,' I say, 'but I must have, I suppose. I remember dreams.'

We step down out of the train. On the platform is a row of old-fashioned metal streetlamps, the globes of light seemingly suspended in a dense and swirling darkness. The station is a low white building, with ARKHANGELSK spelled out in giant dilapidated letters on the roof. Of Sergei and Konstantin there is no sign. These people you see once, and never again.

Since it's still so early, just after seven, Yevgeny suggests we share a taxi. In front of the station he approaches a driver and negotiates a price, then we climb in. I ask to be dropped at the Pur Navolok hotel.

As we set off down a wide bleak avenue, tyres crackling on the snow, Yevgeny gives me a puzzled look. 'I thought you were staying with your father's friend.'

'He was called away unexpectedly,' I say, 'on business. He'll be back tomorrow.'

Turning to face the window, I wipe a hole in the condensation. Sheer apartment blocks, low-voltage neon signs.

When we reach the Pur Navolok I try to say goodbye inside the taxi but Yevgeny climbs out and leans on the open door, gripping the top edge with his gloved hands.

'I'm probably a little old for you, but I'd like to give you my number.' He removes his right glove and fumbles in his pocket for a pen and paper. In shaky handwriting he jots his number down. 'If you need a companion or if you'd like someone to show you the city.' He pauses. 'Or if you're in trouble.'

'That's very kind,' I say. 'Thank you.'

He glances up at the hotel's modern blue-and-white facade. 'It's a good place. Expensive, though.'

We say goodbye and Yevgeny lowers himself back into the taxi. I wait until the car has turned the corner, then I consult the map Vladimir printed out for me on my second night in Moscow. I have lied to Yevgeny from the beginning. I won't be staying with my father's friend, since he doesn't have a friend, and I won't be staying at the Pur Navolok either. I have booked a room at the Best Eastern Dvina, which is cheaper and just as central.

The Pur Navolok overlooks the river, but all that shows in the darkness is a strip of snow-dusted beach and a pinpoint of green light in the distance. I follow the promenade for half a mile, a cold wind blowing off the water, then I turn inland. In twenty minutes I reach the Dvina, a huge pale-pink block set back from the road. The blonde woman on reception – Olga – speaks a little English. After the long train journey I feel like a swim, but when I ask if there's a pool she laughs.

'We can build perhaps,' she says.

In my room on the fifth floor I part the net curtains. Below are a few parked cars. Off to the right is a supermarket with a red neon sign on top. I turn from the window. Yellow walls, a 13-inch TV. A small bland painting of a coffee cup. I could be anywhere in Russia – or anywhere at all. I arrange my Richter postcards on the mirror above the desk, wedging them between the glass and the frame, then I go downstairs again. In the shopping mall across the street I buy myself an Arctic parka and a scarf.

Later, when it's light, I walk along the river, back towards the Pur Navolok. On the long grand esplanade is a stone-and-metal monument that reminds me of the prow of a fighting ship from the Dark Ages. The beach below is wide and flat. Pieces of driftwood lie about on sand that has frozen hard as concrete. Somehow I never imagined sand could freeze. The sky is vast and overarching, a limitless dreamlike mauve-blue. In its upper reaches are the strangest clouds I have ever seen – identical soft-edged cubes of white which fit together in a loose mosaic.

* * *

Back in my room I switch on the desk lamp and look at the scrap of paper Yevgeny gave me. It's odd how closely it resembles the messages I came across earlier in the year, messages that were either misleading or irrelevant, meant for somebody else, or no one at all. Though the scribbled number seems to be prompting me to pick up the phone I know I will do nothing of the kind. I don't need any guidance or comfort. That stage is over.

I tear Yevgeny's number into pieces – quickly, without thinking, the way you swallow medicine – then walk to the window and turn the handle. Cold air knifes into the room. I reach out with my fist and open my fingers. The bits of torn paper are sucked sideways into the dark. For a moment I see them as plasma. Blood draining from my body. Life leaving. I pull the window shut and lie down on the bed. Just the pyramid of lamplight on the desk. *Arkhangel'sk.* My heart starts beating faster, as if I'm waiting for a lover. I have come so far.

In my mind I track the fragments as they whirl off into the bitter Russian night. I picture a boy out walking, hood up, hands shoved deep into the pockets of his jeans. When he glances up and sees the scraps of paper he knows what he must do. He must collect each and every one of them or something terrible will happen. He's an only child. He's always playing games like that. If he kicks a stone and it doesn't stay on the pavement his father will lose his job. If he's on his bike and the traffic light turns red before he reaches it his parents will separate, or die. How can he hope to pick up all the pieces though? They scarcely show up against the snow, and there must be at least a dozen of them. My thoughts are dogs, he tells himself. Keep them on a tight leash. One piece at a time. He's methodical, obsessive. Even though it's close to freezing. Some of the bits of paper he finds do not belong. They're part of another puzzle, a different challenge. His hands go numb. He doesn't care. And finally, when he has gathered them all, every last one, he takes them home and shuts himself in his bedroom and fits them back together. Only then does he realise it's a phone number. He waits until his parents are asleep – they're still alive, still married – then he tiptoes to the phone and dials.

A man answers. 'Who's speaking, please?' The man sounds old.

The boy says his name.

'Do I know you?' the old man says.

'No.'

The old man lowers himself on to a chair and stares out across the room. On the wall above the phone is a calendar showing the rooftops of Oxford. 'How did you get my number?'

The boy describes how he saw the little bits of paper flutter from the window of a tall building in the city centre, and how he chased them down until he had them all.

'Which tall building?' the old man asks.

'The Dvina.'

'That's a hotel – near the river.'

'Yes.'

The old man falls quiet, thinking. Then he says, 'Ah yes. I see.'

'I stuck the pieces together,' the boy says. 'Like a jigsaw. It took me ages.'

The old man smiles. He tells the boy that he has enjoyed talking to him and thanks him for calling and then hangs up. The smile drains from his face like water sinking into sand. He remains on his chair, staring out across the room.

'Yevgeny,' he says, 'what were you thinking?' And then, a few moments later, 'Stupid old man.'

Lying on my bed, I feel bad. My imagination has become my conscience.

What does the boy do? He puts the piece of paper in a safe place, along with his other treasures. It's proof of something – of what he isn't entirely sure. His urge to make sense of things, perhaps. His tenacity. At some point in the future, when he has grown up, he will come across the piece of paper and stare at it. He will remember the old man's voice and he will call the number again. Will the old man answer? Or will the number ring and ring?

My imagination might be acting as my conscience but it's also a thread that reaches all the way back to the beginning of the journey. It's my only contact with the world I've left behind.

It's a kind of lifeline.

They have come for me. They're milling around downstairs, in the lobby. I can't see their faces and I don't know their names, but I can hear them murmuring. They ask Olga for my room number, then they gather by the lifts and draw lots. They use cigarettes, some with filters, some without. The losers will have to climb the stairs. They want to cover all the bases, make sure that I don't slip away. One of them steps forwards and presses the call button.

I need to leave my room as soon as possible but I'm only half-dressed and I can't find my shoes. They're not in the cupboard or the bathroom. I kneel on the floor. They're not under the bed. Was I even *wearing* shoes? I can't recall. And all the time the lifts are rising through the building, and the footsteps in the stairwell are growing louder. Is there another way out? A fire escape? It's the law, surely – even here. The notice on the wall next to the door is written in Cyrillic. I manage to decipher the words EVACUATION – FIFTH FLOOR but can't make sense of the floor plan. It bears no relation to the hotel I'm staying in. For what seems like minutes on end I move my fingertip from one room to another, from one stencilled box to the next, trying to discover how it works, trying to orient myself, but I can't even tell which room is mine, let alone find an emergency exit.

I look again, more closely. There must be something I have missed. Then I realise. It's the floor plan from a different building altogether. An office block maybe. A shopping mall. Why hasn't someone brought it to the management's atten-tion? How can people be so careless? I'm wearing a T-shirt and nothing much else. My feet are numb. I wish I could go back to sleep but the lift doors are opening and there are voices in the corridor. A red light wobbles through the window and settles in the room.

I jerk awake. The room is cold but I am soaked in sweat. My T-shirt clings to me. The red light is coming from the supermarket's neon sign. Shivering, I wriggle out of the T-shirt. I drop it on the carpet, then I dry myself on a towel and drink some water from the bathroom tap. It's five a.m. I'm worried that Yevgeny might appear at the Dvina – or that someone might. What are the chances of that happening? Practically zero. But I can't afford to take *any chances at all*.

After a breakfast of tepid semolina and hard-boiled eggs I pack my case and take the lift down to reception. A woman I don't recognise is on duty. I ask for Olga.

The woman seems offended. 'Olga not here.'

When I tell her I want to check out she consults her computer. 'There is problem?'

'No problem,' I say. 'I just need to leave.'

'What is problem? Room?'

'Room good. Room OK.' I smile and give her the thumbs-up. '*Skólka stóit?*' How much do I owe?

She doesn't answer. Instead she picks up the phone and dials a two-digit number. While she talks she keeps looking at me, her eyes magnified by her glasses, like goldfish when they swim too close to the side of their bowl. Not long after she hangs up a door opens behind her and a man appears. He is short and bulky and his grey suit jacket, which is shiny, almost lacquered, is tailored in such a way that it makes his upper body look square. Between his lips is a wooden toothpick which he manoeuvres using just his tongue and teeth. This man has the patient lethargic air of somebody whose job is to resolve disputes. He's probably the manager. Outside it has begun to snow.

'You book two nights,' he says.

I nod. '*Da.*'

He seems to inflate like a prosecutor who has exposed a flaw in a defendant's case. 'You book two nights, you pay two nights.'

'No problem,' I say. 'I pay two nights.'

After more discussion, during which the two hotel employees break off once or twice to stare at me – did they expect me to argue, lose my temper? – they allow me to pay. I say goodbye, then leave through the revolving doors.

I make for a travel agency I noticed the day before, when I was returning from my walk along the river. The light is muffled, grey. Soon there won't be any light at all. I feel drunk, even though I haven't had a thing to drink. Heads turn as I pass. A snowflake settles on my tongue and melts.

The woman in the travel agency speaks broken English and has an unlikely tan. She was recently in Sharm el-Sheikh. Behind her are two shelves of souvenirs from her travels.

'What's your name?' I ask.

'Elena.'

'I'd like to go north, Elena. I'm looking for a place that is very far away. Obscure.'

'Obscure?' She doesn't know the word.

'A place with not too many people.'

She glances sideways, through the window. 'Not so many people here.'

'Smaller than here.'

'Smaller?'

'Like the end of the world,' I say. 'Like nowhere.'

She tilts her face upwards and backwards until she seems to be looking at me through the bottom of her eyes. Though her gaze is eerie I take it to mean that she is confused by my request. Also that she's beginning to understand what I'm after.

'Where can I go,' I say, prompting her, 'that is further north?'

It's so quiet in her office that I hear her spine click as she turns in her chair. She begins to tap away at her keyboard. A map of Northern Europe and the Arctic appears on her screen.

'Maybe here,' she says at last.

I lean over the desk, my head next to hers. She has zoomed in on a cluster of islands with shattered or serrated coastlines.

'Svalbard,' she says.

I have heard of Svalbard, but the name sounds fantastical, like El Dorado or Atlantis.

'This.' She points to a settlement located halfway down an inlet and surrounded by miles of nothingness.

'What's there?' I ask.

'Very small place. Very—' and she makes a humming sound that reminds me of the man in the Peking Hotel, 'very *obscure.*' She gives me a thin smile. She seems daunted by her own suggestion.

'How many people?'

'I don't know. Maybe three hundred.' She frowns. 'They look for coal.'

'It's a mining town?'

'Mining. Yes.'

'And the name?'

'Ugolgrad.' She explains that although the archipelago belongs to Norway the settlement is Russian.

My heart leaps as I look at the screen again. I didn't realise such a place existed. 'How do I get there?'

'Not so easy.'

A complicated journey, then. Good.

While Elena makes phone calls and trawls through the Internet I stare out over the rooftops. The next step of the journey is taking shape. All I have to do is leave as soon as possible, before the people in my dream catch up with me. I hope it's not too late in the year to be going so far north. I hope I have sufficient funds.

The travel arrangements take hours – Elena also books me into a new hotel – and when I finally step out on to the street it's dark again. The lack of daylight makes me feel giddy, breathless, as if time itself is speeding up. I cross Chumbarovka, with its historic houses and its young mothers pushing prams. Fog thickens the air, reducing visibility. Elena told me to catch a bus on Troitsky Prospekt. The number 61 goes directly to my new hotel, which is over a bridge, in a different part of the city. The two connecting flights have cost me close to twenty thousand roubles but I know it will be worth it. The only drawback is, I have to wait four days.

I come out on to Troitsky Prospekt. On the far side of the road is a church, its walls caged in scaffolding, two golden domes abandoned on the ground. A bus with purple curtains in the windows comes to a standstill near me. Behind the misty glass is Yevgeny. When he sees me his features widen. He points towards the door, then signals that he will get off at the next stop. As soon as the bus surges away from me I double back and cut down a sidestreet, my suitcase bouncing behind me on its tiny wheels. I take the first left turning, past a sauna, then turn left again on to a path that divides two rows of old wooden buildings.

As I flatten myself against the side wall of a house, a door opens behind me, or seems to give, and I'm drawn backwards into a kind of porch or anteroom, coats heaped shapelessly on hooks, a spade propped against the wall. Beyond is a dimly lit interior that smells of solvents. The room is about the size of a railway carriage, with bare boards on the floor and a tin ceiling. At the far end a low-voltage bulb dangles above a glass-topped counter. The shelves that line the walls on either side of me are crammed with small round objects that reflect the meagre light.

I take a few quick steps into the room. The objects are snow globes, some made of plastic, others of thick discoloured glass. I pick one up at random and wipe off the dust. Inside is a replica of Lenin's mausoleum. I shake it gently and watch the white flakes shower down on to the famous revolutionary's face. I look at the base. No price tag. I put the snow globe back and pick up another. This one contains a murky sea encrusted with ice floes. Resting at an angle on the ocean bed is the slim shape of a submarine. The figures of survivors float on the surface – or are they casualties, the bodies of the drowned, the dead? I have a dim memory of a news story about the sinking of a Russian submarine. It happened around the time of the millennium. Thoughtfully, I return it to the shelf. The third snow globe I look at holds a stand of birch trees, a frozen pond, and a couple skating hand in hand. I sense a heightened innocence, a pleasure that seems intense but fragile, as though the small glass dome has captured the moments preceding a catastrophe. I have never seen such an extraordinary collection. Is this a toyshop or a museum?

I look towards the end of the room again, aware of some sort of shift or change yet unable to describe it. The naked bulb above the counter sways. There's a draught perhaps – or else a truck went by outside and shook the building. I don't see the man until he moves in his chair and I have the feeling he only moved in order to relieve the tension. It reminds me of something I haven't thought about in years. When we were living in London I would often sit so still that people would walk into the room and out again without noticing that I was there. It was as if I was able to find a wrinkle in time or space and hide in it. I used to believe I could become invisible. Inanimate. The man huddled in the shadows to one side of the counter is dressed in a brown suit that looks too small for him. His elongated head is covered with a sparse grey fuzz. Behind him is a heavy pleated curtain.

I say good afternoon in Russian. He responds with a sweeping gesture which I assume is an invitation to browse. One of the snow globes is much larger than the rest and contains the whole of Arkhangel'sk. I can see streets fanning out from the centre, and the industrial zone beyond. There is the Pur Navolok, and there, further east, is the Dvina. There is the bridge I will have to cross to reach my new hotel. I can see buses with purple curtains in their windows. I can see people too. One is wearing a black cap. Deep lines bracket his mouth. I step back suddenly as if from a cliff edge.

The floorboards groan and I glance over my shoulder. A second man is standing beside me. He says something in a voice that makes me think of a homeless person begging for loose change. With his narrow face and pale eyes he resembles the man in the armchair, though he has wispy hair that falls to his shoulders, and his style of dress is more traditional or archaic – a cardboard-coloured leather waistcoat, a maroon shirt embroidered with meadow flowers. The man in the armchair nods, then speaks. *That's my brother. We're twins.* At least that's what I understand him to be saying. The man in the waistcoat repeats part of what his brother said, dim light glinting on teeth that are minute and stained, then he motions towards a wooden cabinet and pokes a key into a lock. As he tugs on the brass handle and the door shudders open there's a wincing sound and then the smell of dust and walnuts. Inside the cabinet are more snow globes, each of which houses a solitary, detailed figure. The figures are much larger than those in the replica of Arkhangel'sk, three or four centimetres high at least, and uncannily lifelike, as waxworks often are, and I realise that every one of them is a recreation of a real person. I don't have any evidence or proof. It's just an intuition.

Katherine Carlyle

The man in the waistcoat plucks at my sleeve and breathes a question into my ear. Once again I have no idea what the words mean, only that he seems to be making an offer or a proposition, and when I look into his face, which is much closer than I would like it to be, his eyes have a surface gleam, like balls on a pool table. In the meantime the other man has risen from his chair and is positioned at his brother's elbow. They appear to be united in trying to exert some kind of power over me. I understand that they want me to accompany them beyond the curtain. I also understand that what happens behind that curtain isn't something I should contemplate, or even know about.

I free myself, then reach for my suitcase and move across the room towards the entrance. Thank you, I say in Russian, more than once – *Spasiba, spasiba* – as much to paralyse the two men as anything else. To keep them from coming after me. To keep them from speaking. Where's the door? I search among the coats. Cut my hand on a protruding nail. The spade clatters to the ground. At last I find a doorknob and wrench it open. Darkness pours in. A different darkness. Keener, colder.

As I hurry back towards the road I hear shutters being closed, bolts being driven home. The sign above the sauna flickers like a tic in someone's eyelid. On Troitsky Prospekt the fog is thicker than before, turning headlights into haloes. I suck the gash at the base of my thumb and spit the blood into a bank of dirty snow. If I happen to run into Yevgeny I will tell him that my failure to appear had nothing to do with him. I left my purse in a museum, I'll say. I had to go back and get it. The museum is owned by two men who might or might not be brothers. They specialise in snow globes. Does he know the place?

I approach the bus-stop where we were supposed to meet. Now I have a story I'm almost disappointed to discover that he isn't there. He's a kind man and I have behaved badly; I would like to make it up to him. A gravelly reverberation fills the sky. It sounds like an avalanche, but there aren't any mountains. Is it thunder? Possibly. Or maybe just a plane coming in to land, a plane hidden by the fog that is smothering the city. The 61 appears. I flag it down.

The Meridian sits on a piece of waste ground to the east of a red bridge, in an area of the city known as Solombala. The hotel is modern but curiously empty. In the lobby there are paintings of sailing ships, and ceramic fish in alcoves. The café has a stone fireplace and diaphanous turquoise curtains. Fixed to the ceiling is a huge curving piece of pale-green fibreglass or plastic, like a swimming pool suspended upside-down. My room is on the third floor, facing back towards the river. Though I'm still in Arkhangel'sk, somehow I'm separated from it too. I'm grateful to Elena. She couldn't have found me a better hiding place.

During the next three days I only leave the Meridian once, to collect my plane tickets. It's a simple precautionary measure; I can't risk any more coincidental meetings. Sometimes as I pass through the lobby on my way to breakfast or dinner the hotel staff try to interest me in tourist attractions. There is Malye Karely, for instance, an outdoor museum of ancient buildings. If you don't been Malye Karely, the woman on reception says in broken English, you don't been Arkhangel'sk. Malye Karely is beautiful. The White Sea is beautiful. And the Solovetsky Archipelago, with its historic monastery. That is also beautiful. And what about the Kola

Peninsula? There is beauty on all sides, apparently. I leaf through a brochure and admire the wide expanses of blue water, and the tundra, devoid of trees and people, and then I shake my head. I can't, I say. I'm too busy.

I spend most of my time in my room, poring over the map I have spread on the floor beneath my window. According to a print-out Elena gave me, Svalbard is only thirteen hundred kilometres from the North Pole. Permanent night descends at the end of October and lasts until the middle of May. Since the darkness is more absolute than on mainland Norway or in Russia, Svalbard is an ideal place for observing 'celestial bodies'. In January the average temperature is -16, but the lowest recorded temperature is -46. The name 'Svalbard' means 'cold edge' or 'cold coast'. It's hard to describe the way these earnest factual sentences affect me. I stand on my balcony looking out. Once home to shipyards, Solombala feels neglected, melancholy, the dark wooden houses sinking, lopsided, into the earth, the river a grey strip in the middle distance. I veer between rushes of adrenaline – a rollercoaster thrill – and a sweetness that is laced with pain, a delicious cloying poignancy. What it resembles most closely – what it actually *feels like* – is nostalgia.

The day before I fly to Svalbard I'm jumpy from the moment I wake up. I'm the only person having breakfast in the café. The turquoise curtains hang motionless, a world of grimy monochrome beyond. When I look at the ceiling it seems to undulate, and I'm not sure I don't hear the trickle of a water filter. I could dive upwards. Disappear beneath the surface. My clothes would be found next to my chair, a few telltale splashes on the floor. ENGLISH TOURIST VANISHES AT BREAKFAST.

Later I pace up and down on my balcony. Scrapyards, graffiti-covered walls. The dull red bridge. At first I imagine it's impatience. I'm desperate to leave, and yet I'm being forced to wait. But then, in the early afternoon, I realise. It's October 17th, the day I'm supposed to meet my father. I check my watch. One forty-five. Arkhangelsk is two hours ahead of Berlin, and my father is always punctual. He will be walking into the Einstein at any moment.

My legs start trembling. I go back inside and sit down on the bed. I have imagined it so many times but what's going to happen – really? My father will meet Lydia, that much is certain. It seems unlikely he will get hold of Oswald – and even if he does all he will discover is that I boarded a train to Moscow. I could have got off in Warsaw, though. Or Minsk. Not such a good lead after all.

What about Cheadle?

Opinionated and belligerent he may be, but he is also inquisitive. Suppose he took a look at my passport while the Russians had it – or even before that, one day when I was out? His eyes will have been drawn to my father's name and address, since my father is listed as the 'friend or relative' who should be contacted 'in the event of an emergency'. I imagine Cheadle studying my father's details, the jealousy stirring and curdling inside him. *To be contacted in the event of an emergency.* What if Cheadle wrote to my father? What if he were to raise the subject he has already raised with me? He would be quite capable of such effrontery, and would conceal his own address by using the American Express office near the Gendarmenmarkt, which is where he often picks up mail.

Katherine Carlyle

c/o American Express
Friedrichstrasse
Berlin

Dear Mr Carlyle,
Following a number of conversations with your daughter in which
your shortcomings as a father have become apparent, I am propos-
ing that you henceforth waive your rights and responsibilities in that
department. Cede them to me without further delay, and I will make
the necessary arrangements for her legal adoption here in Germany.
   Should you feel inclined to discuss the matter, I can be reached at
the above address, and would be prepared to meet with you at your
own convenience, though pressing business prevents me from leaving
Berlin at this time.
   If I fail to hear from you, I will assume you have no objection to
my proposal.
   Sincerely,
   J. Halderman Cheadle

If my father were to receive a letter like that not long after
mine, he would be bound to believe the two were connected,
even though they don't refer to each other, not even obliquely.
He would reply by return of post, taking care to hide his
outrage and his disbelief, since he knows from experience that
they would only inflame a situation that is already volatile.
Shortly afterwards he would fly to Berlin for a meeting with
– what's his name again? – *J. Halderman Cheadle*. Ridiculous.
Cheadle would suggest a dodgy venue. A bar or a casino.
Even a sex club of some kind. Not because he's determined
to make my father uncomfortable or to create a bad impression – though, given the circumstances, he might find that

prospect irresistible – but because he wants to highlight my father's failings, his unsuitability. After all, if Cheadle considers himself the more appropriate parent, despite belonging to a world inhabited by addicts and strippers, what does that say about my father? That's the point Cheadle would be making, even before a single word has been exchanged. He'd wait in a dark corner in his plastic raincoat and his filthy tennis shoes, a Maker's Mark on the rocks in front of him, and the look on his face would be steady, with just a hint of the combative, the kind of look that sorts the wheat out from the bullshit.

Suspecting himself to be the victim of a hoax – or even, perhaps, of blackmail – my father approaches the appointed venue with extreme caution. I see him in the back of a taxi, leaning forwards to talk into the driver's ear. To whisper instructions. They pass the club in second gear. A girl lounges in the doorway, smoking. Behind her, black stairs lead down into a basement. My father asks the driver to go round the block. They pass the club again. The girl, the stairs – there's nothing to be learned by looking. He might as well go in.

On arriving at Cheadle's table he remains on his feet. To sit down would be to acknowledge Cheadle as an equal. The last thing he wants to do is give the man any respect or credibility.

'I'd like to speak to my daughter,' he says.

Cheadle extracts a thin cigar from the flat tin on the table and then leans back in his chair, considering my father. 'You seem – I don't know – upset . . .'

'Of course I'm upset. My daughter's missing.'

'Interesting you say that—' Cheadle breaks off to solicit a light from a passing topless waitress. 'You see, your daughter wasn't sure you'd be upset. She wasn't even sure you'd *notice*.'

My father makes an exasperated sound and looks out across the dingy dance floor. 'That's absurd.'

'Is it?'

'I don't have time for this. I'm going.'

'Why? Is there somewhere you have to be?' Cheadle's voice is heavy with sarcasm. When my father fails to respond he says, 'That's what you always do, isn't it. Look the other way, use your work as an excuse. How do I know? She told me.'

My father places both hands flat on the table and looks straight at Cheadle. 'Where is she? Where's Kit?'

Cheadle laughs. 'You don't even know her name.'

'Her name's Katherine. People call her Kit.'

'You're never there for her, are you. In fact, you're hardly there at all.' Cheadle slits his eyes and feels the air, the way a blind man might. 'Where are you? Are you there? Hello?'

My father stands back. 'I have a job. Do you have a job?'

'Yeah, right. You have a job. The only time anyone can see you is when you're on TV.'

'Tell me where my daughter is or I'll have you arrested.'

'What for? Writing a letter?' Cheadle signals for another whisky and it arrives in seconds. 'I don't know where she is. She could be anywhere.'

'You don't know. But I thought—'

'I don't know where she is *exactly*. I think she went to Russia.'

'*Russia?* What on earth for?'

'You tell me.'

'I'm asking you.'

'You're a real pain in the ass. Didn't anyone ever tell you that?' Cheadle glares at my father, then shouts, 'Fucking *sit down.*'

Startled, my father does as he is told.

Cheadle passes the flat of his hand over the surface of the table as if removing crumbs. 'She's got some idea about how her life ought to be.' His voice is quieter now, more patient. 'That's why she went.'

'But Russia's dangerous.'

'So they say.'

'I thought you cared for her.'

'I do.'

'And you let her go?'

'More than that. I made it possible. I helped.' Cheadle stubs out his cigar. 'She was making for a place called Cherepovets. It's a steel town, about an hour north of Moscow.' He pauses. 'An hour by plane.'

My father sits at the table, staring at his hands.

'That's all I know,' Cheadle says.

The liar. There's another name, which he has kept concealed. Why? So he can come for me himself? Or is it simply that he wants my father to suffer?

I see Cheadle weigh the options. He is tempted to withhold information, make things difficult, but if he imparts – no, flaunts – his knowledge he will be asserting his own superiority.

'Actually, there was somewhere else she mentioned,' he says as he rises to his feet, his voice casual, indifferent. 'Arkhangel'sk.'

He buttons his raincoat, then heads for the stairs that lead up to the street. As he circles the dance floor, bits of silvery light from the mirror ball whirl across his back, making him look, for a moment, like a man caught in a blizzard.

My father goes on sitting at the table, even after Cheadle has gone. He doesn't move. He doesn't even blink.

A girl in a floaty negligee approaches. 'Something I can get you?'

He doesn't look at her. 'Arkhangel'sk,' he whispers.

She shrugs, then walks away.

Outside, the weather is dry but very cold. In my room on the third floor I sit by the window and watch the lights come on in buildings on the far side of the river. Cars ease over the bridge towards me. In a nearby yard or garden somebody has lit a fire. The drifting smoke looks blue against the snow.

The plane is small, with old-fashioned propellers, and the other passengers are all men. The man seated next to me ignores me, transfixed by the card game on his phone. No sooner have I fastened my safety belt than the propellers start to click over. They hum, then roar. The whole interior vibrates.

We bump along the runway and then suddenly, almost haphazardly, lurch up into the air. As the plane banks, Talagi airport appears, the dark runway in stark relief against the whiteness of the landscape. Some distance to the east is Arkhangel'sk, the city sprawling on a big bend in the river. Creamy smoke pours from chimneys in the industrial zone. I think of Yevgeny, who I befriended, then avoided. He's speaking to his mother on the phone. *Yes, I'm home . . . I met a girl . . . No, she was English . . .* The plane banks again. Far below, the White Sea is a colour that reminds me of my childhood, the muddy grey-blue I used to get if I mixed too many paints together.

Once, when I visited my mother in hospital, a wind was blowing, something that hardly ever happens in Rome, not in the summer. It was one of those days when it's impossible not to imagine being intensely, unthinkingly, alive, and yet there she was, propped in a chair, her face slack and grainy from the pain relief they had given her. The blanket had slipped on to the floor, and her feet and ankles, which were swollen, no longer seemed a part of her. Every now and then she would appear to fall asleep. She was adrift between two states, neither completely there nor completely gone.

'Do I look awful?' she said that afternoon. 'I do, don't I.' She glanced down, past her knees. 'My feet are purple!' She let out a laugh, somehow both astonished and disgusted. Then her eyes closed again. Even the smallest outburst could exhaust her.

My father went to refill the water jug, though it was still half full. He couldn't stand it, and had to get away, if only for a few moments.

'I killed you,' I murmured. 'It was all my fault.'

My mother's eyes opened wide. 'Of course you didn't. What a thing to say! And anyway, I'm still here, aren't I?' She looked around, trying to make light of her predicament. 'It wasn't anybody's fault. It was just bad luck.'

That last exchange didn't happen. Instead, we sat in silence, her hand in mine. The pulse on the inside of her wrist was weak and feathery; it didn't beat so much as flutter. Through the half-open window came a smell of resin from the umbrella pines on the main road. Then the harsh tearing noise of a plane going overhead. Rome's second airport, Ciampino, was close by.

My father returned with the water. He stood at the end of the bed, clutching the jug.

'Are you going to give me some of that or aren't you?' my mother said, her eyes still closed.

Later, as we drove back into Rome, my father remarked on how tiring the treatment was. But that wasn't the whole story. I see that now. If my mother let go, it was because she suspected there would be no more good days. There was nothing to look forward to, and everything to dread.

The plane tilts sharply. The land beneath us looks unoccupied, unyielding. Bare black trees stick up out of the earth. It's like flying over a bed of nails. I check my watch. In twenty minutes we'll be landing in Norway.

I remember the two customs officials in Talagi airport studying my passport.

'You leave Russia?' the woman said.

I told her I was flying to Tromsø and then on to a place called Longyearbyen.

'You don't like Russia?' The question was gentle, but pointed. She had noticed that I was leaving the country three weeks before my visa expired.

'Yes, I do,' I said. 'I like Arkhangel'sk very much, but it's not cold enough.'

The woman laughed. Once she had translated for the man sitting next to her she turned back to me. 'Is joke, yes?'

'Not really. Svalbard will be colder.'

The man spoke quickly, then signalled for the woman to translate.

She looked at me. 'He says, maybe next time you try Siberia.'

The flight from Tromsø to Longyearbyen takes approximately ninety minutes. For the first hour thick white cloud reaches all the way to the horizon where it blurs and softens like the edge of a wool blanket. The Barents Sea is thirty thousand feet below but you wouldn't know it. Tucked into my window seat I study Russian verbs and speak to no one.

At last we begin our descent and spits of land appear,

ghostly white with dark streaks where the rock shows through. There are dirty-looking glaciers and long tongue-shaped fjords, and in the distance, in the northern sky, there's a single strip of purest pale-green. In some places the ground is frozen to a depth of five hundred metres all year round. Permafrost, they call it. Not many people live this far north but I'm going to be one of them. One of the few.

I'm in my mother's Alfa Romeo, racing up the slip-road that leads off the *autostrada*. Bright sunlight flashes through the inside of the car like something splintering. A petrol station, the grating of cicadas. My mother's eyes behind dark glasses. Blue-grey irises, black lashes. I know what she wants me to say, so I say it. *Are we there yet?*

She smiles. *Nearly, my darling. Nearly there.*

Four

Wedged into a narrow river valley between two mountain ridges, and sloping gently down to a fjord, Longyearbyen has a magnetic quality I can feel in my bones. People tell me I could find a job – in a hotel, or a restaurant – but I stick to my original plan and after three days I hear about a tourist ship that can drop me in Ugolgrad, the Russian mining settlement Elena mentioned. The man who sells me the ticket works out of a large scale Nissan hut on the water-front. I'm lucky, he says. The season is almost over. It's likely to be the last boat of the year. The skin around his eyes is wrinkled, a pattern of miniature diamond-shapes, but the eyes themselves are a clear washed pale-blue. The voyage will take three hours, he tells me. Though daylight is limited, I might glimpse a ringed seal – even, perhaps, a whale. I'm curious to know how long he has lived in the town. Twenty years, he says. Everyone in Longyearbyen has a story, he goes on. Either they've run away from something or they're looking for something. He studies me for a moment, as if wondering how I might fit into the equation. I ask him about Ugolgrad, and there's a subtle shift in his face that reminds me of a gust of wind moving across a lake.

'It's interesting,' he says.

'When English people use that word,' I say, 'it often has a negative meaning.'

'Yes.'

His ambiguous response only fuels the mystery and makes me still more determined to see the place. Longyearbyen, Ugolgrad . . . These, after all, are the names I pored over in the Meridian. Polysyllabic, clumsy, they seem appropriate to me, like numb fingers trying to grasp something in the cold. Ugolgrad is part of Russia, but it's also nowhere at all, adrift in sub-zero waters, virtually unreachable during the winter months. In a travel agency near the Radisson I notice a poster issued by the Norwegian Ministry of Tourism. *You are welcome to Svalbard*, it says, *as long as you leave no trace of your visit behind.* They are doing their best to protect the pristine environment, of course, but they might be talking directly to me. It's as if they knew I was coming.

My hotel is by the docks. Converted from a row of miners' cabins, it has a wide gateway with antlers arranged along the top. At the back is a conservatory where you can sample Arctic delicacies like smoked whale. On my last night in Longyearbyen I take a seat by the window and write to Oswald. The postcard has a picture of a husky on the front. *Not a patch on Josef*, I scribble, then sign my name and add two kisses. Later, I start talking to Natasha, the girl with the tongue stud who runs the bar. Within minutes, our conversation becomes intimate, even confessional. She's from Ukraine, and has been living in town for about nine months. During the day she works in a hairdressing salon. Two years ago she lost her boyfriend in a crash on the outskirts of Kiev. She was in the car at the time, but escaped without a scratch. 'He died in my arms,' she says. 'On a roundabout, in the rain.' Then she smiles and says, 'I don't know why I'm telling you all this. I don't even know you.'

While Natasha pours drinks and takes food orders from the tables behind me, I sit at the bar. We keep talking, and half-way through the evening she looks at me sideways and upwards – she is loading dirty glasses into the dishwasher – and asks if I would like to go on an expedition after she has closed up.

'An expedition?' I say.

We leave at eleven-thirty with Klaudija, the Latvian girl who works on reception. Klaudija has an ear-cuff with an ivory pendant and a silver chain, and her dyed red hair is long on top and shaved at the sides. After spending five years in casinos in Oslo and Stockholm she came to Longyearbyen to be with her boyfriend. She only sees him every other week – he has a job in Svea, a Norwegian mine half an hour away by plane – but he's the love of her life and she's hoping to have his baby.

Natasha fills her car with petrol, then drives east, into the dark. I lean forwards, my head between the two front seats, such an excitement in me that I feel like a child again. In the headlights the unpaved road looks black, as if made from coal, and it is raised like a causeway, with water on both sides. On our right is the town's reservoir. On our left, the Adventfjord, which becomes more and more shallow until it merges into marshland and tundra.

Ten kilometres out of town, at the foot of a mountain, is an old trappers' camp. Natasha parks, but leaves her headlights on high-beam. In the foreground stands a tall triangular structure fashioned out of wood, a kind of gibbet. Four huge dead seals hang upside-down from the apex, the ground beneath them stained red and black with congealed blood. Along one of the horizontal struts are twenty or thirty glinting cod, also upside-down, with nails driven through their tail-fins. There are huts with antlers fixed upright above their doors, and rows of metal sledges, and boxes filled with empty bullet casings. Inside a fenced compound are dozens of wooden hutches raised up on legs, each with a husky's name on it. The nearest – Borneo – sits quietly, his eyes coin-flat in the glare of the headlights.

Back in the car, we drive up the mountain to Mine 7, which crouches on a steep slope above the valley like a spider in the top corner of a room. Several reindeer graze some distance off, and higher up, on the rounded summit, are two squat telescopes belonging to an observatory. I go over to Natasha, who is standing by herself, looking out over the valley. Far below, Longyearbyen shows as a handful of lights.

'This is a healing place,' she says. 'Here you can just be.'

We stand quietly, side by side. Green shapes begin to appear above us, faint at first, but gradually increasing in intensity.

Klaudija joins us. 'They say you're looking at the armour of the gods.'

The breath stops in my lungs. Tilting my head back, I stare up into the sky. I think of veils, smoke. Waves breaking. I think of curtains. I think of ghosts. When our necks begin to ache we lie on our backs in the snow. Time has slowed down, or else it has been suspended altogether. There isn't anything for it to measure. It no longer applies. I feel I'm at the very centre of the world, and at the same time I don't count. I'm everything and nothing, the gap between the two collapsing like the pleats in an accordion.

Here you can just be.

Later, as we drive round Longyearbyen, Natasha picks up a tourist who is hitching. His name is Martin, and he comes from Utrecht. We ask if he wants to go dancing. He says he can't. He has to be up early. He's climbing Hiortfjellet the next day.

'Hiortfjellet?' I say.

He points through the back window, at the mountains on the far side of the fjord.

'I think you should come with us,' Klaudija says.

Natasha agrees. 'You only live once.'

'How often does this happen,' I say, 'three beautiful women asking you to go out with them?'

We are all laughing, Martin too.

'I can't,' he says. 'Really.'

When we drop him in Nybyen, where he is staying, he thanks us for the lift and hurries towards the entrance to his building. He doesn't look back.

Natasha stares through the windscreen, both hands on the steering wheel. 'He thought we were crazy.'

We're strangers, Natasha, Klaudija and I, but our brief acquaintance with a *real* stranger makes us realise how well we know one another, and how rapidly the understanding has come about. This is the way we're supposed to live, I think to myself. Adrift and yet together, elated but at peace. Natasha drives us to a club called Huset, and we dance until three in the morning.

I board the ship the next day, at midday. Apart from me, there are only seven passengers. Once the guide, Torgrim, has taken us through the safety procedures and the itinerary we cast off. I stay on deck, gripping the thick black lip of the bow. I have bought myself a fur hat with earflaps, and new socks, boots and gloves. Ugolgrad is basic – there are no shops at all – and it's vital I should be properly equipped.

Behind us Longyearbyen gradually shrinks, the colourful A-frame houses swallowed by a landscape that is vast and jagged. We pass a gantry left over from the mining days, then the airport with its single runway. We pass a beach where I found pulpy green-gold banners of seaweed and square grey stones as flat as plates. The Isfjord lies ahead of us. The pinched mauve light makes the water look translucent, dense, almost congealed, like vodka when you keep it in the freezer. In the distance, on the western horizon, is a ghostly range of mountains, cloaked in snow. My heart dilates with a pleasure that is pure and undiluted.

We have been under way for at least an hour when a man in a red oil-stained baseball cap approaches me. His skin has a rough, pocked texture, like pebble-dash. He is Captain Axelsen, he says. Am I the passenger who is going ashore in Ugolgrad? That's me, I say. He asks how long I plan to stay.

'I'm hoping to live there,' I tell him.

He reaches beneath his baseball cap and scratches his wiry hair. 'You're hoping to live in Ugolgrad?'

'Yes.'

He stares at me.

'It's something I've been dreaming of,' I say.

'Strange dream.'

'Really?'

'You haven't been there,' he says. 'You don't know what it's like.'

'I know enough.'

'After a day or two you'll want to leave.' He wags a prophetic finger at me.

'No,' I say. 'I won't.'

'Yes,' he says complacently.

The surface of the water is ruffled now. We must be getting closer to the open sea. To the east, the Bird Cliffs tower above us, more than a thousand feet high. Carved into the sheer rock, and worn smooth by the harsh climate and the passing centuries, are huge repeating shapes that resemble ancient kings or warriors.

'It's getting cold,' Axelsen says.

I follow him to the bridge, a narrow room with a polished wood floor and a rifle hanging on the wall. Once inside, he picks up where he left off. 'Tomorrow,' he says, 'or maybe the next day, the phone will ring, and there will be a voice on the other end, a little English voice. Please, the voice will say. Come with your ship. You have to take me away from this place.'

He makes it sound simple, sentimental, like a story for children, and I'm not sure whether to be insulted or amused.

'It won't be the first time,' he says, 'that I have heard those words.'

'So you make a habit of rescuing young women?'

He gives me a sharp look, then adjusts his baseball cap and peers through the window. I watch as he decides to attack the subject from another angle. He's a stubborn man, and won't be put off. It's important to him that I see things his way.

'The weather's good today,' he says. 'Soon it will be much colder, and it will be dark all the time.'

'You don't understand,' I say. 'That's what I'm looking for. That's why I came.'

He looks at me again, and his eyes flare. 'No, it's you who do not understand. It's not like Longyearbyen, where you are going. It's a sad place. They don't have money or respect for the environment. Also it's dangerous, especially at the week-ends. The men are always drunk, and fighting. There's no law. And you, you're only a girl—'

He breaks off to answer a call on the radio. While he talks in Norwegian, I put my face close to the glass. His depiction of the mining town feels exaggerated, the fruit of prejudice and superstition. He might as well be telling me that Russians eat their offspring or have six fingers on each hand. Directly overhead, the sky is a swirl of brooding black, but a smoky glowing strip of orange in the west has turned the water all around us steel-blue. A gull glides past, flush with the horizon.

'We stay in Ugolgrad for an hour and a half,' Axelsen says a few minutes later, when the call is over. 'There's enough time for you to walk around. You can see everything in an hour and a half. Then you can come back, with me.'

Not wanting to upset him, I pretend to be considering his proposition. The rumble of the engines, the dull gleam of the cream paint on the walls . . .

'It can be a strength,' Axelsen says, 'to know when to change your mind.'

That's probably true, I think to myself.

'I will not think less of you,' he says.

I thank him for his advice and his kind offer, then I tell him I'm going out to get some air.

Standing on the upper deck, I watch the water peel back from the hull, fold after fold. The cold has a weight to it. The cold feels solid. In the far reaches of the fast-encroaching darkness the mountains are dim white shapes. From studying the map I know I'm looking north-west, towards Oscar II Land and the research station at Ny-Ålesund.

Walking over to the other side, I find Torgrim with his hands in his pockets, a knitted wool hat pulled down to his eyebrows. He jerks his chin towards a few scattered lights.

'The airport for Ugolgrad,' he says.

As we round the headland more lights appear. A tall chimney stands close to the shore, dark smoke trailing out across the water. I ask Torgrim what he knows about the town.

'You hear some strange things,' he says. 'I don't know if they're true.'

'Like what?'

He tells me about a man who was wanted by the Russian Mafia. He fetched up in Ugolgrad. Found work in the mine. It was so far away and so isolated that he thought he would be safe.

'And was he?' I ask.

Torgrim shrugs. 'I never heard any more about him.'

Despite my warm clothes I'm shivering. *Ugolgrad*. It's hard to believe this is the place I have been making for, hard to believe I have almost reached my destination. Because that's what it is. My destination. After Ugolgrad there's nowhere left to go.

The shoreline shocks me with its mood of baleful dereliction, and just for a moment I'm tempted to follow Axelsen's advice and take the boat straight back to Longyearbyen. The buildings on the waterfront have corrugated-iron roofs and broken windows. Rusting containers stand about in the glare of the floodlights, and coal has been dumped in careless heaps, staining the snow. A truck is parked at an angle, a knot of workers gathered at the back. Two or three of them wield shovels. Beyond them, wooden steps zigzag up to the town, which huddles on a ledge about a hundred feet above the sea.

The boat bumps against ridged tractor tyres that are held in place by rusting chains, and then a rope is flung through the air and looped round an iron bollard. Torgrim unshackles a metal walkway and lowers it on to the quay. I let the other passengers go first. As I follow with my luggage I hear Axelsen's voice.

'Something I forgot to say,' he shouts down from the bridge. 'There's only one hotel, and it's full of rats.'

'I don't believe you,' I shout back.

Though combative, he's honest and reliable, made of the same durable material all the way through. He would fiercely defend anything he loves. He would make a good father.

I approach the workers, who are patching up a hole in the quay with old car tyres, smashed-up bits of concrete, and shovelfuls of coal.

'*Gastinitsa?*' I say. Hotel?

A bearded man moves his hand in the air to show me which way I should go. It seems straightforward enough. I thank him in Russian and set off for the steps.

Halfway to the top, my heart pounding from the climb, I stop to rest. I seem to hear the crunch of my footsteps on the shallow crust of snow, as if my brain is lagging, out of kilter. I glance back down. The dockside swamped in silver light, the boat the size of a toy. Darkness all around. No stars, no moon.

I pass several houses with planks nailed over their windows, and then a large brown-and-white building, also boarded-up, that has the word STOLOVAYA above the entrance, and come out into a sort of square. There are park benches and streetlamps, and the side of one of the buildings is covered with a mural of a forest. Birch trees with speckled trunks. Green grass. There is nobody about. Still walking uphill, I cross the square and turn into a street paved with uneven slabs. Yellow spotlights shine down from the rooftops. The rumble of my suitcase fills the silence. In between the buildings are areas of waste ground, bits of buckled metal fencing, and warped lengths of wooden boardwalk. I've never seen – or even imagined – a place like this.

The hotel is a four-storey block raised off the ground on concrete piles. I climb a flight of steps to the front door and suddenly I'm at the end of my strength. It's partly all the travelling – the journey, which has always felt driven and yet open-ended, has taken it out of me – but it's also the conversation I had with the captain. There's nothing more exhausting than having to listen to people who think they know what's best for you.

Once through the entrance I stand in a hall that is small, brightly lit and deserted. A glowing sign above the glass-panelled double-doors to my left says BAR. To my right is another set of doors, also with glass panels, a dim yellow corridor beyond. When a woman walks up the corridor towards me, her presence feels supernatural, since she appears suddenly, from nowhere, like a jump-cut in a film, and her approach is silent, the sound of her footsteps deadened by the doors that stand between us. She offers me a key, then says something about 'dinner' and 'seven o'clock'. Her eyes keep slanting downwards and to my left, as if I have a child with me.

I climb the stairs to the third floor. In a corridor that is bright as the entrance hall and just as empty I put down my case and look around. There's a strong smell of paint. With its grey doors and its imitation parquet floor the building reminds me of a show-house – somewhere no one has ever actually lived. I stand quite still and listen hard, but can't hear any sounds. No TVs, no voices of any kind. No running water. I unlock the door to my room, switch on the light. The twin beds have shiny blue covers, and the pale wooden furniture looks new, unused. Above the desk is a photo of an iceberg-studded sea, as if the management felt guests needed reminding of their whereabouts. A vent near the ceiling breathes warm, slightly musty air into the room.

I part the curtains. My view is of a rugged snow-encrusted hillside that lifts from right beneath my window, a number of heavily lagged pipes snaking up the slope to the top of the ridge. Like the hotel – like the room – I feel new. I'm a blank slate. A gamble. Axelsen told me there will be one last boat before the season ends. He said that when he returns, in a week's time, he expects to find me waiting on the quayside with my case. He's sure I will have had enough by then. I'm already looking forward to seeing his face when he hears that I'm staying.

That evening, at seven, I go down to the bar. A woman in a royal-blue tunic emerges from the kitchen and shows me into the far room through doors whose glass panels are engraved with polar bears and crossed pickaxes. There are maroon tablecloths, and walls of lacquered pine. The TV is switched off. Only one table has been laid, and dinner is already waiting. A scoop of Russian salad, some sliced white bread. A jug of processed apple juice. No sooner have I sat down than two more dishes are put in front of me, a bowl of hot clear soup with globules of fat floating on top and a small plate containing a thin piece of meat and a spoonful of plain rice.

I eat in silence, and alone. My vision blurs. A disco ball spins wearily. Its rails of silver light make the matt-black walls look dusty. A girl in high-heels and a sparkly thong climbs awkwardly on to a low stage and begins to dance. Her solid, surgically enhanced breasts only serve to emphasise how thin she is; the tendons stand out in her neck, and behind her knees. This is the dive Cheadle chose for his confrontation with my father but Cheadle is long gone. My father sits with his head lowered, ignoring the tacky 80s music and the gyrating girl. He's trying to process the information Cheadle has just given him. *Cherepovets, Arkhangel'sk . . .* But what if Cheadle never wrote to my father? What if he never summoned my father to that dingy club? Is there any other way my father could learn of his existence?

I replay the Berlin scenario. When my father reads my second letter, the letter Lydia hands him, he is bound to be concerned, but he takes Lydia back to his hotel and they make love. He falls asleep. An hour later, he jerks awake. *Of course. Why didn't I think of it before?* While Lydia showers, he puts in a series of calls to fellow journalists. Using his contacts – his influence – he makes a televised appeal that goes out nationwide. This is a version of my father I have rarely seen before. For once, he isn't an authority. He's just an ordinary man, helpless and weak. Still, I don't doubt he will bring a certain flair to the role. His voice will falter at exactly the right moment; he might break down, or even cry, which is what a parent who has lost a child is supposed to do. *My daughter, Katherine Carlyle, is missing . . . She's all I've got . . . Kit, if you're listening, please come home . . .* Most important of all, they will show a photograph of me, though hopefully it won't be the one in my passport. Taken when I was fifteen, I have dark rings under my eyes, and hollow cheeks. When Massimo first saw it he laughed and said I looked like a junkie.

Cheadle will miss the broadcast – he doesn't own a television; *TV's for losers* – but Klaus Frings, who has three, one in the kitchen, one in the living room, and one in the master bedroom, sees my picture and almost chokes on his profiteroles. Still coughing, he calls the number given at the end of the appeal.

My father appears at the door of his apartment later that same evening. Klaus offers him a drink, which he declines.

'She lived here for about ten days,' Klaus says. 'She often sat where you are sitting now.'

'When was this?'

'September.'

My father surveys the apartment – the coffee table books, the soft furnishings, the art. At last his gaze comes to rest on the big unlikely German.

'I don't understand,' he says. 'How do you know my daughter?'

Klaus looks past him, at the mysterious grey painting. 'I also don't understand.'

He describes how he first saw me, at the *café-konditorei* round the corner, on a foggy Tuesday morning. He says he suspects me of having followed him.

'*Followed* you? Why would she do that?'

'I have no idea.'

Klaus relays the explanation I gave him. It sounds even less plausible the second time around.

Impatient, my father asks for an account of the time I spent in the apartment. Klaus describes our evenings together – how we drank good wine and talked, and how he sometimes took me to restaurants. He doesn't know what I used to do during the day, while he was out at work. I was deliberately vague. Elusive.

'She was like a lodger, then,' my father says.

The idea that Klaus and I might have slept together doesn't occur to my father, but Klaus, who is still tortured by the memory of his impotence, squirms on his chair.

'Yes,' he says miserably. 'I suppose.'

'And when she left, where did she go?'

'I don't know. She didn't tell me.' Klaus gets up and walks to the window. 'She said she'd met someone.'

My father holds up the photo of me and Oswald. 'Was it him?'

'I don't know,' Klaus says. 'Who's that?'

'His name's Oswald.'

'It's not a name she mentioned—' Something occurs to Klaus and he stares at the floor, one hand wrapped around the lower half of his face. He remembers me talking about the man I was going to stay with. *He's older – more like an uncle . . .*

My father notices. 'What is it?'

Klaus's thoughts move back in time, back to the night in the Gendarmenmarkt when, heart still aching from the muted finale of Tchaikovsky's *Pathétique*, he walked out of the concert hall. He looked for me in the main bar, and then in the smaller bar. He looked in the lobby. I was nowhere to be seen. Just as he was beginning to despair, he spotted me outside, at the foot of the steps, deep in conversation with a middle-aged man. In the taxi on the way back to Walter-Benjamin-Platz I showed him the card the man had given me. I mentioned the man's name as well. Something foreign. Complicated. What, though? And then it comes to him: 'Cheadle!'

'Is that a last name?' my father says.

Klaus nods. 'Yes. I think.'

'Cheadle. You're sure?'

'Absolutely.'

After dinner I return to my room and switch the TV on. I select a Russian news channel – no Norwegian channels are available – and watch a soldier reporting from the scene of a flood. I walk to the window. A snow-covered hillside, sheer as a wall, and half a dozen lagged pipes. That sense of isolation again. Oddly familiar. Comforting. What surprises me, in retrospect, is my efficiency, my focus, as if I have been following a particularly clear and comprehensive set of instructions.

Cheadle!

When my father asks where Cheadle lives, Klaus can't help. All he can do is give my father a physical description. Would that be enough to go on? Were my father to wait outside the Konzerthaus every evening, would Cheadle eventually appear? In fact, what was Cheadle doing there in the first place? The more I think about it, the more out of character it seems. But he wasn't easy to know, or to predict. He didn't like to talk about himself – *I don't do the past*, he told me once, when I questioned him about his life – though I did manage to find out that his parents were Austrian Jews who had fled the country shortly before the *Anschluss*, settling first in Milwaukee, then in Madison, Wisconsin, and that he had developed a passion for icons from a Russian émigré he had met in San Francisco in his late teens, a man who, as he said teasingly, had taught him 'pretty much everything'. If I were to ask Cheadle why he was in the Gendarmenmarkt that evening, his answer would almost certainly be mischievous or flippant – *I was looking for you, baby* – but there would be a reason, and it would be unguessable. I imagine my father standing on the steps of the Konzerthaus, coat buttoned to the neck against the chill, on the off chance that the American might once again pass by . . .

Is there anything else he could do?

Hold on.

Everyone who lives in Germany is required to register with the police, especially if they come from outside the EU. Then again, Cheadle prides himself on being a renegade, and is unlikely to have paid much attention to the law. Knowing him, he will have engineered a degree of invisibility – as far as the authorities are concerned, at least. More fundamental still, there's the matter of his identity. I have kept his card – it's glued into my notebook – and I study it from time to time. Is J. Halderman Cheadle his real name? I wonder. I never saw his passport, only a bank statement that I suspect is fake. But if anyone can trace Cheadle my father can.

I reimagine the showdown. This time it's Cheadle who is summoned, Cheadle who is put under pressure. What kind of venue would my father choose? An embassy, perhaps – or even a police station. Somewhere that would serve to underline the gravity of the situation.

A windowless room. Bright lights. The table and the two chairs are screwed to the floor. In this encounter Cheadle is less enigmatic, more aggressive. He isn't accustomed to forfeiting control. The door opens and my father walks in.

Cheadle toys with an unlit cigar. 'You don't look half as good in real life.'

'I'm sorry?'

'You look better on TV.'

My father smiles, then takes a seat.

'You must be – what do they call it? – *telegenic*.' Cheadle makes it sound like something you could catch.

My father leans forward. 'Tell me about my daughter.'

Within seconds of turning off the lights and the TV I sink into the deepest sleep, my dreams overlapping, incomplete, and when I wake, nine hours later, only fragments of an oddly luxurious state of anxiety remain – not enough time, too much luggage, a plane to catch . . . I lie on my side in bed, the darkness absolute. There's a distant, dull tumbling sound that reminds me of a cement-mixer. When I think about where I am, on that steep slippery curve near the top of the globe, I experience a few moments of vertigo. Things are precarious, and I feel I might slide sideways or backwards, like someone clinging to a roof-rack in a car chase. I doze for another hour. I'm tired, of course, but perhaps my body has realised I have reached my final destination and has decided to relax. Though I have met new people and visited new places, those aspects of the journey never had much relevance. What has inter-ested me right from the beginning – what has preoccupied me above all – is the prospect of arrival.

When I walk into the bar at nine o'clock, an hour after the appointed breakfast time, a dark-haired woman I have never seen before steps out from behind the counter. She seems angry or exasperated as if my appearance constitutes an infringement of some kind. Her face is round and white as a dinner plate, and the spaces below her eyebrows are swollen and slightly moist, like hard-boiled eggs without their shells. She tells me breakfast is finished.

'Finished?' I say. 'There's nothing to eat?'

'No, nothing. You're too late.' She points at an electric kettle on a low table by the wall. I can make myself a cup of tea or coffee, she seems to be saying, but that's all there is.

Before returning to my room I arrange to have my evening meal at seven. I would like to crack a joke about not being late, but I lack the vocabulary and I suddenly remember something Torgrim said about it being impossible to get a smile out of the woman who works in the hotel. This must be her.

That day I make my first reconnaissance of the town, surviving on TUC biscuits and Toblerone bought from the bar. Though it's eleven o'clock when I step outside, it feels more like dusk or twilight, except for in the east, beyond the mine, where the clouds are a garish chemical yellow, like the flames in a gas fire. I follow an unpaved track that runs parallel to the fjord, passing buildings with smashed windows, an olive-coloured van on wheel-blocks, and several sledges propped upright against a wall. It's hard to tell where the settlement ends. There are no markers or boundaries. The place just peters out in a tangle of smokestacks, gantries, conveyor belts, and sheds, the ground littered with wooden pallets and bits of metal whose purpose is obscure, coal everywhere, blackening the snow. A woman in Longyearbyen told me polar bears outnumber people on Svalbard, and that I shouldn't venture out of town on foot unless I was armed. In Longyearbyen there were signs warning of the presence of polar bears. There are no signs here.

I turn back, moving past the hotel. The settlement occupies a narrow shelf of land between the fjord and a steep craggy ridge. Though the buildings mostly face the water, they seem randomly arranged as if they were dropped from a great height and then allowed to remain where they landed. Some look traditional, with intricate white fretwork around the doors and windows, their clapboard exteriors painted in yellows, blues and greens that have been bleached and ravaged by the weather, but there are also larger, more utilitarian blocks made of bleak grey-brown brick. Municipal buildings like the school, the canteen and the museum are to be found on or around the square. The naïve, almost visionary murals on many of the facades – explorers, castles, whales, longships, domes – stand out against the landscape, like wishful thinking or white lies. There are very few people about – just, sometimes, a woman hurrying along with a plastic bag, or a man wearing an orange helmet with a light on the front.

I walk down a path and across a football pitch, the goalposts rusting, netless, then I climb a slope to a road that is flanked by long low warehouses, many of them open-ended. One contains an enormous eerie heap of sawdust. Another is piled high with bags of cement. A third warehouse is filled with small green tiles, some of which have spilled on to the ground outside. There's a faded red building with a row of cages attached to the exterior wall and a sign that says PIG HOUSE in English, and when I stop and listen I can hear the animals inside, snuffling and squealing. I'm about to knock on the door when a man appears, cradling a piglet in his arms. With his blue-grey complexion and his sunken cheeks he looks like an undertaker, or one of the undead, but I sense a gentleness in him.

'*Angliyski*,' I say, pointing at myself.

He points at the piglet. '*Russki*.'

When I ask whether I can see the pig house he seems to caution me – I think he's telling me the smell is bad, and that it will stick to my clothes – but then he shrugs and unlocks the door. Once inside, he leads me from pen to pen, introducing each of the pigs by name. Using a combination of words and sign language I ask if he slaughters them as well. Of course, he replies. That's his job. Heated by banks of ancient radiators and lit by large dim bulbs, the atmosphere in the building is soupy, sickeningly sweet, and it's a relief to step outside again. He makes a joke about how we both smell bad now, then he invites me into his house, where his wife offers me a glass of juice and some hard biscuits that taste like dust. My hunger is such that I'm thankful for anything.

By the time I leave their house it is two in the afternoon, and the light has altered dramatically. Though the sun itself isn't visible, it has risen high enough to illuminate the rugged land on the far side of the fjord. The top half of the mountains is a rich orange, the colour of marmalade, and the lower slopes, which remain in shadow, are a muted, atmospheric mauve.

'Amazing,' I say out loud, even though I'm quite alone.

At the far end of town I come across a building with the words GREEN HOUSE on the side. The door has been left ajar. I look both ways, then step inside and find myself beneath a huge slanting roof of glass panes, many of them broken or missing altogether. The round columns that support the roof have been painted silver-white, with horizontal flecks and streaks of black. This nostalgia for birches, which I first noticed in the mural, seems especially poignant in this town, not just because of its extreme isolation, but because it's a place that has no trees at all. The greenhouse looks to have been abandoned for some time, the raised area where vegetables once grew now covered with spongy moss and rust-coloured grass on which a ragged dummy sprawls, half scarecrow, half voodoo doll, its blank stuffed bag of a face topped with a trilby. Sitting on a chair I sketch the interior – the trailing, desiccated plants, the pipes tangling on the far wall, the fall of grey light through the smashed glass panes. I draw until my feet go numb. When I leave the building, the sun has withdrawn from the mountains, and the air is so cold that it seems to creak and snap like an old man cracking his knuckles. I hurry back to my hotel room where I run a bath. The water that gushes from the tap is brown and slightly sticky. I lie there for half an hour, my body only hinted at.

That evening I appear in the bar on the stroke of seven. The dark-haired woman remains expressionless, her face Kabuki-like, though I sense an air of grim satisfaction, as if she thinks she might have taught me a lesson. I don't see her as vindictive or malicious, only impatient with those who fail to abide by what is, for her, completely normal practice. She might also resent foreigners, since we have enough money to come and go as we please.

I eat dinner in silence, as before. It's so quiet that I can hear the blood circling round my body – or perhaps it's the fizzle of the lights behind their plastic panels. Afterwards I make a cup of instant coffee and go up to my room where I watch a Russian film in which men gallop about on horses shooting each other.

At breakfast on my third morning a man of about thirty-five is sitting at a table just inside the door, bent over a bowl of dry cereal that looks like puffed wheat. The moment I sit down he looks across at me and asks me, in English, where I'm from. I'm Misty, I tell him. From England. His name is Anatoly, he says, and he comes from Moscow. He works as a doctor in the hospital, which is the red-and-white building opposite the hotel. His contract terminates at the end of the month. When I remark on his meagre breakfast, he tells me his stomach troubles him. The pain keeps him awake at night. I ask if he's on medication. He indicates the mug next to his bowl. Tea, he says. His eyes are red-rimmed and haunted, like a figure in a painting by Munch, and his posture is stooped, his shoulder-blades poking through a thin striped sweater.

As I eat, he tells me that the town's drinking water is taken from what he calls 'the lake'. Many local people have problems with their stomachs. Also with their teeth and bones. He recommends that I buy water, and points at the bottle on my table, imported from Germany. He will be glad to leave Ugolgrad, he says. The place isn't good for him.

Since I never expected to meet anyone who could speak English I view Anatoly's presence as a stroke of luck, a kind of blessing, and I have so many questions suddenly that I can hardly choose between them. The other places I have visited only engaged my interest obliquely, but it's important I learn everything I can about Ugolgrad, since I am already thinking of it as home. I start by asking about the miners. Most come from Ukraine, Anatoly tells me. They earn 6000 roubles a month – which is more than he earns, he adds ruefully. They eat in the canteen, using a card issued by the mining company. They buy groceries there too. No money ever changes hands. When I probe him about safety in the mine, he tells me there are many accidents. The ground is

– and he holds one hand above the other, then moves them both backward and forwards.

'Unstable?' I say.

'Yes. Two months ago, death. Four months ago, death.'

He spoons more cereal into his mouth. The individual pieces are so light that the simple act of lifting them through the air dislodges some of them, and they spill on to the floor. It doesn't seem to occur to him to pick them up.

I ask if he could show me round the hospital.

He nods. 'Tomorrow.'

Checking his watch, he rises to his feet. His faded jeans look too big for him, and there are gold buckles on his shiny black loafers. When I wish him a good day he gives me a fatalistic look.

'We will see,' he says.

As I leave the bar a few minutes later, the woman who handed me my key on my first night emerges from the double-doors on the far side of the entrance hall. On the spur of the moment I ask if I can change rooms. Move to the front of the building. The woman's lower lip sticks out, like someone who is sulking or feeling rebellious, and her eyes drift sideways and downwards, fixing once again on the space a child would occupy if I had one with me.

'No,' she says, then rattles off a couple of sentences in Russian.

'No?' I say.

'No.'

This is such a perfect snapshot of the Russia I have heard about that I can't help smiling. After all, as we both know, the hotel has three floors and I'm virtually the only guest. But she says nothing else, only pushes past me, into the bar. Climbing the stairs, I feel hard done by. I'd like to be able to look out over the town and watch the snow-covered mountains in the distance change colour. Later, though, I realise she was right to turn down my request. For a few moments I forgot why I came to this place, and it was her job to remind me.

I'm not a tourist.

I'm not here for the views.

As I hesitate at the entrance to the hospital Anatoly appears, wearing a white coat over his faded jeans. There is nobody on duty in reception. I follow him down an empty corridor and into what he calls his 'cabinet', where he has an electric kettle, a sink, and a desk with a phone and a computer.

He indicates the phone. 'Direct line to Moscow.'

I'm not sure if he's showing off or trying to be funny.

'*Kharashó*,' I say. Very good.

He walks to the cupboard in the corner and returns with a tray heaped with bunches of keys.

'Let's go,' he says.

Like the hotel across the road, the hospital feels recently completed or refurbished. The walls and ceilings have been freshly decorated – eggshell blue, lilac, pale-green – and the floors are spotless. But there are no patients, no nurses. The rooms' only occupants are pieces of furniture and medical equipment, all seemingly brand-new. I suddenly remember somebody in Longyearbyen telling me that Putin visited the settlement not long ago, under pressure from the Norwegian government, and that he was so appalled by the conditions that he promised immediate and substantial investment. What arrived, a few months later, was a shipment of paint.

On the first floor Anatoly shows me into a room that

contains nothing except a large machine, and Klaus Frings comes to mind, Klaus Frings in his luxury apartment. I bear him no grudges. On the contrary, I hope he finds someone who shares his passion for Tchaikovsky and Heinrich Heine, someone whose beauty will not disempower him.

Anatoly rests a hand on the machine. 'For sterilising clothes. Very expensive. Same price as a car.'

We leave one empty room and enter another. A desk stands by the window.

'No chair,' I say.

Anatoly smiles.

I'm beginning to feel complicit in a fiction of his own inventing. It's as if the sole purpose of the tour is to have me authenticate an enterprise that doesn't actually exist. But then I remember that it was my idea.

The only time we encounter any people is when he opens a door at the far end of the building. Enveloped in a swirling mist of fumes are two men wielding brushes, rollers, and trays of paint. A third man, dressed in a black fur hat and overalls, sits in a half-built shower, smoking. Russian folk music hammers out of a ghetto-blaster wrapped in see-through plastic. The man in the hat looks at me steadily. Nobody speaks.

'The alcoholic department,' Anatoly says as we back out of the room, and this time it's clear that he is joking.

Later, in his 'cabinet', I ask if I'm allowed to use the local sports facilities. I would like to start swimming again, I tell him. He says I'll need a certificate of health from a doctor.

'Then I've come to the right place.' I give him a bright smile.

'Yes,' he says, 'but you are young. It will not be necessary to examine you – or . . .' Something about the way he leaves the sentence dangling unnerves me.

I move past him, to the window. The snow blowing off the hotel roof is fine as smoke.

'You have health problems?' he says, almost hopefully.

'No.'

Perhaps I was too eager when he first spoke to me. Perhaps he mistook my curiosity about the settlement for an interest in him – and then I asked if I could see the hospital, *his* hospital.

He mutters to himself in Russian, then takes a seat in front of the computer. As he clicks and scrolls, he tells me that the water in the pool comes from 'the lake'. I should be careful not to swallow it. He prints out a single sheet of paper, signs it and hands it to me.

'Soon I will be leaving,' he says.

This second reference to his imminent departure feels loaded, and his gaze lingers on me, hangdog and oddly ravenous. I thank him for the tour and the certificate, then I return to my hotel. I hoped he would be a source of information, a kind of guide, even perhaps a friend, but from now on it will be difficult to talk to him or learn from him. It might be wiser, in fact, to avoid him altogether. Though he has put me in an awkward position I still feel for him, and will go on feeling for him, even after he has left for Moscow or wherever it is that he's going, and I know that when I think of him in the weeks and months that lie ahead I will picture him standing beside that machine for sterilising clothes, as if posing for a photograph, the run-down sickly employee with his red-rimmed eyes and his faded jeans, about to be reassigned, and the expensive, superbly engineered piece of medical equipment, recently installed and still unused.

October is drawing to a close, and it's only light between eleven in the morning and three in the afternoon. If the skies are clear, sunrise merges into sunset, the transition so gradual and smooth that it's hard to tell them apart. On cloudy days there's a glow that is spectral and diffuse, as if an eclipse is happening. It's during these elusive dream-like hours that I map the town – its streets and buildings, its footpaths, its forgotten spaces. I often walk out along the straight paved road that heads due west. Beyond the warehouses, with their hoards of sawdust, tiles and cement, is a monument that harks back to the Soviet era, a tall tapering concrete obelisk topped with a faded silver star. Nearby is a sign that says UGOLGRAD, a red line drawn diagonally through the name to indicate that you are leaving. But no one ever leaves, not unless they're going to the heliport. The road doesn't lead anywhere else. If you want to go to Longyearbyen – and for years, during the Cold War, the Russians weren't welcome there – you have to go by boat. Overland, the only option is a snowscooter, but it isn't advisable until January, when the snow is hard and packed and the darkness begins to ease, and then only with someone who is familiar with the terrain. I lean against the sign, my face turned to the south. Across the water the mountains loom, their flanks a milky lilac-white, like yoghurt flavoured with forest fruits. It looks ethereal over there, difficult to believe in, like an imaginary kingdom.

With two days to go until Axelsen arrives, I decide to embark on a series of drawings of derelict properties, beginning with the pink house that stands close to the shoreline, to the west of the steps that lead down to the quay. To reach the house I have to climb down off the steps and on to a frail wooden walkway that cuts sideways across the slope and over a gulley. If the walkway gives I will drop three or four metres to the steeply sloping ground below. I could break an ankle, or even a leg, and end up in that creepy hospital, with only Anatoly to care for me. Ignoring the hand rail, which looks as though it has rotted clean through, I hurry across the thin buckled planks and step on to the equally fragile moss-encrusted verandah. The front door is padlocked. I look around, making sure no one is watching, then climb through an open window at the side. I check my watch. Just after twelve. Three hours of daylight left.

I choose a small room at the back of the house. The window, half hidden by a threadbare orange curtain, looks back up the slope towards other, grander properties, including the brown-and-white building, which used to be the miners' canteen. Scattered about on the floor are a number of random objects – among them, a bone-handled knife, a single mattress and a crumpled Pepsi can. On the windowsill are five stubbed-out cigarette butts. Four have brown filters. The other one is white. I imagine a tryst where the man was nervous and smoked more than the woman. The gap between the white filter and the brown ones suggests the couple didn't quite connect – it seems unlikely they made love on that soiled mattress – and the man left the house frustrated and alone. I draw the cigarette butts, then I draw the knife. This takes a good couple of hours, and I keep myself going with biscuits, chocolate and bottled water. When I have finished I climb back out of the open window, hoping no one sees me until I'm back on the grey wooden steps.

* * *

The day before Axelsen is due, I enter the building that houses the museum. On the second floor is a library. When I walk in, a young woman is sitting at a desk, sorting through slips of paper. Her dark hair is cut straight across, stopping just short of her eyebrows, and a close-fitting black sweater shows off her slender arms. Her movements are slow, as if she's sedated.

'Can I help you?' The woman speaks English in a low slurred voice I feel I could have predicted.

'I thought the doctor was the only person who spoke English,' I say.

'You know the doctor?'

'He eats breakfast in the hotel.'

She nods, then gathers up the paper slips and puts them in a drawer.

'You have a great voice,' I tell her. 'Do you sing?'

'Only when I drink too much.'

I smile. 'How did you know I was English?'

'Somebody tell me an English girl arrive. Everything is news here. Small town.'

'Do people read a lot?'

'Not so much. But we have one or two people, they like books. The winter is very long.'

Later, when I have walked round the library, which seems to specialise in technical literature – books on geology and engineering predominate – I ask the woman about herself. Her name is Zhenya. She came to Ugolgrad with her husband on a two-year contract. Her husband works for the mining company. She sighs, then adds, Like everybody else. They left their six-year-old son in Donetsk with his grandparents. It was a difficult decision, and there's hardly a moment when she doesn't think of him, but it isn't for much longer. They plan to return to Ukraine in the summer, and it will have been worth it. You make good money here, she says. More than back home, at least.

'And there's nothing to spend it on,' I say,

'Phonecalls,' she says, 'and vodka.'

I'm smiling again.

'You're curious about our town?' she asks. 'You are – how to say it? – a voyeur?'

'Not at all. No. A voyeur is a person who is on the outside, looking in. I want to become part of the place. I want to live here.'

'You want to *live* here?'

'Yes.'

Zhenya's deep-set eyes and the dry way in which she expresses herself give her a haughty condescending air, and yet she seems happy to talk. It's possible she is grateful for the company. I imagine her days must pass in silence – unless one of the few people who reads books happens to appear. An idea occurs to me, and I decide to try it out on her.

'Perhaps I could work here,' I say, 'in the library.'

'I don't think so.' Zhenya looks past me, towards the curtained doorway, with that distant gaze of hers. 'There is not enough even for me to do.'

'Not as a librarian. I could clean. With books, there's always dust.'

She looks straight at me, and her eyes are focused suddenly, and clear. 'Strange you say that.'

She tells me that Mrs Kovalenka, the cleaner, has recently been taken ill. The poor woman had a stroke, and was airlifted to the mainland.

A scene from *The Passenger* comes back to me. Jack Nicholson and Maria Schneider are having drinks on the terrace of a hotel that appears to be in the south of Spain – the décor is flamboyant, Moorish – and they're both smoking, their glasses of rosé offset by the pale-green of the tablecloth. He's curious to know whether she believes in coincidence. She says, *I never asked myself.* Then she smiles, but only with her eyes, which are mischievous and smudged. *I never used to notice it*, he says in his slightly nasal drawl. *Now I see it all around.*

'I'm sorry to hear that,' I say. 'But I could fill in for her, perhaps – until she returns.'

'She's old,' Zhenya tells me. 'I don't think she will return.'

My heart speeding up, I wait to see what she says next.

'We don't pay so much – not what you are used to.' She smiles faintly. 'This is not England.'

'I only need enough to live,' I tell her.

'I will talk to the authorities.'

'Thank you. You don't know what this means to me.'

'No.' And she glances at the papers on her desk, her eyebrows raised. 'I do not know.'

At three o'clock the following afternoon I pull on my parka, my fur hat and my gloves and I leave the hotel. It's light outside, but only just. A grey sky blankets the town, and flakes of snow stick to my clothing as I hurry down to the dock. The temperature is dropping every day. Though I haven't seen a thermometer I can tell it's below freezing, and October isn't even over yet.

I descend the two hundred-odd steps, passing the viewing platform and the house whose interior I have begun to document. The ship from Longyearbyen has already docked, its black hull flush against the quay. I shield my eyes and peer through the rapidly darkening air. Axelsen is in the cabin on the bridge, his head and body framed in the side-window, the light a murky aquarium green.

Once the tourists have disembarked – there's only a small group, all wrapped in waterproofs – I say hello to Torgrim, then I climb on board and pass through the door that leads to the bridge. The smell is the same as before. Oil, metal. Brine.

When Axelsen sees me, he adjusts the peak of his baseball cap, then folds his arms and leans against the wall, partially obscuring a chart showing various species of whales. Next to him are three pairs of binoculars in upright brackets.

'No suitcase,' he says.

'No.'

'So I was wrong.'

I go to the window. The floodlights are on, and snowflakes whirl and jostle in the brittle sodium glare. Beyond, there is nothing but greyness, impenetrable, chaotic, all-enveloping. 'I'm going to stay for a while. It suits me here.'

When he doesn't say anything I face him again. I sense him repeating the words to himself, testing them for authenticity.

'I found a job,' I tell him.

That morning the humourless woman from the bar handed me a note from Zhenya asking if she could see me. After breakfast, when I called in at the library, she told me I had been hired as a cleaner. We went through the paperwork together. Later, she walked me round to the mining company's main office, where there were more forms to fill in. While in the office, I learned that Mrs Kovalenka's family have contacted the company to say there are medical complications, and that she won't be coming back. Zhenya has suggested I move into Mrs Kovalenka's apartment. It will cost much less than the hotel.

'You will work as a cleaner?' Axelsen's voice lifts in disbelief.

'Yes. Why not?'

'You don't look like a cleaner.'

'You think I don't know how to clean?'

'I didn't say that.'

'You'll see. Next time you come—' I break off, thinking. 'When *is* the next time?'

He picks up a manual and slowly flips through pages that are thin as onion skin. 'I will be back in April.'

'Five months.'

He nods. 'And even then the winter will not be over. The winters are very long up here.'

'So everybody keeps saying. But that's why I came – for the winter.'

He seems to lose patience, letting his breath out fast and turning towards the window, then he checks himself and looks at me steadily, sideways on. 'There are things you can't tell me.'

Startled, I'm reminded of Adefemi, and how he used to talk sometimes. *Somewhere there's another version of us that got married, and had children, and lived together for the rest of our lives*, he told me on the night we agreed to separate. He would say things that were so perceptive, so *right*, that I would gaze at him with eyes that felt wide and liquid, like a Manga girl, but he never seemed to appreciate the significance or value of his words, and he wouldn't be able to remember them after-wards, nor would he have any idea of the effect they had on me. They were involuntary and obvious – to him, at least

– and it was in his nature to allow them to pass through him. He was thriftless in that way. Axelsen, also, doesn't seem to be entirely in control of what he's saying. It's as if he knows something he should not know. As if he momentarily became a medium. He even *looks* slightly dazed, like someone waking from a trance.

'I brought you something.' He opens a cupboard, takes out a flat package and hands it to me. The wrapping paper has Santas on it.

I smile. 'Christmas is early this year.'

'It was the only paper I could find.'

I tear off the wrapping. Inside is a red hot-water bottle, just like the one my mother used to put in my bed when I was little. I feel tears coming.

'Did I do something wrong?' Axelsen asks.

'No, no. It's all right.' I sniff, then wipe my eyes. 'I haven't seen one of these for years.'

'Just something for the winter.'

'So you knew all along. You knew I wasn't going to change my mind.'

'Sometimes, if you do one thing, you can make the other thing happen.'

I understand the principle. Like the opposite of tempting fate.

'I'm sorry it didn't work,' I say. 'But thank you, anyway. It's a lovely thought.'

He looks away from me, adjusts his baseball cap.

'What's your first name?' I ask.

'Olav.'

I step back, towards the door. 'Enjoy the winter, Olav. I'll see you in April.'

247

'And your name?' he says. 'You won't tell me your name?'

'I'll tell you – on one condition.'

Folding his arms, Olav turns back into a figure of authority – decisive, unruffled.

'If somebody asks about me,' I say, 'or shows you a photo of me, you must say you haven't seen me.'

'What if it's the police?'

Once again he catches me off guard but I don't hesitate. 'You haven't seen me. It doesn't matter who it is.' I pause. 'You have to promise.'

'That's a big condition.'

But he promises, and so I tell him.

'Misty?' he says in a voice that suggests he would never have guessed. 'It sounds like a country and western singer.'

A boat on a lake, three men in tartan shirts. My mother up on her feet, singing a song about the coal mines of Kentucky and the secrets of her soul.

Lights glittering all along the shore.

Then later, in a motel outside Milan, a man shouting *Maledetta putana* in the car-park at four a.m., and my mother murmuring *Go back to sleep, darling*, and then, half to herself, *It's just some drunk.*

'Do you like country and western?' I ask Olav.

'Actually, I do – and Röyksopp.'

'I'm sorry?'

He grins. 'It's Norwegian music.'

Later, back in my room, I wonder why I didn't tell him who I was. I owed him the truth – surely. But perhaps I didn't feel I could bank on the fact that such an honest straightforward man would lie successfully on my behalf. At least now, if someone asks him about Katherine Carlyle, he can say, with his hand on his heart, that he has never heard of me.

I gaze down at the dull pewter-coloured key Zhenya gave me, unmarked except for an unevenly stamped number. A few weeks ago, Klaus asked me what I was doing in Berlin and I told him, rather pretentiously, that I was 'experimenting with coincidence', and now, as I stand in the corridor outside Mrs Kovalenka's apartment, the walls a hospital green, the air smelling of reheated food, I realise my idea has become a reality. I would prefer her departure to have been less traumatic – a lottery win; a golden handshake at the very least – but once again I have the impression that I only have to apply the slightest pressure to the fabric of the world and it will give. It's as though I forged the key through sheer force of will; I wanted it so much that it came into being. Is it any wonder I feel powerful? I haven't met the cleaning-lady, and probably never will, yet I'm about to wrap the remnants of her life about me like a cloak. I could take her name, adopt a new persona. Complete my disappearance. *Misty Kovalenka*: less like a country and western singer than an ice-skater or a tennis star.

Facing the stairwell, Mrs Kovalenka's cheap wooden front door has been treated with a clear varnish and fitted with a Judas eye. I insert the key into the lock and feel it engage. The door clicks open. A gust of air moves through the gap like someone breathing out. A final sour exhalation. The door's bottom edge catches on the floor as I enter, and I have to push it with both hands. Expecting similar resistance when I close it, I give it a good shove. It slams loudly, then stares at me with its Judas eye. *What?*

Inside the apartment it's colder than in the stairwell, so cold that I can't smell anything. The hallway is L-shaped, with a glass light-shade in the ceiling. Just inside the front door, on the left, is a windowless kitchen, its walls the scorched yellow-brown of nicotine-stained fingers. A half-full glass of tea in an ornate metal holder stands on a work surface. I open a cupboard. A jar of pickled mushrooms, a tin of sprats. A few packets of rice and crackers. At the end of the hallway or corridor, on top of a chest of drawers, is a kind of shrine, with china animals, church candles, and a tin jug filled with plastic flowers. Tacked to the wall above is a picture of Jesus, his soulful eyes gazing skywards, a red heart bleeding through his robes. There's also a photo of Putin, cut from a magazine, and one of Marcello Mastroianni, as he appeared in *La Dolce Vita*. The bathroom, which is also on the left, has the white tiled walls and floor of a slaughterhouse. The mirror above the sink is cracked, but the tube of toothpaste on the shelf below has been carefully rolled from the bottom and isn't quite empty. A pink towel hangs on a rail. One moment I feel like a detective, clear-eyed, forensic, looking for evidence or clues. The next, I'm one of Mrs Kovalenka's relatives, feeling for her. Missing her. I asked Zhenya about the cleaning-lady but she didn't give too much away. Quiet, she said. Lived alone.

On the other side of the corridor are two more rooms. The bedroom isn't much bigger than the kitchen, with a single bed and a wardrobe, and the walls are papered with a recurring pattern of blue flowers and brown autumn leaves. On the bedside table is a cheap alarm clock, a pair of glasses, a radio, and several bottles of pills. The clock is half an hour slow. The window overlooks the football pitch, and the road that leads to the heliport. A renovated apartment block stands on the high ground to the right, snow piled at its base in dirty sculpted heaps. I face back into the room. Open the wardrobe. Enclosed in see-through plastic is a jacket and skirt of a synthetic green material, which Mrs Kovalenka probably kept for special occasions. At the bottom is a pair of fur-lined ankle boots worn down at the heel. I have a flickering sense of the woman, a twinkly, half-suggested image, like a hologram. She keeps her own company, and doesn't ask for much. I wonder what brought her to this place. I wonder if she'll survive.

In the living room, too, the wallpaper is oppressive – a psychedelic design of orange-and-yellow swirls. On the sideboard is a TV with a framed picture of a boy and a girl on top. Though they're dressed in matching fleeces, they don't appear to be twins. The boy has a pudding-basin haircut. The girl is smiling, but her lips are clamped tight shut, as mine often were in photographs when my milk teeth started falling out. On the other side of the room are two brown armchairs, and a sofa covered in a crocheted blanket. Above the sofa is a large creased map of the world. Given how far north I am, it's hard to believe in all those countries, especially the warm ones, but maybe that's exactly why the map is there, to link the cleaning-lady to the mainland, her past, the children in the picture. Vertigo grips me for a second, just as it did on my first morning.

I should air the place, as Zhenya advised. I open the cupboard between the kitchen and the bathroom and flick the switch. The boiler responds with a reassuring *whoomph*. I listen to the radiator pipes begin to tick. It will be a relief to move out of the hotel, away from the woman with the white mask-like face, though I feel differently about her now Zhenya has told me something of her story. The woman's name is Ivonna, and her husband is serving a long prison sentence in Ukraine. That, perhaps, Zhenya said in her deadpan way, is why she does not smile.

There are some things you can't prepare for. When I realised I would never see my mother again I locked myself in the bathroom. *Now what?* Thinking I should be sick I knelt on the floor, leaned over the toilet-bowl and retched. Nothing came up. I breathed the musty coolness for a while, then I got to my feet again and studied myself in the mirror. My face looked misshapen, sloppy, as if the two halves didn't fit together properly. *For fuck's sake*, I said, watching my mouth. It was something I'd heard my father say, when my mother accused him of not loving her, or not being around enough, or having an affair. *For fuck's sake*, I said, *you knew this was coming*. It didn't help, though. Nothing helped.

The morning after my mother died I heard the doctor say that her body would have to be removed from the apartment. Seized by a kind of terror, I hurled myself from one room to another, picking items up, then putting them down again. I couldn't allow my mother to be taken. I had to stop that happening. But how? I stood in the kitchen, a pair of scissors in my hand, the two blades overlapping, knife-like. My father was on the terrace. He had his arms round Auntie Lottie and held her carefully, as if she were not one thing but several, as though she had come apart. Her shoulders were shaking. He stared over the top of her head and out across the tiled roof-tops. He had the face of a statue, his features gritty, dry.

I crept back to where my mother was. The doctor had

gone, and the door stood ajar. The silence coming from inside the room was exaggerated, artificial, as if there were people hiding. As if they might suddenly jump out. *Surprise!* I found it hard to believe that she was not alive and yet still there. I slipped round the edge of the door. She lay on her back with a sheet pulled up to her neck, her lips slightly parted. She might have died in mid-sentence or mid-song. *I Fall to Pieces. Crazy. Help Me Make It Through the Night.*

'It's only me,' I whispered.

Since she was gone it seemed tasteless or insensitive to look at her, but it was impossible to look anywhere else. All forms of looking were problematic; it would have been easier to have no eyes. I kept thinking she would come back to life. Sit up, smother a yawn. Run a hand through her hair, which was stiff and coppery. She would glance round the room, puzzled, but also mildly entertained. *I must have dozed off. What time is it?*

At first I thought I might cut her fingernails and keep the clippings but I couldn't bring myself to disturb the sheet. Instead, I climbed on to the covers and was kneeling over her, snipping off a piece of hair, when my father walked in.

'No,' he cried out, and pulled me roughly off the bed.

I landed on the floor and hit my head on the edge of a chest of drawers. There was no blood but I felt a bruise form, the kind of swelling my mother would have called 'an egg'. The scissors lay in an X-shape on the tiles, the blades blue with reflected sky.

'Oh God,' my father said. 'I'm sorry.' He walked to the window. 'I'm just so tired.'

I picked myself up, a lock of my mother's hair clutched tightly in my fist. That was why I hadn't been able to break my fall. I hadn't wanted to let go of her hair, or let him know I had it.

He faced back into the room and took a step towards me. 'Forgive me, Kit.'

'Yes,' I said. 'All right.'

But I didn't forgive him. He hadn't earned it. Why didn't he understand that I couldn't bear to lose my mother, and that I wanted to keep a part of her for ever? Why couldn't he see that a black wind was blowing through me, wreaking havoc? All I was guilty of was loving her too much. Like him.

The weather is becoming unpredictable. One afternoon at the beginning of November the sky has a green glow to it, a subterranean colour that turns the fjord below a sulky charcoal grey. The next day there's a white-out. It's as if someone stuck blank paper over my windows. I can't see the short flight of steps leading to my building, let alone the football pitch. Sometimes the light is so delicate – primrose, oyster, eyelid-mauve – that the landscape looks hand-tinted, like a photo from the early 1900s. Then, in the second week, polar night descends, a cloth thrown abruptly over the town. The footpaths that remain unlit are hazardous, and time is difficult to gauge. Under the spotlights the snow on the ground is brownish-yellow, the colour of burnt butter.

Though still an object of curiosity to the miners and their families, I feel I'm beginning to earn their respect. I'm not like all the other foreign visitors, who spend an hour gawping at the town, then scuttle back to the comfort of the tourist ship. I'm not a voyeur, as Zhenya would say. I live in a residential block. I eat in the canteen. I work long hours. I'm even learning the language. People are surprised by my commitment. Flattered. I *chose* this place. I'm making it my own.

On the morning of November 15th, my twentieth birthday, I arrive at the library, as usual. Zhenya hands me a blue envelope and a small package wrapped in drab green paper.

'You're supposed to be saving your money,' I tell her, 'not spending it.'

She shrugs. 'It didn't cost so much.'

On the card are two white kittens in a wicker basket. Inside are the words 'Happy Birthday – from Zhenya'. It's so undemonstrative, so matter-of-fact. So very like her. I unwrap the present. Inside is a guide to Svalbard, written in English, and something that looks like a tube of toothpaste. She found the book in the library, she says.

'And this?' I hold up the tube.

'It's cream.'

She takes my hands and looks at them. The sides of my fingers are hard and shiny, like plastic, and the skin has cracked open in several places. It's partly my cleaning job, partly the cold.

She asks if I would like to come home with her that evening. She has invited some friends round to her apartment, she says. There will be plenty to eat and drink.

'Will you sing?' I ask.

She smiles, but doesn't answer.

After work, I follow her down a path and across the football pitch. We climb the slope to the newly renovated block, our heads bent against a wind that tears out of the north-east.

Zhenya's apartment is far more spacious than mine, her living-room filled with pine furniture that could have come from Ikea. There is a 30-inch flatscreen TV, and an old-fashioned stereo with a record deck and wooden speakers. Pinned to the wall is a huge orange-and-black flag featuring a pickaxe crossed with a hammer. Shakhtar Donetsk, Zhenya tells me. The football team her husband supports.

'He's crazy about that team,' she says. 'I think maybe he loves it more than me.'

She introduces me to Svetlana, who is in her twenties. Svet teaches the children. She has limp blonde hair and sits with her hands wedged between her thighs. Her purple sweater has a white reindeer on the front. I try out a few of my Russian phrases but all she does is nod or shake her head. Zhenya tells me she is very shy. Most of the other guests are in their thirties or forties and none of them speak English. Zhenya's husband, Gleb, sits on the sofa drinking beer with two other men.

For dinner we move to the table. Once we have finished the main course – pork escalopes and potatoes in a sour cream sauce – Zhenya leaves the room. The lights go out and she returns with a cake, her face made golden by the candles. She stops in front of me. The white icing has been sculpted to resemble the landscape that surrounds the town, while the buildings are huddled blocks of yellow, brown and green. People sing *Happy Birthday* in Russian and when they come to the end I blow the candles out. Loud applause, and a piercing whistle from one of Gleb's friends.

The lights flicker on. I get to my feet.

'Thank you, Zhenya,' I say in Russian. 'Thank you for this beautiful—' I can't remember the word for 'cake', 'this beautiful pastry.' Everybody laughs. 'I'm very happy. This town is like a home to me.' I say thank you again and sit back down.

Later, vodka is served, and the guests sing traditional folk songs from Russia and Ukraine, one of which – *Kalinka* – they insist I learn.

'Your Russian is very good,' Gleb says, the first words he has addressed to me all evening.

Everyone dances, even Svet.

It's the strangest birthday I have ever had.

The next day I wake at seven, and though my head aches from all the vodka I pack a bag and walk over to the pool. Ever since Anatoly gave me my certificate of health I have been meaning to start swimming, and this seems as good a time as any.

A still morning, the air like aluminium. Snow crunching and wincing beneath my feet. I pass a lighted ground-floor window. A woman in a green sweater stands at a kitchen sink. Her hair hangs past her shoulders, straight and brown. She appears to be looking at me but her face doesn't alter and I realise I'm invisible to her. All she can see is her own reflection – though if I had to guess I would say her mind is somewhere else, a past she misses, a future she's hoping for. Feeling I'm intruding, I move on. On reaching the square, I tilt my head back. Breathe in deeply. Whole galaxies scattered across the sky, like cocaine on a smoked-glass table. The life I used to live in Rome seems overblown, preposterous. Made up.

I cross a red entrance hall that is empty apart from a wooden bench and a well-stocked trophy cabinet. The TV is showing a wild-life programme, but no one's watching. As I hand my certificate to the woman in the office I think of Anatoly, who left without saying goodbye. Was he angry with me? Did he feel rejected? Or am I overestimating my own importance? Probably he knew most of the people who lived in town, and he would have had a lot on his mind, as you do when you're moving. The last time I saw him, at breakfast, he told me he collected coins. I ran up to my room and came down with some loose change left over from Berlin. As he took the money his fingers touched mine and he looked me full in the face, then he lowered his eyes and turned the coins over on his palm. *Beautiful,* he said.

The woman mutters what sounds like a caution, but I don't understand the words. Only when I leave the changing-room do I notice there is no one in the pool. There's no lifeguard either. I walk to the deep end. The water is murky, almost brown, like the bathwater in the hotel, and I remember Anatoly telling me it's piped in directly from the fjord, and that I should be careful not to swallow it. Perhaps the woman was saying that if I get into trouble it will be my own responsibility.

I haven't swum since the end of August and I reel off half a dozen lengths of languid freestyle, feeling the chill on my skin. Then, when my muscles have loosened, I switch to breast-stroke. The musty muddy flavour of the water isn't entirely pleasant but I gradually get used to it.

After thirty laps my body finds a familiar rhythm. I started swimming laps the year my mother died. It was a way of not talking. Not thinking. Some of my wealthier friends had pools in their gardens – one even had a rooftop pool that overlooked the Colosseum – but I preferred the high hollow echo of a sports complex like *Belle Arti,* where I could swim unobserved, among strangers, or the *Piscina delle Rose,* open to the Roman sky, and surrounded by surreal neo-classical buildings and bursts of purple bougainvillea. I was soothed by the going up and down, from one end to the other. All that repetition. It was like crossing something out. It was like forgetting. By the time that summer drew to a close I could swim for an hour without stopping. When I finally hauled myself out of the water after one of those sessions I would feel exhausted and relaxed and curiously unformed, half muscle, half liquid. I spent so much time in the pool that my body began to change, my shoulders widening, my limbs longer and more toned.

Once in a while I notice things – a row of rust-red radiators, three reindeer picked out in dark tiles on the wall above – but mostly my mind floats free. Then something alters, and I have the sudden conviction that somebody else is in the pool. When I turn at the deep end and peer ahead of me there's no one there, just a wide shifting box of green-brown water. I struggle to explain the rush of apprehension and euphoria. As I keep swimming up and down, the sense that I'm not alone intensifies, becomes specific. There are people on either side of me, and slightly behind me, just out of range of my field of vision. Turning at the shallow end, I look left and right. The pool is empty. But as I swim back towards the deep end I have the feeling once again that I'm accompanied. We're in a loose V-shape, like geese flying south for the winter. A shiver ripples through me. I'm remembering a conversation with Aunt Lottie, in her house in Norfolk. This was a few days after my father took me to the restaurant in Kensington. We sat in armchairs by the fire, with cups of tea nearby. *You weren't alone when they put you inside your mother's body*, Lottie said. *There were three of you. Three of me?* I didn't understand. *Three embryos*, Lottie said. *I know. I was there.* Outside, the wind hurled itself at a row of conifers. *On the Ultrasound you showed up as small specks floating side by side. Something so brave about it – like spaceships launched into a huge uncertain universe.* She prodded the logs with a poker and the chimney sucked up all the sparks. *Your mother was worried none of you would make it. Because that was what happened before, more than once, and it nearly destroyed her. You were the last throw of the dice.* Lottie reached for my hand and squeezed it, her eyes wide open, almost scared. *You know what she told me later, after you were born? She told me she was amazed by you. Why?* I said. *Why was she amazed? You were the strong one, the charmed one.* Lottie's eyes found mine, flames leaping in her pupils. *You were the one who wanted to live.*

After forty-five minutes my body begins to tire. I should build up slowly. Not overdo it. As I climb out of the pool I glimpse something in the corner of my eye, a shadowy scissor-movement that might be someone's legs, a person walking quickly, but when I stand dripping on the tiled edge and look around there's no one there. I think of the thawed embryos implanted at the same time as me. I imagine them looking for stability, security, but failing to connect, their cells degrading, their gorgeous yellow darkening to a grim doomed black. How to remember them? They had no names, no faces. There were no funerals, no graves. No ashes to be taken by the wind or washed away by rain. They left nothing in the minds of those from whom they came, nothing except – what? The memory of those white grains in the pulsing gloom, and a sense of regret, as indescribable as the taste of water.

I'm leaving for work one day when a man comes up the stairs as I'm going down. I hear him before I see him, each footstep harsh and gritty, like a spade being driven into gravel. Then he appears below. He's wearing a dark-green jacket, and his boots wouldn't look out of place on a parade ground if they weren't so scarred and scuffed. So far as I know, there's no military presence in the town, though I remember people in Longyearbyen telling me that the Russians continue to occupy Ugolgrad not for its coal, which has long ceased to be profitable, but for its strategic position. The mine is just an excuse, they say. A smoke-screen. But this man looks too dissolute to be a soldier. Even from a distance I can smell the alcohol on him, and it's only eight-thirty in the morning.

He stops and gazes up at me. His eyes are puffy, and his black hair is receding. His lips are livid, cracked. I lower my eyes and move on down the stairs. When I reach him, he blocks my way, leaning close to me and swaying slightly, the reek of spirits overpowering. He mutters a few words, then lurches back and lets me pass.

Later, at the library, I repeat the words to Zhenya.

'Who said this?' she asks.

I describe the man.

Zhenya nods slowly. 'I think it's Bohdan. He has some problems.'

'Does he live in my building?'

'Yes. Sometimes.'

After lunch, we sit in Zhenya's office drinking black tea with sugar. I question her further about Bohdan. She tells me that he fought in Chechnya. When he was discharged he discovered that his wife had been seeing someone else. In a fit of jealous rage he set fire to his apartment. He was arrested. Spent time in prison. Later, he started drinking heavily and lived on the streets. This was in Kharkiv. Somehow, he ended up in Ugolgrad, working as a security guard for the mine. She doesn't know whether it was the horrors of war that unhinged him or the fact that his wife betrayed him.

'You said he isn't always here,' I say.

'Sometimes he's in Pyramiden.'

Pyramiden is another mining concession, she tells me, built at the foot of the angular mountain from which it takes its name. Once home to a thousand Russians, it was closed down a decade ago. It's a ghost town now, she says, with only three inhabitants – the men who guard the place. A bust of Lenin still gazes out over the water, and there is grass in the streets, imported from Siberia. She shakes her head. Some say Pyramiden is being turned into a tourist destination, and that Bohdan is involved in the salvage work.

'Where is it?' I ask.

'About one hundred kilometres north of here,' she says. 'At the top of the Isfjord.'

'Sounds pretty isolated.'

Zhenya nods. 'I don't know how he survives.'

I finish my tea.

Zhenya advises me to avoid Bohdan. Some people carry catastrophe around with them. She turns her cup on the table thoughtfully, then looks up at me.

'Are you frightened?' she says.

That night, in Mrs Kovalenka's apartment, I open my silver locket for the first time in weeks. As always, the sight of my mother's hair sparks memories – her kissing me goodbye on a rainy school morning, my toes tucked into the back of her knees when my father was away and I was allowed to share her bed, her face during chemotherapy, drained of all colour, timeless and terrifying, like an oracle, a seer . . . I fetch the kitchen scissors and walk into the bathroom. Standing in front of the cracked mirror I snip off a piece of hair. If I place it next to hers I will always be near her. It will be like being buried together, in the same small grave. The piece I've snipped off is too wispy, though. The ends are split. I cut another piece. Now one side's longer than the other. I'm about to try and even things up when I realise that long hair makes no sense in a place like Ugolgrad, especially given my new job. I keep on cutting, and soon the sink is full of hair. I study myself in the mirror. My eyes seem prominent, my ears stick out. I have become a waif. I select a piece of hair and fit it into the silver heart, between the two locks of my mother's hair, then I snap the lid shut and turn on the shower.

Later, I stand at my living room window. Outside, the air is motionless. In the distance I can hear a steady, hollow roar that must be coming from the power station or the mine. Fingering the locket absentmindedly, I hear my aunt's voice. *You were the strong one, the charmed one.* The snow is so thick and perpendicular that it reminds me of a curtain coming down after a performance, a curtain continually falling, a finale that never ends . . .

Three thousand kilometres away, my father is also standing at a window, his hands in his pockets. It's a cold wet evening in Berlin. A police car speeds past below, bits of blue light flung recklessly across the road. Weeks have passed since our failed rendezvous, and yet he has stayed on. Is it the thought of me that keeps him there, in the last place I was seen? Is he still trying to solve the mystery of my disappearance?

'Arkhangel'sk,' he murmurs.

My heart heats up. What will he do?

Still standing at the window, my father selects a contact on his phone, then puts it to his ear.

'Lydia?' he says. 'It's David.'

* * *

One day in late November, when I'm having lunch in the canteen, the door swings open and Olav appears. His eyes find mine even before the door has shut behind him. He glances down quickly, taking off his gloves, then he removes a couple of outer layers, hangs them on a hook on the wall and walks over. There's a wariness in his face and also a kind of pride, which makes him look younger, almost boyish.

'This is a surprise,' I say.

'Yes,' he says. 'I was just passing through.'

But Ugolgrad isn't on the way to anywhere, as he knows perfectly well. No one just 'passes through'.

'How did you get here?' I ask.

'Snowscooter.'

'Isn't that dangerous?'

He watches me, half-smiling. 'How would you know?'

'They told me. In Longyearbyen.'

'I did it before.'

'It's completely dark, and the snow hasn't frozen properly. You could hit a rock. Or there could be an avalanche.' I push my empty plate away. 'It's crazy.'

'Now who's worrying?'

'I have good reason, not like you. This place isn't as terrible as you made out.' I pause. 'There aren't any rats in the hotel.'

Still smiling, he looks away, across the canteen. The silence is filled by rap music coming from the TV on the wall.

'I need a coffee,' he says. 'How about you?'

'OK. Thanks.'

He walks up to the counter. Though I'm upset about the risk he has taken, I'm happy to see him. There's something about his gaze that anchors me. Olav, Zhenya . . . These new friendships feel deep-rooted, resilient, and yet we hardly know each other.

'It was my birthday last week,' I tell him when he returns.

His eyes drop to the brown sweater I found in Mrs Kovalenka's wardrobe. 'Was that a present?'

'This? No. I borrowed it.'

I talk about the party at Zhenya's and about my speech and how I made everybody laugh.

'They are treating you well,' he says. 'I'm glad.' But he doesn't look glad. He hunches over his coffee, lines stacked up on his forehead. 'You could leave now and come back in the spring. It's beautiful in the spring. You wouldn't believe the sky.'

I tell him I'm staying. Apart from my job, which takes up more time than I expected – I now clean the museum, as well as the library – I'm determined to become fluent in Russian. I also swim most days. I'm recovering my old fitness.

He has nothing to say to this.

'And you?' I say. 'What are your plans?'

He shrugs. 'My ex-wife lives in Bergen, with my children. I will visit them.'

'You have children?'

'Two boys. Six and nine.'

I ask if he has pictures.

He takes out a wallet and slides a small photo across the table. The nine-year-old is the image of his father, with rugged features and crinkly rust-coloured hair. The other one has a round smiling face and his hair is greenish-blonde. All of a sudden I can picture Olav's ex. I think of the children on top of Mrs Kovalenka's TV, their soggy complexions, their matching fleeces. No one looking at them now.

'They're lovely boys,' I say.

'Yes.' He turns the photo on the table and studies it dispassionately as if he has been asked to make some kind of appraisal. As if the children aren't actually his.

'Will you take them sailing?'

He smiles faintly, bitterly. 'Their father, the sea captain.'

'It's not something to be ashamed of.'

'My ex-wife wouldn't agree.' He sighs. 'In any case, in Norway we sail only in the summer.'

'Of course.'

He looks at me and something tightens in his face.

'What's wrong?' I ask.

'You look so different.'

'My hair, you mean? I know. I didn't do a very good job, did I?'

'No.'

'It's more appropriate – for my work. Besides, no one's going to see me, are they, not out here.'

'I see you.'

Not sure what to say, I let my eyes drift past him. A man is sitting near the door, under a mural of a knight on a white charger. I think I recognise the man from the birthday party. He's one of Gleb's friends. Oddly, though, he doesn't acknowledge me. No smile or wave. Not even a nod. When I look at Olav again he's gazing down into his empty coffee cup.

'You look younger,' he says at last.

'Is that bad?'

'No, not bad. Only . . .' He tails off, unable to grasp hold of his feelings, uncertain how to put them into words.

'It will grow again,' I say.

He glances at me, as if he disagrees with this, then checks his watch. 'I should be going.'

Outside, the air is sharp, abrasive. You could almost graze yourself on it. Light from the canteen windows lands on the square paved area in yellow slabs. As Olav walks to his snowscooter I notice that he's limping. I ask if he has hurt himself.

'It's sciatica,' he says. 'I'm getting old.'

We embrace quickly. We're wearing so many layers that it feels chaste and faintly humorous. He fits a pair of goggles over his eyes, then climbs on to the machine and turns the key in the ignition.

'You're not old,' I call out over the urgent high-pitched buzzing of the engine.

He grins. 'See you in April.'

The red glow of his tail-light dissolves in the grainy darkness. It will take him at least three hours to get back. I hope he will be all right.

Standing in the cold, I think about Natasha and Klaudija, who I met in Longyearbyen. I should have asked Olav to call at the hotel and give them a message. They were good to me. I don't want them to think I have forgotten them.

Not long after Olav's visit I stay up late, leafing through my guide to Svalbard, the TV on in the background. Girls in glittery bikinis twirl behind a host who is more than twice their age, his hair peach-coloured, his teeth all capped. I wonder which girl he's sleeping with. If this was Italy, he probably would have had them all. Who watches these shows? I reach for the remote. In the sudden quiet after I turn the TV off I hear a sound I don't recognise at first. When it happens again, I realise it's my front door shaking in its frame, as if someone just collided with it.

I creep up the hall and peer through the Judas eye. My breath rushes into me, abrupt and shallow. Standing up against the door is Bohdan, the man I spoke to Zhenya about. I don't dare move. He's unshaven, as before, and the snow in his black hair is beginning to melt and trickle down his face. His cheeks are covered with a patina of grime. He looks like someone who was on fire and has only just been extinguished. Above his left eye is a deep cut in the shape of a crescent moon, the edges crusted and black. He brushes at the wound, smearing blood across his face, then he stares at the ground and mutters a few incoherent words. All I can see is the top of his head, the scalp showing through his thinning hair. He fought in Chechnya and his only reward was to lose his wife. Is it any wonder that he drinks?

Once, as if intent on catching me off guard, he tries to look through the Judas eye. Idiotic, of course, since that's what Judas eyes are designed to prevent. In that moment, though, we're only three or four centimetres apart, and my heart is beating so hard that I worry he might hear it. After a few long seconds he stands back and fiddles with the front of his jacket, then he swings away and walks into the stair-well. At last I can see the whole of him. His shoulders are wet – the green of his jacket has darkened to a sodden black – and snow sticks to the heels of his boots. His back still turned, he glances over one shoulder, in the direction of my door. He thinks he forgot something, perhaps, or that something changed while he wasn't looking. His cracked lips move. He's talking to himself again.

Standing near the stairs, he undoes his flies, then he takes out his penis and stares at it, as if he wasn't expecting to find it in his underpants and is wondering how it got there. A dark greyish-mauve, it reminds me of certain vegetables – a beet-root when it is first lifted from the earth, or purple sprouting. He tries to masturbate but he's too drunk to get an erection. Leaving his penis dangling outside his trousers, he reaches into his jacket pocket and brings out a bottle of vodka. He lifts the bottle to his mouth. The vodka lurches left then right as he takes two or three fierce gulps, then he lowers the bottle and wipes his mouth on his sleeve. His eyes veer towards my door again. I back away. This could go on for hours.

Later, lying in the dark, it's hard to put the drunk man out of my mind. Noises keep coming from the corridor outside. The chink of glass on concrete, the shuffle of boots. Muttering, and more muttering. Shouting. Then a crash. He must have fallen over. I switch on Mrs Kovalenka's radio. The classical music station she used to listen to is playing a song cycle. I turn the volume down and leave it on all night.

In the morning I go and look through the Judas eye. The stairwell appears to be deserted. I crack the door open. Bohdan's gone. The vodka bottle lies next to the wall, and there's a pool of vomit on the floor. The poor man. He's such a mess. What can I do, though?

The Moscow–Arkhangel'sk flight lands on time, and my father follows Lydia down the metal steps and across the tarmac. Outside the airport they climb into a waiting taxi. They have reserved a room at the Best Eastern Dvina, which is where I stayed. It's not such a big coincidence; the city only has a handful of decent hotels. All the same, I wonder if my father can sense my presence as he walks towards reception. Is that what brings him to a halt halfway across the lobby?

'What are you doing, David?' Lydia says.

He pats his pocket, then appears to relax. 'Sorry. I thought I left my passport in the taxi.' But he knows exactly where his passport is. He's lying to her and he's not sure why.

The next day, as they scour the city for evidence of me, they take a short cut between some old wooden houses. Lydia stops by a window. Between the net curtains and the glass panes, arranged on the thin shelf of the sash, is a row of snow globes. Lydia suggests they go inside. Though my father is eager to keep moving he doesn't want to seem inflexible or stuck in his ways – and it's hard at this stage in their relationship to deny her anything. Reluctantly, he agrees. The two men are there, just as before, one folded into the armchair by the counter, the other curved against the shelves, oddly boneless. Despite himself, my father feels a stirring of curiosity. The atmosphere intrigues him. Something other-worldly, anachronistic. The tin-lined ceiling, the dark boards on the floor.

'How old is this place?' he asks the man who is leaning against the shelves.

The man surveys him, the glitter in his eyes reptilian and cold, then he turns and speaks to the other man, who might or might not be his brother. He fails to answer my father's question. Probably he didn't understand.

My father doesn't pursue it. Looking round, he finds himself drawn to the left side of the room, and then to one snow globe in particular. Inside the plastic dome is a replica of the airport where he and Lydia landed the day before, every detail faithfully recreated. The long low terminal building. The blue-and-white light aircraft mounted on a pedestal outside and placed, bizarrely, in among some birch trees. The chunky pale-pink control tower. Tiny passengers thread their way across the tarmac towards an old-fashioned turbo-prop that is preparing for take-off. My father is about to call out to Lydia when he sees something that almost stops his heart. At the top of the steps that lead up to the plane is the figure of a young woman with hip-length hair. Dressed in a dark-brown coat, she glances over her shoulder, taking one last look at the place she is about to leave behind. The air between my father's eyes and the plastic dome seems to contract, congeal.

'David?' Lydia says. 'What is it?'

He doesn't reply. Instead, he snatches up the snow globe and carries it over to the man sitting by the counter. He points at the inside of the dome.

'This girl,' he says. 'Have you seen her?'

The man looks past my father at the other man, and his lips draw back to reveal receding gums.

My father pushes the snow globe up against the man's face, too close to focus on. 'You've seen her, haven't you. Where did she go?'

Lydia touches my father's arm. 'He doesn't understand, David. He doesn't know what you're talking about.'

He shakes her off. The man *does* understand. *Both* the men understand. He's convinced of it. They're communicating, all three of them, at a level beyond language.

'Tell me where she is,' he says, 'or I'll call the police.' He searches for the word in Russian. '*Militsaya.*' He seizes the man by his lapels, hauls him to his feet and shouts into his face. '*Militsaya!*'

The man begins to shake, as if he has a fever – he's shaking all over – then he opens his mouth, showing all his teeth, some of which are thin as matchsticks, and he's shouting too, in a high-pitched voice, like a bird.

Lydia steps back into the shadows. She's used to thinking of herself as practical, efficient, but the situation frightens her. She has no idea what to do.

The snow globe slips from my father's hand and smashes on the floor.

Everything stops.

My father lets go of the man, who slumps back in his chair. The man's chin rests on his chest, and he's panting. His hair has fallen over his eyes. It occurs to my father that the man might be a cripple, or an epileptic. Or even mentally deficient. The other man leans down and straightens his brother's clothes, then whispers in his ear. There's a thin acrid smell, like blown light-bulbs or melted fuse-wire. Lydia still hasn't moved.

The man in the chair is saying something in Russian. The same words, over and over. This time it's my father who doesn't understand. The man reaches for a pencil and paper. With a trembling hand he begins to scribble.

It's a number.

A price.

He says the words again, then aims a finger at the shattered globe. He seems to be pointing at the tiny figure in the cashmere coat. She is still poised at the top of the metal staircase, still glancing nostalgically over her shoulder, but the plane has lost a wing, and the airport is in pieces, and the granules of snow are scattered across the dark wood floor.

As my father stares at the broken globe, the man comes out with a simple quiet sentence. My father doesn't know what the man is saying. I do, though. I know exactly what he's saying.

If you don't pay, your daughter will die.

* * *

A few nights later I rise up slowly through several layers of sleep. My feet are so cold they feel separate from the rest of me. The clock says twenty to three. A symphony is playing on the radio. Stealthy apprehensive music. Feelings that aren't permitted. A cleansing wash of sound from the strings, but then anxiety and turbulence from the brass instruments. I turn the volume down and listen. There are no noises in the corridor, not tonight. Bohdan is in Pyramiden, perhaps. Once I have rubbed some warmth into my feet I leave the bed and walk to the window. I never tire of looking out at this unlikely place; I still marvel at the fact that I am here. The smooth white sports field, spotlights casting soft-edged circles on the snow. Buildings that seem unnaturally motionless, as if braced against the cold. One of the older houses sinks, lopsided, into the earth. To the left and lower down, not far from the old canteen, is the wooden church with its blunt black spire. The lights have been left on, and the two windows glow, sinister as the eyes in a Halloween pumpkin.

I'm about to turn away when a shift in the shadows to my right distracts me. A polar bear shambles down the slope, moving like an athlete, with a loose easy muscularity, its coat a musty yellow-white. The breath stalls in my throat. Once on level ground, the animal rears up on its hind legs. Head swaying on its powerful neck, it lifts its muzzle and sniffs and scours at the air. Then it drops lightly back on all fours and disappears into the darkness beyond the football pitch, and I'm left standing at the window, buds opening inside my body, a tingling on the surface of my skin. Torgrim told me that polar bears do most of their hunting on drift ice. From April onwards, though, the ice begins to melt. Polar bears can survive without eating for eight months, but they are so hungry by late autumn that they will go almost anywhere in search of food. All the same, I can't quite believe what I've seen. Back in bed I reach for the radio and turn the volume up again. The symphony isn't over yet. The music has an insistent rhythmic quality – risks are being taken, avenues explored – and I lie awake until it finishes.

When I walk into the library the following morning Zhenya's eyes are swollen and I suspect she has been crying. I ask if she's all right. She shrugs and doesn't answer. Later, over a cup of dark sweet tea, she tells me that she and Gleb had an argument the previous night, and that she couldn't sleep for hours afterwards. It was about money, and about their son. She wants to return to Ukraine but Gleb thinks they should stay on, perhaps beyond the summer. He claims it would be an investment in the future. If you don't have a present, she told him, there *isn't* any future. After that he said cruel things, hateful things. He'd been drinking, of course.

'It's hard to be in this place.' Zhenya gives me a direct, almost accusing look. 'Sometimes I don't understand why you are here.'

'I don't have a husband,' I say, 'or any children either. I'm free to go where I want.'

'You have no boyfriend?'

'There was someone.' I sigh, then look away. 'It's over now.'

'Your heart is broken? That is why you came?'

'No, no. Nothing like that.'

Zhenya's eyes are still fixed on me. 'Strange you have no boyfriend,' she says, 'a girl who looks like you.'

Outside, the darkness is absolute, even though it's the middle of the day. It has been like this since November 12th, when the last of the light disappeared. I pick at a loose thread on Mrs Kovalenka's sweater, then reach for my cup. The thin clean smell of tea.

'I can't tell you why I'm here,' I say, 'not now.' I hesitate. 'Perhaps if I get to know you better.' And then, in an attempt to lighten the mood: 'If you stay for long enough.'

'So that will be my reward,' Zhenya says matter-of-factly, and without a trace of sarcasm. 'To hear your story.'

'It's a long story. I'm not sure how to tell it yet.'

'Does it have an end?'

'No. But it has two beginnings.'

'A story with two beginnings and no end.' She looks beyond me, into the library, where all the books sit undisturbed. 'That's something new.'

Her dry delivery makes me laugh. 'You're very funny, Zhenya.'

'Really? No one told me that.'

'It's true.'

'My husband doesn't think I'm funny.'

'Well, he's wrong.'

She takes her cup over to the sink and stands with her back to me for a few moments, not doing anything, and I worry that I might have caused offence. Then she looks at me, over her shoulder. 'I feel better. Thank you.'

I finish my tea and join her at the sink.

'Guess what I saw last night,' I say.

Winter grips. Satellite images show the town from above, blurred, buried, close to being obliterated by whiteness. A south-easterly rushes between the buildings, shrill and relentless, and the cloud cover is dense and low. I ask Zhenya if the wind has a name. In most countries, I tell her, winds have names. *Chinook, meltemi. Tramontana.* Maybe it does, Zhenya says, but she isn't aware of it. The streets are deserted except for when the miners return from their shifts, lights shining on the front of their orange helmets, faces wrapped in scarves or balaclavas. The temperature has plummeted twenty degrees since my arrival, though the wind-chill factor makes it feel more like thirty. In the evenings I make endless cups of tea and coffee and sit in bed with my hot-water bottle, learning Russian or listening to the radio. If Bohdan's keeping vigil in the corridor I haven't heard him.

On the first Saturday in December I arrange to have dinner in the bar of the hotel. It's an extravagance – I will have to pay in Norwegian kroner, like a tourist – but I'm tired of cooking for myself and I feel like a change from the canteen. That night, as I pass the half-open door to the kitchen, Ivonna looks round. We say good evening to each other, but Ivonna's expression is neutral, as always. Everything is the same as I remember it – the dark-red tablecloths, the pine-clad walls that gleam like glass, the vodka and Toblerone behind the bar. What I'm unprepared for is the presence of two middle-aged men, seated where the doctor used to sit. One of them is balding, with a beard. The other has fair hair and pink cheeks. They're deep in conversation, though they fall silent and look round when I walk in. My old table is set up for me, with three or four *pirozhki*, some sliced white bread and a jug of processed apple juice. As soon as I sit down Ivonna brings the hot part of the meal – a small plate of *cannelloni,* and a piece of grilled meat.

Later, when I'm standing by the electric kettle, waiting for it to boil, the man with the beard asks if I'd like to join them. They are scientists, he says. From Denmark. I thank him, then introduce myself and take a seat.

The fair-haired man pours me a vodka. 'You're American?'

'No, English.'

'Bottoms up!' He raises his glass. 'That's what you say in English, no?'

'Not very often,' I tell him. 'Usually we just say Cheers.'

'Oh.' He smiles ruefully, then drinks.

'But it's not wrong,' I say.

The man with the beard tells me he works as a botanist. The two men have been to Svalbard on many occasions, though this is their first visit to Ugolgrad. I'm surprised to see them, I say, transport being virtually non-existent at this time of year. They were lucky, the bearded man tells me. Their university contacts in Longyearbyen managed to secure them a lift on the Russian helicopter. They are regular visitors to Ny-Ålesund, he goes on, the scientific community that acts as a centre for research into climate change. I ask if it's true that the Norwegian government have built a doomsday vault on Svalbard.

The fair-haired man breaks in. 'It's near the airport. You didn't see it?'

I shake my head. 'I didn't know it was there.'

'That's a shame. It's beautiful.'

Since the materials used in the top half of the vault include mirrors, stainless steel and prisms, he tells me, it reflects light throughout the summer, acting as a kind of beacon or focal point in an otherwise bleak landscape. In the winter it's even more spectacular. A network of two hundred fibre optic cables means it gives off a constant, muted white-and-tur-quoise glow. A Norwegian artist by the name of Sanne designed the installation.

The botanist takes over. Svalbard was chosen for the project on account of its comparative security, he says. Permafrost is one factor, but the absence of tectonic activity is also significant. The vault itself is located 130 metres above sea-level, in the side of a sandstone mountain. Even if the polar ice cap were to melt, the site would remain dry. Locally mined coal provides power for the refrigeration units that cool the crop seeds to the recommended minus 18 Celsius. Four and a half million seeds will eventually be stored inside the vault, to be used in the event of global catastrophe.

He hesitates. 'You're smiling.'

What he's saying reminds me of my own origins. He might almost be describing me.

'Sorry,' I say. 'I was thinking about something else.'

Worried that he's boring me, perhaps, he changes the subject. The flora is astonishingly varied on Svalbard, he tells me, partly due to the warming influence of the Gulf Stream, and partly on account of the seabird colonies, which provide natural fertilisers. Roughly a quarter of the flowering plants are completely unknown in Scandinavia. There are twelve different species of Whitlow-grasses, for instance, though he has only ever spotted seven. The fair-haired man interrupts. He works as a marine biologist, he says, but his real passion is bird-watching. On Svalbard you can see King Eider ducks, grey phalaropes and fulmars. You have to be careful with fulmars. If you encroach on their territory they spit a rancid liquid at you.

The two men are enthusiasts, and eager to share their knowledge, but after a while, inevitably, the conversation shifts. They are amazed to find someone like me in such a remote place, especially at such an inhospitable time of year. They couldn't quite believe it when I walked into the bar. Am I alone? Surely not.

I tell them I have come to Svalbard for the peace and quiet.

'Peace and quiet?' the botanist says. 'That is – how do you call it in English? – an understatement, no?'

The two Danes are laughing. They're both a little drunk. The marine biologist is curious to know how I spend my days.

'I work as a cleaner,' I say, 'and I'm learning Russian in my spare time. I'm keeping a journal too.' I talk about my drawings of abandoned interiors. The pink house near the quay, the old canteen. 'Now it's dark all the time, though, I've started writing.'

The botanist exchanges a look with his colleague. 'We must be interesting. Then she will write about us.'

'I'll write about you anyway,' I say.

The two men find this very funny.

'Ah yes,' the botanist says, shaking his head. 'The English humour.'

The marine biologist lifts the vodka bottle. 'Another drink?'

I thank the men for their company, but plead tiredness and rise out of my chair.

'Can we walk you home?' the botanist says.

'That's very kind,' I say, 'but there's no need. It's really close.'

Outside, the night is so cold that breathing is difficult. My throat and lungs feel scoured by the air. I tip my head back, and the sky towers above me, layer on layer of blackness. The moon is a round hole, small and brilliant. Light streams through it from another, brighter world.

I take my usual short cut, behind the back of the school, then through the playground with its warped collapsing hut and its marooned blue rowing boat, and up past the new canteen. The vodka simmers deep inside my body. I'm already looking forward to being home and lying in the dark with the radio on. The botanist's words come back to me. *We must be interesting.* Smiling, I climb the short flight of steps that leads up to the front door of my building.

I'm standing at the foot of the stairs, by the fire extinguisher, feeling for my key, when somebody grabs me from behind and clamps a hand over my nose and mouth. Without looking, I know it's the man in the green jacket. Bohdan. He must have been waiting in the shadows just inside the door. His palm is rough, like the heel of a foot. It smells of nicotine. He wraps his other hand round my middle, trapping my arms, and drags me away from the stairs. I kick backwards. Catch him on the shin. He twists my head so violently that colours explode before my eyes. White, then purple. I can't cry out, though. I can hardly breathe. I think about biting his hand but it would be like sinking my teeth into cardboard or leather. It's hard to believe that his hand and my face are made of the same thing.

He hauls me back outside, into the dark. I let myself go floppy as a doll, as if I've passed out or given up. My weight doesn't seem to trouble him, though he's breathing noisily, through his mouth. The reek of vodka hangs around him in a cloud. He's drunk, as always. I have to use that to my advantage. He might be strong but he's bound to be sloppy, careless, unsteady on his feet. I'm sure I'm faster than he is. More nimble. If I can just wrench free of him I don't think he'll be able to catch me. Where's my door-key, though? I no longer have it. I remember a chink and then a tinkle as it bounced off the fire-extinguisher and landed on the floor. I see it in my mind's eye, pewter-coloured, lying on the concrete.

The sky tilts, its blackness sooty, dense. The moon is

nowhere. It seems a different night to the one that hypnotised me earlier. The man drags me backwards across a stretch of waste-ground. My hat has fallen off; cold air scalds my ears. Though I've been mapping the town for weeks, I can't tell which way he's going. Will anybody see us? Probably not. It's too dark, too late. Their TVs will be turned up loud, their curtains drawn. Shouting won't do any good. It's the wind, they'll say. It's just the wind.

My heels bump and scrape over hard snow, and my neck aches from when he twisted it. I want to take a deep breath but his hand's still clamped over my face. I glimpse a park bench, then a lamp-post, then I seem to disappear into myself. Everything shrinks, and I turn inwards, crumple, drop away. I keep falling, but never land, and there's a dragging, chain-mail sound, like waves on shingle. I can't feel my body or the cold, and I've lost all sense of where I am.

I come to in a derelict room, the floor covered with sheets of paper, dust and broken glass. A single beam of light shows me a doorway and part of a wall. At the far end of the room is an overturned piano, the rows of white hammers tightly packed as the gills on a fish. All manner of things are scattered about. A tin bowl, a boot, a dumb-bell. A red book lies face-down, its spine split open. There's nothing that isn't incomplete or out of place, nothing that hasn't been tampered with or damaged.

All of a sudden I'm laughing.

I have just remembered a conversation with my father. I was staying with a family in an idyllic Alpine village as part of an exchange programme. I would have been sixteen at the time. During the first week my father called from Libya.

'How's it going?' he asked.

'There have been violent clashes between the security forces and the protestors,' I told him, 'but we're hoping order will be restored quite soon.'

My father sighed. 'Are you learning any French?'

I notice, almost incidentally, that I'm naked below the waist, except for my socks. My trousers and boots lie in a tangled heap nearby. The man stands over me, swaying slightly. There's no cut on his forehead, and his hair is not receding. He's younger than Bohdan, with a bulbous nose. I have never seen him before.

It's sometime in the future, late spring or early summer. The sky is a high hard blue, the sawtooth peaks still capped and patched with snow. The fjord is blue too, smooth and polished as a glaze. The coastal plains and tundra blaze with Arctic bell-heather, purple saxifrage and mountain avens. I have never seen a landscape that has such a clear empty beauty. People often cry at the return of the light.

My father has arrived by ship. He always scoffs at the kinds of holidays that are advertised in the windows of travel agencies or the back of Sunday colour supplements – *Experience the magic of the Midnight Sun!* – but as I watch him step out on to the deck I sense a change in him, a relaxation of his principles. Lydia appears. Her red hair, long and loose, streams sideways in the breeze. When it blows across his face, half blinding him, he laughs. She tilts her head and twists her hair into a rope. Her ring finger glints. Ah yes. I see. He may have lost a daughter but he has found a wife.

The cruise ship anchors in the fjord, and passengers are encouraged to go ashore in Zodiacs. The museum is worth a visit. They can see a polar bear's heart preserved in alcohol, a chess set carved out of driftwood by an early settler, a range of elegant harpoons. They can stop at the hotel bar and drink hot tea or local beer or sweet champagne. There's also a shop that sells Russian souvenirs. Though my father disapproves of groups and tours it's unlikely he will pass up the chance to explore such a strange and desolate place. Is it sheer coincidence that has brought him here? Or is he still looking for me, still following leads, no matter how tenuous they might be?

As he stands at the guard rail, a little girl collides with him, then runs on up the deck. A woman calls after her to be careful. In her late forties, she has sleepy eyelids and an erect, almost military bearing. She apologises for her daughter's clumsiness, then asks my father if he ever read the story of what happened here.

'What story was that?' he asks.

'A girl was murdered.'

'*Murdered?*'

'Yes.' The woman surveys the town. Her drooping eyelids give her a complacent air. 'It was in all the papers.'

'Was she a local girl?'

'That's just it. She wasn't from here at all.'

My father frowns. 'I don't remember it,' he says half to himself. 'Perhaps I was away.'

'She was English,' the woman says. 'Like us.'

A sudden sickly churning in his heart. 'What was her name?' But he keeps his eyes on the town, with its rusting containers, its gantries and its messy coal-spills. He can't bear to look at the woman for fear of what she might say next.

'Her name? I don't remember.'

Lydia takes my father's arm. 'Are you all right, David?'

He doesn't answer.

I turn my head to the right, away from where the piano is.

A door opens into another room. On the faded green wall someone has transcribed a poem in black felt-tip, some lines tilting upwards, others sagging in the middle. I feel the poem might hold the key to everything, but it's too far away to read, and anyway it's written in a language I can't understand.

'I know this room,' I murmur.

I've drawn this room. I'm in the old miners' canteen, on the first floor.

The man has rolled me over, on to my stomach, my left cheek pressed into the dust and dirt. I'm face-down, gagged with a cloth that tastes of bleach and oil. My locket is lying a few feet away, just out of reach. The chain must have snapped during the struggle. The man unfastens his belt. Everything is taking a long time but there are gaps too. Breaks in the continuity.

My father came to me one spring afternoon, while I was reading on the gold sofa in the living room. He wanted to know what I had done with my mother's ashes. He seemed gentle, inward-looking, like a bird with its wings folded.

'I told you,' I said. 'I scattered them.'

'Would you show me the place?'

We drove to Testaccio with the windows open. It was late afternoon. Warm air filled the car. As we turned right, on to the Ponte Garibaldi, I looked across at him. He glanced at me and smiled.

Once in the cemetery I took him to the cypress tree, its shadow like a spill of ink, darkening the daisy-studded grass. He asked if this was where I had put the ashes. He wanted to be able to imagine it. I had emptied them in a circle round the trunk, I said. I told him about my panic, and about the rain. He asked how I came to choose the tree. It was somewhere she liked to sit, I said. The sense of peace, and life going on just beyond the walls. She said it was like being cut off from the world but still a part of it.

He nodded, then looked away towards the pyramid. 'It's a good spot. I wouldn't mind being here myself.'

'But it's illegal.'

'Yes.'

As we left the cemetery, I took his hand. Neither of us spoke. When we reached the car he turned to face me.

'Thank you,' he said.

I wasn't certain what he was thanking me for – I could think of at least three things – and I didn't mind not being certain.

When summer arrives at last, with its endless days, its surfeit of light, I will walk in the hills behind the town and out along the shore, and I will search for the twelve types of Whitlow-grasses, and also for Moss campion, its dense pillows scattered over the ground, and Jacob's ladder, with its shadowy blue flowers and its thin fragrance. I will go fishing on the Isfjord at midnight and catch mackerel as long as my forearm. I will see Barnacle geese fly overhead, with their black necks, the air full of the rush of their wings. I will sail to the high needle-shaped rock in Hornsund, known as Bautaen, and to the ice cliffs of Austfonna, the longest glacier front in the northern hemisphere. I will see everything there is to see, know everything there is to know.

You can't bury people, not out here. Bodies are forced up out of the ground. They surface of their own accord. On the west side of Longyearbyen white crosses cluster at the foot of a ridge but no one has been buried there since 1950.

When someone dies in Ugolgrad, the body is flown to Longyearbyen, and then on to mainland Norway, or Russia, or Ukraine. The nearest graveyard is probably a thousand kilometres away.

My mother's speaking, and her voice is really close. She might be talking in my ear, as she used to when she woke me on school days. I feel the fleeting heat of her breath on my cheek. *You're the strong one. You're the one who wanted to live.*

The man's face looms above my shoulder. He's using both hands to support himself. Even so, his bulk bears down on my hip-bones and my ribcage, crushing me into the floor.

Now Olav. *It can be a strength to know when to change your mind.* Antlers tangled above a wooden gate, waves breaking in the sky. Stones like plates. A black road unwinding in the head-lights, the laughter of new friends.

Here you can just be.

My father sits with his hands over his face, the tips of his fingers thrust into his hair, his head outlined in gold. He's not in Rome or in Berlin. There are no hotels, no lovers. His hands fall away and he looks straight at me, his eyelids swollen. He has been crying. Not for her, for me.

For me.

The movie is nearly over. Jack Nicholson sprawls on his bed in a flyblown Spanish *pensión*, his girlfriend gone, the hitmen closing in. He's alive when the camera leaves the room, but dead when it returns, his murder discreet, unnoticed, an event that happens in the wings. My attacker bites down on his bottom lip. The smell of vodka and cold sweat. This is the moment when the camera leaves, but I will be unscathed when it returns, without a single scratch on me. I reach out and feel my hand close round one end of the dumb-bell. I need to smash the mirror. Step through it, towards my future – all the whirl and glitter of a life . . .

I grip the weight and swing it backwards, as hard as I can. I feel it connect with the side of the man's head, the tender bone above his ear. He grunts, falls sideways. I rip off the gag and struggle into my clothes.

The broken piano, the poem on the wall.

My father's tears.

I snatch up the locket and begin to run, along a corridor, down a flight of stairs, then through a half-open door and out into the night. I collide with two men who happen to be passing. One is fair-haired, the other has a beard. The Danes. When they see me, all the laughter drains out of them. Their smiles disappear. The bearded man wraps his coat around my shoulders. His mouth is moving but I don't understand. Everything's just noise. Then one or two words get through.

'You're all right now,' he says. 'You're safe.'

They take me back to the hotel. The bar is darker than before, one tube-light where the vodka bottles are, the maroon of the tablecloths almost black. Ivonna stands against the wall, in the shadows, her arms folded. The man with the beard boils the kettle, makes some tea. Ivonna watches him but says nothing. She looks the same as always, except around her eyes, perhaps, where there's a tightness – confusion, or concern. The other man walks this way and that, one hand in his fair hair. He seems to blame himself. The bearded man is talking to Ivonna.

I sip my tea.

Steam lifts past my face, and I can feel dirt on my hands, dirt from the canteen floor, a gritty layer between the china and my skin. The fair-haired man is still walking up and down, up and down. It's difficult to bear. I ask him if he has a phone.

He stops, then looks at me. 'You need to call someone?'

'Yes,' I say. 'I'd like to call my dad.'

Acknowledgements

I would like to thank the following people, who were a great help to me during the writing of this book: Mariann Albjerg, Christiane Bauermeister, Evgenia Belousova, David Bickerstaff, Ted van Broeckhuysen and the crew of the *Noorderlicht*, Mick Brown, Elena Bukay, Mary-Ann Dahle, Dara Faramani, Rory Farquhar-Thomson, Rebecca Horn, Lea Iversen, Joanna Kavenna, Eva Koralnik, Anne Marczinczek and the staff of the Kempinski Hotel Bristol in Berlin, Viktorija Mauvik, Olga Maximova, Luca Merlini, Dr. Kaye Mitchell, Francis Pike, Ilka-Carina Rhein, Emanuela Siciliani, Sir Richard Temple, Hunter Thomson, Angelina Voronina, Dr Maria Vourliotis, and Gray Watson. I would also like to thank David Austen, Robin Farquhar-Thomson, Calvin Mitchell, Jean Norbury, and John and Maria Norbury for their support and encouragement, and James Gurbutt, Tamsin Shelton, and everyone at Corsair for their passion and commitment. My gratitude and love, as always, to Katharine Norbury and Evie Rae Thomson.